"You're wrong, you know…"

"But you can still build this business. We had plans, and we'll have to adjust, but—" Jenny stopped talking. She couldn't make Adam want this any more than she could make him want her, want life in general. He had to want those things himself.

He watched her for a long moment. "We?"

Her gaze met his, and it didn't matter that she'd asked him to move out. That their marriage might be over. What mattered was the look in his eyes. The green darkened to nearly emerald, and seemed to cut right through the confusion she felt at what she wanted, professionally and personally. All that mattered was that for this moment, the two of them were together.

He'd come out of the shell she had begged him to exit.

Adam was back.

Jenny swallowed. "I have the draft of the contracts in my office. All you have to do is sign."

"I'll sign anything you want me to sign."

She was in so much trouble.

Dear Reader,

Some books don't want to be written, but they just won't let you go. *Breakup in a Small Town* is one of those books. I first met Adam and Jenny in *Famous in a Small Town*—they were fun and silly and seemed to have life perfectly in place. So much so that I had to just roll my eyes at them. A lot. I fully expected to kill Adam off in the tornado that devastated Slippery Rock, but Jenny refused to let Adam die...and I'm so glad. Because falling in love? Easy. Staying in love, especially when love seems to have left us behind? That is truly special.

Helping Adam and Jenny not only fall back in love, but build a deeper love than they found the first time around has been the best writing experience in my life.

Someone told me once that there is no such thing as an ending, only a new beginning. I like to believe that's true. I hope you enjoy your trip back to Slippery Rock with Adam and Jenny!

I love hearing from readers. You can catch up with me through my website and newsletter at www.kristinaknightauthor.com or on Facebook at www.Facebook.com/kristinaknightromanceauthor, and if you're a visual reader like me, follow my books on my Pinterest boards—you'll get some behind-the-scenes information and lots of yummy pictures.

Happy reading!

Kristina

KRISTINA KNIGHT

Breakup in a Small Town

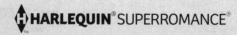

Recycling programs
for this product may
not exist in your area.

ISBN-13: 978-0-373-64043-0

Breakup in a Small Town

Printed in U.S.A.

Kristina Knight decided she wanted to be a writer like her favorite soap-opera heroine, Felicia Gallant, one cold day when she was home sick from school. She took a detour into radio and television journalism but never forgot her first love of romance novels, or her favorite character from her favorite soap. In 2012 she got The Call from an editor who wanted to buy her book. Kristina lives in Ohio with her handsome husband, incredibly cute daughter and two dogs.

For everyone who has found a bright beginning after a dark ending.

For Kyle, who always brings me to the light.

PROLOGUE

Three months ago

THE TORNADO SIRENS began blaring through the downtown area of Slippery Rock as Adam Buchanan raced around the corner of Franklin and Mariner. He glanced behind to see a waterspout out over the lake, visible just over the roof of the Buchanan Cabinetry warehouse. The spout seemed stuck, and he prayed it would stay stuck. Just stay in the lake, away from town, away from people. The wind could still damage property, but strong winds were better than a full-blown tornado any day of the week. A block down Mariner, he rounded the corner to Main Street, and could see the old church, now renovated and housing the day care where his kids spent most summer afternoons.

At the courthouse square, Sheriff Calhoun was urging people into the police station, out of harm's way. A few residents got into their trucks or cars and sped away from the area.

Adam glanced back again as the wind seemed

to increase around him. It was as if time stopped for everything except the waterspout.

The spout moved, becoming bigger as he watched, and the wind roared even louder in his ears. *Move, Adam*, he ordered himself.

He couldn't run; the wind was too strong. Sheriff Calhoun motioned at him, yelling something, but the tornado flung the words into the sky. Adam put one arm up to shield his face and continued on. Just another half block and he'd be at the day care center. He would get the kids over to the police station and into the storm shelter in the basement of the building. They would be fine. Just fifteen more steps.

A piece of roof or siding sheared past him and Adam spun a little to the left, reflexively trying to avoid the debris. A gust of wind rattled the awning of another downtown business, and hail began pummeling the tarp above him.

He looked across the street at the old church's stained glass windows, at the steeple swaying from side to side. No basement. Nowhere for the kids to go to escape all the glass that could explode from the air pressure at any minute.

Adam pushed off the brick wall, running as hard as he could through the gusting wind, until he burst through the front door.

"Frankie, Garrett, it's Daddy. Where are you?" The wind seemed to lessen once he was inside the old building, but he could still hear the windows rattling, and something crashed outside, not far away.

No one answered his calls. Adam tried the old sanctuary first, because it was an interior room without a lot of windows. No kids lined those walls. The converted classrooms were empty, too. He whirled, running through the layout of the place in his mind. When he was a kid, before they'd converted the church, local kids had played endless hours of hide-and-seek or tag-in-the-dark here. No basement, but there were offices on the back side and—

"Kids!" he yelled again, heading for the baptismal area. It was a six-foot by six-foot sunken area that the church elders would fill with water for baptisms several times each year. No windows, and enough space for the kids and adults to wait out a normal storm.

But there was nothing normal about waterspouts, and the radar on his phone had showed a solid blob of red over the entirety of Slippery Rock and the lake area. This was no normal storm. He had to get them out of there and into the shelter at the police station.

"Kids!" Adam called. The door to the baptismal area was lodged shut and he battered his shoulder against it. A long howl of wind seemed to shudder through the church and then the old door gave way. Adam stumbled into the empty room. No kids. And he had no idea where to look next.

Another loud wail of wind shrieked by, rattling the glass in the windows and seeming to make the entire building shake. A loud crack sounded, louder than the wind. The building shook again, and Adam flattened his back against the wall as part of the roof was ripped away.

He could see a green-gray sky where there had once been dark beams of cedar. Other bits of debris sailed past—tree limbs and what appeared to be hubcaps, and— Adam caught his breath. That looked like a telephone pole! And far, far above that, the steeple twisted and turned in the wind, swaying left and then right and then seeming to bend over the gaping hole where the roof used to be.

Pressing his back against the wall, Adam made his six-foot-two-inch body as flat and small as he could. There was nowhere else to go, and at least the kids weren't here. Wherever they were, they were safer than he was now. The steeple bent back, and he watched more debris from the tornado whizz past through the sky above. The steeple surged forward and another loud crack sounded over the noise of the storm. When it bent back again, he'd go. He could make it to the police station, see if the workers got the kids over there before the storm began. If not, he'd figure out where they'd taken them and he'd make sure they were safe.

One. The steeple began twisting again, this time pushing toward the rear of the building.

Two. Just a little more. Just get out of his line of sight, he thought, give him enough space to escape from the baptismal font and slip out of the church.

Three. The steeple disappeared from view and Adam pushed off the wall, running through the old church. Hail pelted him through the ruined roof. He hit the front door with his shoulder, pushing as hard as he could against the winds holding it closed. Stained glass shattered, hitting his legs, back and shoulders in hot little explosions of pain, and still he pushed. The door opened a few inches and he pushed harder.

Another crack sounded and Adam looked up. The steeple bent forward at a weird angle, teetered precariously, then twisted left and began to fall.

Another gust of wind pushed Adam back through the door, slamming the thick oak panel against his knees as the steeple came crashing through what was left of the roof.

And then the world went black.

CHAPTER ONE

ADAM SAT IN his wheelchair, watching life happen outside the picture window of his house. Old Mrs. Thompson carried her gardening basket to her mailbox, talking to Mr. Rhodes as she plucked a few errant weeds from the butterfly bushes lining her walk.

Adam's wife, Jenny, had left the windows open today, so he could hear kids chattering as they walked home from school, and the sound of a passing car up on the main road. And here he was, stuck in the wheelchair that had become his main mode of transportation since he'd woken up in the hospital nearly a week after the F4 tornado tore downtown Slippery Rock to shreds. Not because the crashing steeple had paralyzed him, but because it had messed up his brain. While the doctors adjusted medications to control the epilepsy he hated, Adam was stuck in the chair. Watching the world go by.

God, he hated watching. He wanted to be *doing*. Working with his tools in the workshop at Buchanan Cabinetry, playing with his kids in the yard or taking a walk with his wife. The woman who'd been stopping his brain from functioning properly much longer than the epilepsy.

The woman who now looked at him only with pity in her eyes.

He hated the pity more than he hated the chair.

Adam had no idea how to deal with either one, so he sat, and he watched, and he wondered if they would all be better off without him. Better off without worrying about when the next seizure would hit, better off because then an able-bodied someone could take his place.

He flexed his fingers against the armrests. The thought of Jenny being with another man, of another guy teaching Frankie how to hit a curve ball or push Garrett higher on the swing set had the pretty blue sky outside the window turning red. He didn't want another man taking over any tiny, little piece of the life he'd loved before the tornado. Adam sighed. Did it really matter what he wanted? Letting Jenny and the kids move on with their lives, since his was stuck in the wheelchair, was the adult thing to do.

Jenny wouldn't tell him to leave. If he wanted his family to have a better life, he would have to be the one to leave. Pressure in his chest built up, making it hard to breathe. It was the best option, one that would allow them to heal in a way that his presence never would. Jenny would keep crying herself to sleep. Frankie would still be afraid to so much as hold Adam's hand, and Garrett… God, Garrett would keep looking at him through green eyes filled with terror.

Adam didn't want his kids to be afraid of him. He didn't want his wife to pity him. He just wanted things to go back to normal. To a time when he and Jenny would walk the four blocks to Buchanan Cabinetry together in the mornings. To a time when he'd play with the boys in the backyard before dinner, and wrestle with them before bedtime.

To a time when his touch could soothe whatever troubles made Jenny cry, instead of making those troubles so much worse. He'd been lucky that she fell in love with him before; now it was time to admit that she deserved better. More.

Pushing his hands against the hated wheels, Adam turned the chair from the window and propelled himself to the kitchen. At the step between the kitchen and the living area, he got up, feeling the sharp pain in his knee as he stood. He smiled at the feeling. Pain he could deal with. Pain he could use. He limped across the room, got a glass from the cabinet and poured a beer into it, not caring that he wasn't supposed to mix alcohol with the medications. He held the glass up, closing his eyes as he let the smell of barley and yeast and hops wash over him.

God, he loved a cold beer.

The back door slammed and Adam dumped the full glass down the sink as his kids rushed through the mudroom, chattering about the Panama Canal and the best way to mix paints in art class. The conversation didn't make any sense, but then, his kids' conversations rarely made sense. Frankie, three years older, talked over Garrett, who chattered on whether anyone was listening or not.

Their noise stopped abruptly and Adam turned. His sons stared at him with eyes as wide as quarters.

"Daddy, you're not s'posed to be out of the chair," Garrett said, taking a step into the kitchen. He dropped his little backpack onto the tile.

"I was just getting a drink," he said, rinsing the glass in the sink as he surreptitiously pushed the empty beer bottle into the recycling bin. He limped back to the chair, his injured knee screaming in pain as he went.

"Can I have a snack?" Garrett asked, putting his empty lunch box on Adam's lap, looking at him expectantly. "I ate all my lunch, even the crusts off my PBJ."

"Sure. How about a cookie?"

"Mom doesn't let us have cookies after school, Dad," Frankie said, rolling his eyes as he spoke in that husky voice that made him sound so much older than seven. "Healthy snacks first. Sweets for dessert." He motioned to his younger brother. "How about an apple?"

"With caramel?" Garrett asked, rocking up to his tiptoes and clasping his hands together.

"Sure."

"Cut up, no peel," he said.

Frankie sighed. "You know I'm not allowed to use the knives."

"I'll take care of it," Adam said.

Frankie sighed again, and this time shook his head. "You're not allowed, either, Dad. No sharps because of the seizures."

"Cutting up an apple for your brother isn't going to give me a seizure." And he could damn well do one normal thing today.

Frankie pressed his back to the cabinet drawer holding the knives. "It's against the rules."

Adam gritted his teeth. "I can cut up an apple for a snack," he said, putting steel into his voice and hating himself for it. He'd never raised his voice to the kids, not once, before the tornado. Now, it was as if he couldn't make it through a single conversation without getting angry. He clenched his hands around the arms of the wheelchair and stood up again.

Adam limped across the kitchen, picked up his son and set him aside, then drew a small paring knife from the drawer. He put the apple on the cutting board and set the knife, but before he could make the first cut, the back door opened and his kids were off like shots through the kitchen.

"Mom, Dad's using a knife!"

"It's against the rules," Garrett hollered. "I don't want Daddy to sheeshur because of the knife, Mama."

"I'll take care of it." Jenny's soothing voice washed over him. "I'm sorry I couldn't pick you guys up at school today. How was the bus?"

No answer from either of the kids. Adam sliced the knife through the apple and was rewarded with a perfectly halved green Granny Smith.

"Well? How was the bus?" Jenny asked, and he could hear her heels on the hardwood floor. He continued slicing until he had eight even pieces and then began peeling.

"We missed the bus," Garrett finally said, his voice quiet.

"It's okay, though. I walked us home. It wasn't that far," Frankie said, the words coming in a rush.

"You…" Jenny was quiet for a moment and Adam pictured her running her hands through her hair as she gathered her thoughts. "Okay, well, in the future, don't walk if you miss the bus. Just call Buchanan's and I'll come get you."

"I don't like the bus," Garrett said. "Those big kids are mean."

"It isn't a far walk, Mom. And I'm practically eight now."

And until the tornado had sidelined Adam from work, Jenny had picked up the kids every day at school. Things were different now, he reminded himself. Just one more reason to let them get on with their lives. Without him.

"You won't be eight until next summer. That's more than six months away. And your age isn't the point, kiddo. The point is you're supposed to ride the bus. Was this 'miss' intentional?"

Though his back was to his family, Adam could picture Jenny with her arms crossed over her chest, looking from Frankie to Garrett with her pretty blue eyes narrowed and calculating. She'd hone in on Garrett as the weak link.

The kids didn't answer. Adam turned from the counter to her, back to him, just as he'd imagined. Garrett looked to Frankie, who stared right back at him. Neither said a word, but that look said everything. Yeah, an intentional miss.

Jenny watched them a moment longer, but when it became apparent neither would answer the question, she shook her head slowly, then knelt before them. "What did we talk about when school started? I have to stay at the warehouse now until three thirty. That means a bus ride home. Teamwork, right? You guys ride the bus, I meet you here."

Frankie scuffed the toe of his untied shoe against the tile. "It isn't fair."

Jenny looked at Garrett, who scooted a little closer to his older brother. "We don't like the bus," he told her.

"The bus is the best option we have until Uncle Aiden gets into town in a few days. Papaw is busy with the guys in the workshop, and Mamaw is dealing with the phones and office stuff while I deal with the warehouse shipments. It's just for a little while longer. Okay?"

Frankie shrugged, and Garrett looked at the floor. "Guys?" she asked.

Frankie nodded, and Garrett followed suit.

Adam held the plate out. The kids took it to the table and began to eat.

"Uncle Aiden will be here at the end of the week, and maybe once he's settled, we'll figure out a new schedule. Until then, it's the bus after school." The kids nodded, but kept their attention focused on the table. "I mean it, boys."

Jenny pushed past Adam and began to clean the apple peels off the counter. She rinsed the cutting board and small knife. She didn't even look at Adam. "You shouldn't be standing on that knee. You know what the doctor said."

Of course he knew what the doctor said. The words that damned man said circled around in Adam's mind all day long. *Don't put undue pres-*

sure on the knee. Even the smallest twist or turn could set back his recovery, especially since they couldn't perform the needed surgery on his leg until the epilepsy was under control.

"Cutting an apple isn't putting my knee under any stress."

"Walking on tile and hardwood is." Jenny kept her voice even, but shot him a sharp look then motioned to the living room. She held the handles of the wheelchair expectantly, but Adam was damned if he was going to sit back in that thing and be talked to like he was a seven-year-old. He turned on his heel and walked out of the kitchen, gritting his teeth against the pain in his knee as he moved. When they were out of earshot of the kids, she said, "And what if you'd had another episode? With a knife in your hand? And the boys in the house?"

"It's a paring knife, Jen. It's not going to kill me." And nothing had happened, so what was the big deal?

"It's a sharp blade, and it will cut no matter how little it is."

"Whatever."

"Stop giving me that answer, Adam. You know your limitations—"

"Peeling an apple for my kids isn't going to kill me, Jenny." He threw his arms to the side. "Neither is walking around in my own home instead of wheeling myself in that damned chair." He pivoted, and pain wrenched through his leg when his Nike caught on the hardwood. His knee gave out, and as he fell to the floor, he saw horror flit over Jenny's face as she rushed across the room. She cradled his body against hers the way she might hold one of their kids, and that annoyed him more than the pain in his knee hurt. He wasn't a damned child. He didn't need a damned babysitter.

"It's okay, it's okay," she said, her voice soothing as she ran her hands over his denim-clad leg. Once upon a time, a touch like that from her would have him hard and ready to take things into their bedroom. He pushed away the heat that flashed through him at her touch. Neither of them needed him acting like a horny teenager right now. "I don't feel anything out of position. Let's get you up." She helped him to the chair.

"Stop, just stop," he said, when she started running her hands over his leg again. He didn't think he could keep pushing away his physical reaction to her, not when she was this close to him. Not when he could hear her breathing take on that ragged edge. Part of him wanted her reaction to him. The other part, the smart part, knew physical attraction wouldn't do either of them any good. Not when his body was out of his control. He grabbed her wrists and pushed her away. "I don't need a nursemaid. I twisted the knee—it's not a big deal."

"It is a big deal," she said, but she stepped away from him, shoving her hands into the pockets of her pink capri pants. "It'll be okay, though. Aiden will be here on Friday. I'll figure out a new schedule for the kids, and for you. It'll be okay. It'll be okay," she said again, and didn't wait for him to answer. "I'm just going to check on the boys." She disappeared down the hall.

It wouldn't be okay, Adam thought. It couldn't. Not as long as he was in this chair. Not as long as his brain wasn't working. Nothing would be okay for his family as long as he was sick. And he was tired of being the reason everyone in this house walked around on pins and needles all day.

JENNY BUCHANAN SAT on the pretty, plaid sofa in her living room, staring at the ceiling. She'd gotten the kids to bed a little while ago, and still hadn't heard a peep from Adam. Her husband of six years had retreated to the guest room after the after-school fight. The guest room where he'd been sleeping since coming home from the hospital three months ago.

The guest room where he'd made it clear she wasn't wanted. Or needed. Or even invited.

God, she hated that guest room. If she could, she'd set fire to it so she never had to deal with it again. Burning down part of the home she'd built with Adam wasn't a solution to their current problems, though. As satisfying as it might be.

Her mother's chattering voice continued through the phone line, but Jenny had stopped paying attention five minutes before. She wasn't sure if the occasionally muttered *uh-huhs* and *okays* she offered were for the poor turnout for her mother's annual Coats for Kids drive or for the fact that her father still hadn't fixed the loose downspout on the side of their house. Either way, she didn't really care.

It wasn't even October yet. The first cold snap hadn't hit southern Missouri. In fact, they had yet to see nightly temperatures drop under the seventy-degree mark. And, really, what was the big deal about a downspout that was only slightly off center? There were bigger problems in the world.

Terrorism, for one.

Her husband's continued depression/anger/denial of the very real medical issues facing them since the tornado that nearly destroyed their town, for another. Not to mention the business issues. She and Adam had made big plans to turn Buchanan Cabinetry into Buchanan Fine Furnishings before the tornado hit; his parents had been mostly retired, splitting their time between Slippery Rock and Florida when they weren't traveling the country in their RV. Since the tornado and Adam's hospitalization, though, they'd moved home to Slippery Rock full-time and were now back to running the business. Straight into the ground.

The elder Buchanans had "mislaid" messages from the company suppliers, and when a furniture outlet in Springfield called to ask about a new partnership, they had refused to even consider the option. That was a partnership she and Adam had been working on for months, and his parents had killed the plan without even consulting her. Or Adam.

Adam's response had been to shrug his shoulder, get a bottle of soda from the fridge and wheel himself back into the guest room, where he shut the door and turned on the television.

When she knocked on the door, trying to talk to him, he'd simply turned up the volume until she left him alone.

She didn't know how to reach her husband. She hated her job.

She hated her life.

More than any of those things, she hated that she felt so helpless in this situation. "Mother, I'd like to talk about me, please," she said, detesting the whining note that came into her voice. She wasn't whining; she'd called for advice. But in typical Margery Hastings fashion, her mom had steamrolled right over Jenny's needs and straight into her own.

Margery didn't respond well to whining, though, so Jenny backtracked. "I don't mean to belittle your problems, I'm sure Dad is just focused on work. You know, the bank was hit really hard by the tornado."

"It isn't as if they had to rebuild," Margery said, her voice stiff with self-righteousness.

No, the bank hadn't had to rebuild. They'd had to create loans for local businesses to rebuild, had dealt with construction companies that needed to expand to deal with the devastation, and had to explain to their corporate bosses why capital outlay had increased so much in a single quarter.

"What I meant was that I really do need your advice. I'm just not sure how to reach Adam. He's...not the same man that he was before the tornado." As frustrated with Pre-Tornado Adam as she'd gotten from time to time—she'd begun to refer to him as that—she would take that reckless, carefree, playful man over the dark, depressed man living in her home any day.

"Well, what did you expect, dear? He was in a devastating tornado, trapped in the rubble of a building for nearly a full day before help arrived. Now he's dealing with a debilitating medical condition that is only barely under control—"

"You're right, you're right. I'm being too hard on him."

"You aren't being hard enough on him," her mother said, and Jenny shook her head. She had to be hearing things, right?

"Mother, he's having seizures because of a terrible head injury."

"And you're defending his continued ill behavior. I'm not sure why you expected anything different. He is one of those Buchanan boys. Neither of them took a single thing seriously when they were in school. I still don't know why you had to marry him."

Because she loved him, and she'd been eighteen and foolish enough to believe that no matter what they faced, love would be enough to get them through. She didn't think she could love Adam out of this dark place, though.

She wasn't even sure she wanted to try.

Jenny squeezed her eyes closed. God, she was a bitch to even think those words. Adam was her husband; of course she wanted to try to fix him. Fix their relationship. Fix their family.

"Well?" her mother said, sounding impatient.

"I married him because I loved him," she said, and Margery pounced.

"See, right there. You *loved* him. Not you love him. Loved. Past tense. Jennifer Anne, there are times that you stand by your man, and there are times you have to be honest with yourself. This is one of those times."

One of which times? Jenny didn't know. She wanted to stand by Adam. She loved him—not past tense, but now. As frustrating as it had sometimes been to deal with him being the fun, friendly, never-disciplined-the-kids dad, she loved the man he had been. Sometime in the past few months, though, she had lost that man, and she didn't know if he even existed any longer. It was as if the tornado stole the Adam she knew and replaced him with this angry robot of a man.

"I love him, Mother. Love. Present tense. Being frustrated at our situation isn't a good reason to… to change that." She couldn't say the *D* word. She couldn't. She didn't want to divorce Adam. She wanted to wake him up. To bring him out of whatever place the tornado had left him, and move forward.

"Well, I'm not sure how I can help you, then. I just got in from bridge club, and need to have dinner ready for your father in fifteen minutes. Call me when you come to your senses," she said, and the phone clicked off.

Jenny turned the receiver over and over in her hands. "That was a brilliant move, Jen—call dear old Mom for advice on one of her bridge days." She replaced the receiver and went into the kitchen. She poured a cup of coffee into her favorite owl mug and sat at the counter, drumming her fingers on the granite countertop.

Frankie's army men were strewn around the living room, despite her three warnings that morning for him to clean them up. Jenny sighed and crossed the room. She gathered up the little green men and tossed them into the basket at the end of the sofa. A stack of Garrett's drawings were wedged under the couch and she pulled them out.

Garrett had drawn a picture of their house, with stick figures of Adam, Jenny, Frankie and himself standing before it. Jenny smiled. She and Adam appeared to be holding stick hands in the picture. She put the paper on the sofa, and froze. The next picture was the same house, but black clouds circled the roof and squiggly lines appeared to be attacking it. She swallowed hard.

The tornado. She would reassure Garrett that the storm wasn't coming back.

Jenny flipped to another picture. This time no angry clouds buzzed the pretty yellow house her almost-six-year-old had drawn. Flowers popped up near the feet of the mom and the two kids in the picture, but a big black cloud was attacking another figure. A figure in a wheelchair. A figure with light brown hair and a frown on its face. A figure that was separated from the rest of the family and the house by a gaping black hole.

This wasn't right. She'd thought she and Adam

had been able to hide the rift between them, at least from the kids. She gathered the pictures and put them in a drawer in the kitchen island, and then leaned against the cool granite. Jenny pressed the heels of her hands against her eyes.

She had to fix this.

CHAPTER TWO

ADAM SAT IN the black wheelchair in the guest room of his home and stared out the window. From here he could see the still waters of Slippery Rock Lake, and he wanted to be there. In the water. Floating.

But he couldn't float. He couldn't go in the water. Couldn't take a shower alone. He couldn't do anything that a normal twenty-eight-year-old would do because the doctors didn't know when the next seizure would hit. God forbid he'd drown in his own shower.

He was supposed to be grateful that the damned tornado didn't kill him, but what kind of life was this? Trapped in a freaking wheelchair for the foreseeable future because his brain refused to work right.

Jenny knocked on the door. For the fifteenth time since he'd left the living room, repeating the all too familiar *It will be okay* that she seemed to have on permanent repeat in her mind.

"Do you want something for dinner?"

"No."

She knocked again. "I made the boys grilled cheese and tomato soup."

His stomach growled at the thought. He loved grilled cheese and tomato soup.

"I don't want grilled cheese. I don't want soup or bologna or a freaking rib eye from the Slippery Rock Grill that you've cut into small, little bites for me. I don't want anything," he said.

Or maybe yelled. He wasn't sure anymore. He seemed to be yelling all the time, but then he actually said only about a hundred words a day. Most of the yelling was silent. Internal. Aimed at himself.

Because he'd been a complete fool, and if he'd just obeyed the warning sirens, none of this would be happening. He wouldn't be in this wheelchair. He wouldn't have a wife who looked at him with pity in her eyes. He'd be in his workshop right now, building something with wood and tools, something that would last for decades.

But he'd been a fool. He'd freaked out when those sirens started blaring, and instead of being a normal, healthy man, he was a head case in a wheelchair who couldn't do anything that any other normal twenty-eight-year-old could do.

"Well, we have to leave for the doctor's at ten in the morning, so… I'll wake you before the kids go to school. Let me know if you need anything before then," she said, and her kind, nurse-like voice made his skin crawl.

Jenny's husky voice used to make him hot. All she'd had to do was throw her head back in laughter or say something completely ordinary like *pass the salt* and he had wanted her.

Wanted to kiss her, touch her. Do dirty, dirty things to and with her.

Now all he wanted was to be left alone, and she wouldn't leave him alone. Why couldn't she just leave him alone?

He didn't answer, and she didn't say anything more through the door that he refused to leave open, no matter how many times she or the kids opened it. He didn't deserve an open door, and they deserved more than to have to deal with his brokenness because of an open door.

Adam blew out a breath. Sometimes he wished he could wheel himself down to the lake and just float away. He could borrow a boat—his friend James had one—or he could rent one of the marina boats. Set out from the marina and just flow. If Slippery Rock Lake actually led anywhere, maybe that was exactly what he would do. Man-made lakes didn't lead anywhere, though, except right back to where a person started, and what was the point of that?

Adam twisted the top off his bottle of soda and drank. It was too sweet, and he didn't really like it, but what did like have to do with anything? He finished the bottle and tossed the empty plastic into the wastebasket under the cherry desk he'd built two years before.

It was a good desk. Solidly built, but with enough design elements to also be visually appealing. There were hidden drawers, curved edges. He'd been tempted to create some kind of locking device, so that the hidden drawers would actually be inaccessible, but at the last minute decided that was a little too adventure movie-ish, and simply built them to blend into the desk itself.

A picture of Jenny and the kids sat on the desk and he picked it up, running his fingers over their faces. He'd failed them. He hadn't kept up his end of the bargain. He was supposed to be their protector, their provider. He was neither, and despite that fact, despite knowing that they would be better off without him, he couldn't seem to wheel himself away.

FOURTEEN HOURS AND a million more reasons to let his family go later, Adam was just as uncomfortable as he had been in the guest room of his home. He sat in the exam room of his doctor's office, waiting. Jenny sat in the plastic-backed chair against the wall. He'd left the wheelchair in favor of sitting on the too-short bed thing in the office.

The protective strip of paper on it crackled when he moved, so he did his best to remain still.

Jenny was checking her phone.

"Everything okay?" His voice sounded rough and unused. So, pretty much the new normal.

"Just checking in with your dad. We were supposed to ship the new cabinet fronts for the Wareham project in Joplin today."

"Supposed to?" he asked, because *supposed to* made it sound as if the shipment didn't happen.

Jenny sighed. "He decided to ship them with the countertops next week." She put her phone into her purse. "I'll call the project manager when we get done here, straighten it out."

Adam didn't say anything. What was there to say? He didn't know anything about the Wareham project; maybe it made sense to ship the tops and fronts at the same time.

Jenny watched him for a long while, as if waiting for him to say something or do something more than sit on the edge of the exam table. Finally, she blew out a breath and took her phone from her bag again. While she tapped the keys, he watched the clock on the wall click off two minutes and twenty-five seconds. Then the doctor came in.

"Adam, Jenny, how are you both doing today?" Dr. Lambert wore gray pants and New Balance running shoes. Under his crisp, white lab coat, he wore a pink polo shirt. Adam didn't answer his question.

"We're fine. No seizures since our visit two weeks ago," Jenny said, as if she spoke for him all the time.

"Sixteen days, if you want to be exact." Because sixteen days sounded so much better than two weeks. Two was nothing. Sixteen, that sounded like progress, at least to Adam. Jenny raised an eyebrow but didn't say anything.

"Good, good." Lambert made a notation on his tablet. "We'll keep the same dosage, same meds for now. This could be the cocktail we've been looking for. Adam, how are you feeling?"

"Fine," he said.

"No more headaches?"

Adam shook his head, not caring that it was a lie. The headaches were much better than they had been the first few days after he'd woken up in the hospital. Instead of pounding at his brain like a hammer, they were more of a dull throb. And instead of lasting all day, they were an hour or so at the most. Nothing he couldn't deal with. Besides, his head shake seemed to make Jenny feel better. Her shoulders didn't seem so stiff now.

"What about the vertigo?"

"Nothing." Of course, it was hard to have vertigo when he spent 90 percent of his day either lying on the guest room bed or sitting in that damned chair. He leaned his head forward, and the floor seemed to yo-yo toward him. Adam gripped the edge of the table and closed his eyes. When he looked up, Jenny was tapping at her phone again and the doctor was making another notation in his chart. Good, neither of them had seen through the vertigo lie, either.

"Okay. Let's see how things are looking, then," the doctor said as he turned to face Adam.

He shone a light into Adam's eyes. Looked in his ears. Listened to his lungs and his heart and his belly. Adam wondered what any of that had to do with his malfunctioning brain, but he didn't ask. He didn't want to know. The less he knew, the more he could pretend that this wasn't really happening. That maybe he was still stuck in the rubble of the day care, waiting to be rescued from the worst dream of his life.

Finally, Dr. Lambert finished his examination. He sat on the wheeled stool while he made a few more notes on the tablet.

"I like what I'm seeing, Adam," he said after a long moment. "I think we may be on the right medication track, and your vitals are definitely returning to normal. What's going on with your knee? Still giving you trouble?"

"The rehab doc still thinks he's going to require surgery to fix the knee, but they've talked about ultrasound therapy as a stopgap measure," Jenny stated. "He said it might be enough to reattach the hamstring, which would be a good first step. Or it would be if he was actually going to the physical therapy appointments." She shot Adam a look before he could offer another monosyllabic, false-positive reply. "They won't approve surgery until you give us the all-clear on the epilepsy front."

"I can walk, though—it's just not as comfortable as it used to be."

"Walking mostly comfortable is good. But those ligaments aren't going to reattach themselves, Adam. Rehab will help, especially since I don't feel confident approving the surgery just yet. We need to ensure the epilepsy is under control before we put you under the knife."

Because if his brain freaked out during surgery, chances were the knee surgeon could do more harm than good, Adam supposed. He didn't say that, though. He didn't want Dr. Lambert to refer him to a head-shrinker as well as a rehab specialist.

"Have you given any more thought to a service dog?"

"Yes," Jenny said.

"No," Adam said at the same time. He stared at his wife for a moment.

She shook her head as if to say, "Fine, have it your way."

"I don't like the idea of having a big dog in the

house. We have small children," he said, and he knew even as he said the words that they were a reach. Having a service dog in the house wouldn't be a danger to the kids. It wasn't trained to find drugs or bombs, but to sense his messed-up brain waves or something. Adam still wasn't positive what the service dog would do, other than be another reminder of his new inadequacies. That was enough to put a stop to the dog coming to their home.

Her home. Whatever.

"As long as the children understand the dog isn't a pet, you have nothing to worry about. Even if they don't quite understand it, it isn't as if the dog will go on the attack. These are gentle dogs who are trained to meet your specific needs."

"Well, I don't need a dog." Adam stood abruptly, but the floor did that yo-yo thing again and he quickly sat in the wheelchair.

Dr. Lambert pressed his mouth into a hard line. "Fine," he said after a while. He motioned to the door, and they went into the hallway.

"Thank you, Dr. Lambert," Jenny said, but Adam heard no actual thanks in her voice. There was annoyance, but not thanks. He supposed he was the reason for that.

"Kim at the front desk will schedule you back. Let's go three full weeks this time, unless there is a seizure." He walked beside Jenny while she pushed Adam in the wheelchair. "If there are any issues—" Adam knew what that meant: if the meds stopped working "—please call immediately."

"We will."

The doctor nodded. He paused for a moment, but didn't say anything else, just turned on his heel and went down the hallway.

Jenny scheduled the appointment while Adam sat in the wheelchair. In the parking lot, she turned to him. "You didn't have to be rude about the dog."

"I don't need a service dog. I'm not blind or deaf."

"Service dogs aren't just for the blind or deaf. Did you even read the literature?"

He'd put it in the nightstand drawer, and refused to open that drawer since putting the pamphlets there. "Of course I read the stupid flyers." What was one more lie on the mountain of lies he'd been telling her since the accident?

"Then stop acting as if a service dog means you're permanently—" She covered her mouth with her hand.

"Disabled? News flash, Jen, the doc thinks I am permanently disabled or he wouldn't keep bringing it up."

"Epilepsy isn't the end of the world."

"Well, it sure as hell isn't normal, either," he

said. He got out of the wheelchair, slapped at it until it collapsed into a flat heap, and shoved it into the trunk of the Mustang convertible he'd restored his senior year in high school. The handles stuck out so that the trunk wouldn't close. He shoved at it again, but no matter what he did, the stupid chair wouldn't fit into the trunk.

Jenny pushed him aside. "Let me do it," she grumbled. "If we had a family car, this wouldn't be such a big deal."

"We don't need a family car just because I'm stuck in that stupid chair for another couple weeks."

"Rehab might shorten those couple weeks," she said. "There is no way to rehab epilepsy."

She glared at him for a long moment then started around the car. Adam opened the passenger door, got in and slammed it shut. She slammed her door when she got in, too.

"We need a family car because we have a family," she said, anger making her husky voice even huskier. It sent a thrill down Adam's spine, which was ridiculous. He couldn't walk without a wheelchair; there was no way he could make love to his wife the way he wanted to. "Two kids, all of their school stuff, Frankie is already playing football because he wants to be like you. We need a family car."

"This car is important to me," Adam said, crossing his arms over his chest.

"This car is impractical."

"I restored it. It's a classic."

"Then we'll just get a second car."

"No."

She glared at him again. "No?" she asked, her voice deceptively calm. Quiet.

"No."

Jenny put the car in gear and drove out of the parking lot. She didn't say anything until they pulled onto the highway leading to Slippery Rock. Adam glanced at her. Jaw set. Mouth in a hard line. Hands at ten and two on the steering wheel, knuckles white.

Adam started to apologize. He didn't want to snap at Jenny. He didn't want to fight with her. It was too hard to fight. He leaned his head against the rest and closed his eyes. He didn't like fighting, not with Jenny. Not with anyone. He just wanted everything to go back to the way it had always been. The Mustang was the way things had been.

The Mustang meant everything would be okay again.

THEY DROVE IN silence until the big "Welcome to Slippery Rock" sign came into view. It had taken everything she had not to snap at Adam, not to react when he obviously wanted a reaction. A reason to fight. She wasn't going to be that reason. He hated his diagnosis? Well, so did she, but according to some of the information she'd read online, keeping his world bland and ordinary could help to keep the seizures under control. Something about blood pressure spikes and endorphins, and it didn't make a ton of sense to her, but then Jenny had never pretended to be interested in biology or any of the other sciences. She'd been too busy reading fiction books and daydreaming about Adam Buchanan.

She didn't want to lose him now. She couldn't let him keep walking all over her, though. She was done with that. Everything had been Adam's way since they got married. They'd bought the fixer-upper he wanted, drove the car he'd restored, watched the TV shows and movies he liked best. Hell, she'd taken the job he wanted her to take— and fallen in love with the intricacies of it, true enough.

It never bothered her before the tornado that her life was so closely wrapped up in his. She didn't mind being the one to discipline the kids or pay the bills or make the vacation plans he wanted or bring up the possibility of expanding Buchanan Cabinetry. But now she had the job, and the parenting, and the house upkeep, and she didn't even have Fun Adam to run around with the kids in the backyard while she caught up on the laundry. Or, God, the man she loved to have take her in his arms and kiss her senseless.

God, she missed being kissed.

She'd give anything if he would reach across the car right now to take her hand. To tug on her ponytail the way he'd done a thousand times in her life. Anything, just to let her know he was still there. She'd done all the reaching since the tornado, and no matter what she tried, she hadn't been able to touch him in whatever dark place he lived now.

The Mustang flashed past the town sign, and Jenny slowed. She was through missing things. Missing Adam. Missing picking up the kids at school. Yes, her husband had limitations now, but that didn't mean he could shut himself up in a room and avoid the rest of the world.

Act as if none of them existed anymore.

"It occurs to me that I've been too soft on you." Jenny said the words carefully as she pulled to the stoplight outside Mallard's Grocery. No inflection. No anger. Just words. Calm, cool, concise words. From the corner of her eye, she saw Adam's head snap in her direction. Maybe this change in tactics was a good idea. "I don't like this any more than you do, and I know you have it much worse than me because you're living it. But I'm living it, too."

The light turned green and Jenny continued to

their home. Adam didn't say a word as she pulled into the drive. "I'm watching you fade away and I've tried everything I can to stop it. To bring you back."

"You think this is easy for me?" he asked after a long moment.

"I think this is the hardest thing you've ever done." Her finger traced the small scar at his neck. His skin was warm, and it took all her self-control not to kiss the scar, the way she'd done a million times. She had to be stronger than the attraction she had for her husband.

Jenny pulled her hand back, not wanting to feel the heat of his skin against hers. God, she wanted to kiss him there. Just for a little while, she wanted them to be the Jenny and Adam they'd been since high school. She would kiss the scar and then make her way to his mouth. He would carry her inside the house and make love to her on the living room floor because there wasn't time to carry her all the way upstairs, to that big bed he'd built for her when they were first married.

She pushed the hot thoughts of sex with Adam away as quickly as she'd drawn her hand away from his neck. Made herself remember the phone call that came in the middle of the night when she was fifteen. Aiden and Adam had lost control of their dad's Buick on black ice and totaled it. Adam had cracked two vertebrae in his neck, and had to wear a halo for three months, until the bones were strong again. Then, after the halo came off, he'd needed screws to hold those vertebrae apart.

She'd thought at the time nothing would be harder than that.

God, how wrong she'd been. His life hadn't ended with the car accident, and it hadn't ended when the tornado tore through Slippery Rock. But she had no idea how to reach him this time.

"You'd think God would have been satisfied with one head injury, huh?" he said, and his mouth twisted in that familiar half smile that usually made her heart skip a beat. Instead of sounding like a joke, though, his words were flat, with hard, pointy tips.

"I could have done without either. You scared ten years off my life with that car accident. And when I saw the steeple start to fall during the tornado…" Jenny shook her head. "I know this isn't easy for you. It isn't easy for me, either. But we have to figure out how to get through it, because I can't keep juggling all the balls you keep throwing my way."

"The balls I keep throwing?"

"I've taken up the slack at work. I'm cooking all the meals, cleaning the house, getting the kids to and from school. I'm paying the bills and doing the laundry and chauffeuring you to doctor appointments—"

"I'll call a taxi," he interrupted, but Jenny kept talking. She had to keep talking or she would never get all this out.

"Slippery Rock doesn't even have Uber. And that isn't the point. The point is I'm doing it all. By myself. And you're wallowing."

"I have a deadly disease." Adam narrowed his eyes.

Jenny popped the trunk, got out of the car and pulled the wheelchair from it as if she'd been doing it all her life. Some days, it seemed as if she had. She wheeled it to his door.

"Well, you aren't dying today. And you say you're well enough not to need a service dog. And yesterday you were well enough to use a knife to cut up an apple. You say you have no vertigo, no headaches…" She counted off the lies he'd told the doctor on her fingers. "And here I am, thinking I had to protect you from the world."

"Jen—"

"No. Don't *Jen* me. Don't lie to my face and tell me you're too weak, too scared, too…whatever. You say you're fine, well, I'm taking you at your word." She checked her watch. Still time to make the staff meeting at one, and if she hurried through the rest of her day, she could pick up the kids after school. "I have the Wednesday staff meeting. You know, the one you instituted last summer? We're talking about new product lines, and I've been allowing your parents too much say in what Buchanan's does. I'm going to the meeting, and I'll pick up the kids—"

"I haven't had lunch."

"There is bologna in the fridge—you can figure it out. And while you're figuring it, would you please do a couple loads of laundry? Frankie's out of clean underwear and Garrett wants his favorite dinosaur shirt for school tomorrow."

Jenny hurried around the car before she could chicken out on her demands. She was not going to let the man she loved fade away. Laundry would be her first battleground.

CHAPTER THREE

ADAM GAVE WHAT had been a white T-shirt but was now an odd shade of pink a side-eye as he read the directions on the bottle of detergent one more time. Nothing about the possibility of a color change. He tossed the shirt into the empty hamper and pulled another handful of clothes from the dryer. The jeans looked okay, but there was another T-shirt with odd pink streaks, and a bra that had one pink cup and one white. He was fairly certain none of Jenny's bras were designed that way. Then, at the bottom of the dryer, he found a single red sock. The culprit.

Damn it. Jenny had asked him for one thing. Do a freaking load of laundry, and he couldn't even do that without messing it up. Putting even more work on her plate. What the hell was wrong with him?

The grandfather clock in the living room chimed twice. Two o'clock. The work meeting would be over, and she would probably be back in her office. He had an hour until the boys were through at school to fix this. There was only one thing to do.

Fifteen minutes later, his mother bustled through the back door, chattering into her phone as she let the screen slam shut behind her.

"No, Owen, don't tell her where I went. It's just an errand that I couldn't put off." Nancy Buchanan's voice went quiet, and Adam wheeled himself from the laundry room into the hallway leading to the kitchen.

He waved, but Nancy motioned for him to keep quiet while she spoke to his father on the phone. He felt like he was back in elementary school, with his mom shooing at him like this.

Maybe he wasn't far off. How many twenty-eight-year-old men didn't know how to do a load of laundry without ruining all the whites?

His mother began speaking again. "I'll be back before Jenny has to leave to get the kids. Until then, you keep her busy. And don't let her come home early." Nancy snapped her phone closed—she refused to get a new smartphone, instead choosing to use the older flip model he and Jenny had bought her several Christmases ago. "Hey, honey." She ran a smooth hand over his face, the way she'd done countless times in his life. "How are you today?"

Adam didn't answer, just rolled the chair into the laundry room. Nancy followed, chattering on about the meeting at work. She didn't ask about the doctor appointment, so he assumed Jenny had told her there was no real change to his condition. Before he could explain what he'd done, Nancy picked the pink-streaked clothing from the hamper and clucked her tongue. She muttered something about separating whites and colors.

"This would have been a lot simpler if you hadn't already dried the clothes. Didn't you notice the bleeds when you transferred everything to the dryer?"

Adam started to answer, but Nancy just kept talking. "It's not impossible like this, though," she said, holding the items up to the light. "I'll need some distilled vinegar and more detergent."

Adam had no idea if Jenny kept vinegar in the laundry, but dutifully began looking in the cabinets.

"It'll be in the kitchen, probably," his mother said, but before Adam could wheel past her, she was out in the hall and headed there. She returned a few minutes later with a bottle of something that smelled awful and a measuring cup.

Nancy fiddled with the machine, put the vinegar into the bin along with more detergent, and then tossed the pink-streaked clothing in, too. She waved a box at him, and then tossed what looked like a dryer sheet in with the wash. "Next time, whether you think the colors are going to bleed or not, stick one of these sheets in. It will capture the running colors before they stain the clothes." She looked at him expectantly.

"Thanks, Mom."

"It's nothing, honey. I can't believe Jenny left you with the housework. Did you already fold?"

Adam nodded, and she continued talking. "Then we'll have a little snack while we wait for this load to finish up. Is that the only hamper you have? Your laundry would be much more organized if you had separate bins for colors and whites, towels, and jeans. You'd have fewer snafus like this one." She started down the hallway, and Adam followed.

"It isn't like Jen asked me to paint the house. Laundry is low impact, as far as housework goes."

In the kitchen, Nancy pulled glasses from the cabinet and poured them each a glass of tea. "Yes, but you need your rest. After all that's happened, surely she understands that. How about a sandwich?" The same lunch she'd made him all through school.

Adam wasn't hungry, but when Nancy was in mothering mode, there was no stopping her, so he just sat at the table and sipped the tea while she made a bologna sandwich. She brought it to the table, along with a bag of chips.

"About the laundry room situation. I can have the boys at Buchanan's fix up a temporary system, and I'll order something more permanent when I get home this evening." She eyed Adam until he took a bite of the sandwich. It had tomatoes. He hated tomatoes, but he ate, anyway. "Or I could have our cleaning lady come in once a week and do it for you."

"Jenny doesn't like the idea of hiring help, but thanks. And we really don't need someone to do the laundry."

"Because she's going to keep putting that off on you, no doubt."

"It isn't like that, Mom." Adam pushed away the food.

Nancy rolled her eyes. "You know, we should get a contractor in here to take care of that step into the family room."

"Mom—"

"And I know you use the back door most of the time, but there really should be a ramp for the front, too."

Adam clenched his jaw. He didn't need a damned handicapped ramp in his front yard. "Mom—"

Nancy kept chattering on. "And you and Jenny should really think about turning the guest room into a main floor master suite. You could take some space from that hall closet you don't use—"

"Mother." Adam raised his voice and Nancy turned to him, eyes rounded in shock.

"You don't have to yell. I'm right here beside you."

"I don't want the guys at work to rig some kind of hamper system." Calling his mother had been a mistake. Just like staying here when he wasn't a whole man was a mistake. Just one more mistake added to the long list of mistakes he'd made since the tornado. "And I don't want a maid in my house every day or once a week or once a year. And I don't need a goddamned wheelchair ramp at the front door or to turn the guest room into a suite." He gentled his voice. "Thank you for the help with the laundry, but I don't need—"

"Adam, of course you need. Anyone in your circumstances would need, and your wife should be providing for those needs." His mom squeezed his hand, and he knew it was supposed to be comforting, but only made him feel worse.

"No, that isn't her job. Jenny is doing enough." It was he who wasn't doing what needed doing. While he was sitting here in this chair, she was out there. Doing her job and his, caring for the kids. Caring for him. She was the one who needed, and the first time she expressed that, what had he done? Run to his mother. Just like he'd been running from any kind of responsibility since the tornado. God, he was a jerk. Jenny deserved better than him. So did the kids.

"Go back to work, Mom, and thanks for coming by." He wheeled himself into the hall, and for the first time that he could remember, Nancy followed him. She watched him closely for a long moment.

"It isn't a crime to need other people, Adam."

He knew that. A little piece of him did, anyway. The crime was in pushing against the people who wanted to help him. He'd been pushing Jenny and the kids and his parents away for the past three months. "I know. The crime is in punishing them when they try to help."

Nancy stood at the back door for a long moment, just watching him. "Adam," she began, but he shook his head. He didn't need mothering, not right now. What he needed was to either walk away, the way he'd been telling himself to do ever since the hospital released him, or show Jenny and the kids that he appreciated them.

Unfortunately, he had no idea how to start on either option.

JENNY QUIETLY CLOSED the door to the boys' room as the last rays of sunlight were sinking into the horizon. It wasn't quite eight o'clock, but the kids were still getting used to the school schedule, and both had nearly fallen asleep over their spaghetti at dinner.

"Momma?"

She barely heard Frankie's whispered word through the closed door. Jenny pushed it open and poked her head around the corner. "Yeah, baby?"

"I'm glad you picked us up today. I don't like the bus."

"I know, Frankie."

"And Garrett really doesn't like the bus."

"You were both very clear on that the other day." She slipped inside, ran a hand over Garrett's baby-fine hair. Her younger son was out cold. She sat on the edge of Frankie's bed. "I won't always be able to pick you up, though. You know that."

His mouth twisted to the side in an expression so like his father's it nearly took her breath away. "But you will tomorrow."

"I'm not sure. Uncle Aiden is supposed to get to town tomorrow, but I don't have his flight information yet."

"But you will if you can. And if you can't, it's because you're at work."

"Yes. If I can pick you up, I will, and if I can't, it's because I'm at work."

"It's safe at work. The tornado didn't hurt it at all."

"No, it didn't. Work is very safe."

"And you'll pick us up." He waited a beat, then added, "If you can."

"If I can." She wanted to pull him into her arms

and tell him everything was fine. But everything wasn't fine. The man in the wheelchair downstairs meant things were still not fine for her family. Also, Frankie thought he was too big for hugs, so she ruffled his hair, pressed her fingertips to her mouth, then his forehead.

"Promise?" he asked.

She nodded and smoothed the frown that seemed etched into the little boy's forehead lately. "I'll do my very best."

"But you have to promise. If you promise, I know you'll try."

Jenny sighed. "I promise that I will try. And I'll call the school to let you know tomorrow afternoon. Now go to sleep."

He pulled his full lower lip between his teeth. "Okay," he said, after a long moment of consideration.

Jenny tucked the light blanket around his shoulders and pressed a kiss to his cheek. "I love you, Franklin Adam Buchanan."

"I love you, too, Momma," he said, and his voice sounded drowsy.

Jenny watched her boys from the doorway for a few moments, until Frankie seemed to drift into sleep, then she closed the door softly once more. She waited, but there were no more whispered calls from inside.

Between Garrett's tornado drawings and

Frankie's need to be near his parents—or at least know where they were—at all times, it was clear neither boy had forgotten those tense moments when the tornado had torn through Slippery Rock. Maybe they'd have gotten over that trauma if they weren't reminded of it every day when they saw Adam in the wheelchair.

At least they had hope on that front now. That was how she took the doctor's words from earlier that morning. Staying on the same medication regimen, reminding Adam about the service dog. Those were indications that their lives would return to normal. Weren't they?

In the laundry room, Jenny pulled a load of clothes from the dryer. Jeans were mixed in with T-shirts and underwear, colors with whites. She sighed. Adam had done the laundry, but he hadn't separated the items. She tried to be grateful that he had tried, but when she spotted pink streaks on a few of the whites, the last tiny grain of gratefulness vanished.

She started down the hall, pink-streaked T-shirt in her hand, but stopped near the kitchen. What good would it do? She'd forced Adam's hand. This was her fault as much as it was his.

For their entire marriage, she'd done the cooking, the cleaning, the laundry. Heck, until she'd walked in the door that afternoon to hear the dryer tumbling, she hadn't been positive he knew how to operate either machine.

Sighing, Jenny turned down the hall. She ran cold water into the laundry sink, added a measuring cup of oxygenated detergent, the regular detergent and a bit of distilled vinegar—why was there distilled vinegar in the laundry room?—then set the clothing in the mixture to soak. She'd rewash the clothes in the morning, after they'd had plenty of time in the soaking sink.

After folding the jeans, which were thankfully not pink-streaked, and a couple of the boys' T-shirts, which didn't appear to have streaks, she left the laundry room.

Adam sat in the wheelchair before the big picture window, looking out at the street. The sky was still pink-streaked, much like the laundry now soaking in the sink, and nothing stirred outside.

"You left the vinegar in the laundry room."

He wheeled the chair around to face her. "A red sock got into the washer."

"And you guessed that vinegar would take out the streaks?"

A guilty look flashed across his face. Not his idea, then. Jenny shook her head. Of course the vinegar hadn't been his idea. The question was just how long had it taken him to call his mother after Jenny asked him to help her out.

"I called Mom at the store."

That also explained why, when she'd been trying to finish the new proposal for the furniture distributor in Springfield, all the calls to Buchanan's had been routed to her office phone. Adam's office, technically, but since he wasn't working, she'd taken it as her own. It made more sense than trying to get anything done in the outer office, where she'd worked before the tornado. Between Nancy's constant chatter and Owen's pacing as he watched the work floor below the office, she'd barely been able to concentrate on filling out invoices.

Still, at least Adam had tried to do the laundry. A couple weeks ago—shoot, last week, even—he wouldn't have.

"I set the shirts and things in the laundry sink to soak overnight. That should get the last of the pink streaks out."

"The vinegar didn't work?"

She gestured to the clean clothes in her arms. "Only on some of it."

"Mom suggested a better hamper system, so the clothes don't get mixed up again."

"We've never needed a hamper system before. It's not that difficult to separate on the fly."

"Yeah, I didn't think you'd want a hamper system."

"It isn't that I don't want one, it's that it's unnecessary." Really, how hard was it to throw whites in the wash and leave the colors, jeans and towels for other cycles?

"You seem annoyed."

She wasn't annoyed, she was tired. Tired of… God, she didn't even know what she was tired of. She was just tired. Damned tired.

"I'm going to put the boys' things away and go to bed."

"I did what you asked."

Jenny sighed. "No, you called your mom."

"At least I didn't leave the mess for you to clean up." He folded his arms over his chest. "Isn't that what you were mad about in the car? Me leaving things for you to pick up?"

"No, it isn't. And I wasn't mad." She took a steadying breath. "I can't keep doing this, Adam." Her heart seemed to crack with those six words. She didn't want this. Didn't want to break up with him. But she couldn't help the boys if she had to keep picking up after Adam, too.

"What, the laundry? I'll watch for red socks next time."

"This isn't about the laundry." Jenny smacked her hand against the table and winced. "It's about you not taking responsibility for anything anymore. I'm doing everything I can, but I need help. Can't you see that?"

He just looked at her. Jenny crossed the room, pulled out the drawing Garrett had done of the black clouds over their house, and thrust it into Adam's lap. "Garrett's drawing attack tornados in art class, and Frankie won't let himself sleep until he knows where I'll be the next day. You won't be honest with the doctor or go to your PT appointments. Your parents are doing everything they can to turn the Buchanan's you were trying to build back into what they wanted it to be—"

"At least they're here. Your mother has plenty of time for her bridge tournaments, though, doesn't she?"

"And no time for me or you or the boys or even my father. I've never expected more from her. But I did from you."

Jenny shook her head. She took the picture Adam hadn't bothered to look at and put it back into the drawer, then picked the boys' clean clothes off the side table. "Good night, Adam."

"Jen—"

"Thanks for doing the laundry," she said, and went upstairs before he could tell her he was sorry for something that he probably wasn't really sorry about. Streaking a few shirts was insignificant in the grand scheme of things. Comparing his helicopter mother to her disinterested parent wasn't the point.

The real problem wasn't that he'd messed up the laundry or even that he had called his mother to clean up his mess.

Jenny slid the little shirts and jeans into their proper drawers, then went into her bedroom, sank down on the mattress and pulled her pillow to her chest while she looked out at the darkened sky.

The real problem was that she was alone in this house, despite the little boys down the hall or the man she couldn't reach downstairs. She was as alone now as she had been when she was a little girl. Being talked at by her parents, never allowed to have an opinion or a want that didn't first come from one of her parents.

Doug and Margery Hastings were strict, some might say domineering. They'd had Jenny late in their lives, when they had their routines set in stone, and neither of them once considered that the routines they craved might be oppressive to the daughter they loved. And she'd never told them, because telling them would disrupt their routines more than if she just went along. So she went along with them.

Jenny had thought things would be different when she married Adam. They wouldn't be set in their ways, they would be caring toward one another. But in the end, she had gone along with Adam, just as she had gone along with her parents, and now here she was, adrift.

She had no plan, no goal to work toward.

She was alone in the darkness of this new

life, just as she was alone in the darkness of her bedroom.

She didn't want to be in the dark.

"I don't want to be alone," she whispered into the darkness.

The darkness didn't answer.

CHAPTER FOUR

JENNY CRADLED THE phone between her cheek and shoulder, listening as Aiden, her husband's twin, told her he hadn't gotten on the plane. The flight he'd promised her the day before he wouldn't miss. His voice crackled over the line, and she wondered as she looked at the brilliant blue of the morning sky in Missouri how whatever weather system was moving through California might impact Aiden's travel plans. She needed Aiden here. Adam needed him here.

"Did they shut down the flights out of San Diego?"

"No, I just decided to drive. I'm about to cross into Texas."

Driving. From San Diego to Slippery Rock? That didn't make sense.

"But you'll be in today?"

"More like tomorrow afternoon."

Jenny bit her tongue. She wouldn't lash out at Aiden; he knew the situation.

"I know I said I'd catch the flight, Jen, but I needed a little time alone. You know, Slippery

Rock is like a whole other country compared to California."

And Aiden was a different person since going off to San Diego five years before. He'd been the one adrift then, reeling from a bad breakup, wanting to do more than install cabinets for his father for the rest of his life. Adam had been the rock at that time, the one to tell him to go off and have his fun. Now, when Adam needed him, Aiden was taking his time returning the favor. She didn't understand it.

Not even when the two of them had been in the accident in high school had Adam been this adrift. Both of the men had been sheltered, to some extent, by their helicopter mother. Jenny loved Nancy Buchanan, but before the tornado she had never truly stopped to consider just how interfering her mother-in-law was. To tell the truth, it had been nice having a parent—in her case a parent figure—so involved in their lives. Her own parents were too busy with their own lives to worry much about what Jenny and Adam were doing across town. They'd visited Adam in the hospital only once, hadn't offered to help out around the house. Not that Jenny had expected them to offer. She didn't want them to feel obligated, not really, but it would be nice to know she wasn't so…alone.

She was beginning to hate that word. Since

she'd first allowed it to pass her lips the night before, it had rolled around in her mind on a near-
constant loop.

"He needs you, Aiden," she said.

"I know, Jen." Aiden's voice was a huskier version of Adam's. "But I'm not going to be any good
to him or to you or, hell, the business, if I swoop
in on the morning flight. Why don't I drop by the
house around six tomorrow evening? I'll bring
dinner."

Since she didn't have a choice, Jenny agreed.
She hung up and finished the boys' lunches. One
more day. She could deal with Owen and Nancy
at the cabinetry shop one more day, could keep
Adam's spirits up one more day, could... Damn,
she needed to run that load of pink-striped laundry
again. She shoved the brown bag lunches in their
respective backpacks and hurried down the hall.
Only to find Adam in the room, folding newly
brightened whites. The washer was still going.

"I separated them out this morning. Whites
first, colors are going now."

Jenny blinked, thinking this had to be a fig-
ment of her imagination. But when she opened
her eyes, Adam was still there, standing at the
folding counter with the wheelchair discarded by
the washing machine.

"Adam," she said, and although she wanted to
inspect the clothes he folded, she didn't.

"I made the mess," he said. "I figured I could clean it up."

"Oh. I, um. Thank you. I could have taken care of it."

"I know. But you asked me to do it." He leaned a hip against the counter, the way he'd done in the kitchen a million times. Funny, before yesterday and then this morning, she didn't think he'd ever set foot in the laundry room. He looked at home here. As if he folded the laundry every day.

A man folding laundry should really not make her heart pound in her chest like this, though. Jenny stepped back. She didn't need any heart-pounding moments in a laundry room with Adam. He was just being nice. Folding a load of whites didn't change anything, not really.

Before she could say anything, the boys' stomping feet clattered down the stairway. Frankie was yelling at Garrett, who was chattering as if Frankie were actually listening to him. Typical morning.

"I'll get breakfast and walk the boys to school. We have a client meeting at the warehouse this morning. A new construction company may want to contract with us."

"What about the distributor in Springfield? Can we spare the manpower for more cabinets and still meet the demands for the furniture?"

Jenny shook her head and grimaced. "Your father canceled the meeting while you were still in the hospital. And told him on several other occasions that Buchanan's was only a cabinet shop. I'm still working to get him on board."

Adam blinked as if this was news to him. She'd told him at least three times about his father's meddling in the family business. How Owen had taken their plans to expand Buchanan's and basically spit on them.

"You didn't stop him?" he asked.

"I was a little busy at the time. You know, I had a husband in a hospital two hours away, two boys who were terrified of their shadows, a house and yard to care for. Not to mention a dozen other contracts to protect from your father's helping hands." The words were laced with sarcasm, but Jenny didn't care.

She'd had it with the whole Buchanan clan, as much as she loved every single one of them. Owen and Nancy would never see the business as more than what they had worked to make it, and neither would admit Adam was more than a twelve-year-old who needed their guidance. Aiden had called almost daily, but she'd told him over and over not to come. Until she realized a couple weeks ago that she was losing her grip not only on the business, but her boys. And Adam. Now that he'd agreed to come back, Aiden was taking his sweet time getting here.

And Adam just kept sliding away. He'd been moping around the house for months, rude to the doctors trying to help him, unavailable to comfort or care for their children…and he'd acted as if she existed only to force him to go to doctors' appointments he didn't want to attend.

"It's our business, Jen, not his. Not theirs. We—"

"What's this *we* you're talking about? Yeah, we both signed the papers when they retired three years ago, and yes, we were both working on the expansion. But since the tornado it's been *me*. I've paid the bills, ordered materials, approved layouts and figured out design issues."

She could hear the boys in the kitchen, debating the merits of the mini muffins she'd left on the table for them against the sugary goodness of their favorite cereal. She intentionally lowered her voice. They didn't need to hear their parents arguing, not on top of everything else. "I was the one who got the extension from the distributor in the first place, and I'm the one who has been busting my ass to win him back since your father treated him like a pariah. I begged you to go with me to a meeting last month, and all you did was stare out that damn window, feeling sorry for yourself. And now you're surprised that, because you folded a freaking load of laundry, the life we'd been building is falling down around our ears?"

"What was I supposed to do? Go in this wheelchair? So he could take us on out of pity?" Adam put a hand on her arm, but Jenny jerked away from him.

"No, you were supposed to go as Adam Buchanan, a damn fine furniture designer. A man who, yeah, is temporarily in a wheelchair. The wheelchair doesn't stop your mind from working."

"No, the epilepsy does that," he said, the words dripping with sarcasm.

"Temporarily. They'll figure out a medication regimen—you heard the doctor. You'll get the surgery for your hip and knee, and you'll have your life back." Jenny held her hands out at her sides. What wasn't he understanding about this? "But you couldn't even do a load of laundry without calling your mom for help. You know what that means, don't you? It means for the first hour that I'm at work today, instead of actually working, I'll be listening to her lecture me on your condition, as if I don't already know it by heart."

"I'll call my mom—"

"No. No, I'll deal with it, just like I've been dealing with everything else. But let me tell you one thing that you don't know. I'm done, Adam. I'm done. I've been the supportive wife. I've been encouraging since the accident, and I've tried everything I know to help you deal with this. I still believe they'll find the right medications, and

I still hope that somehow the epilepsy won't be permanent. When they find the right meds, and if the epilepsy goes away, I'll be cheering for you."

Jenny squeezed the bridge of her nose between her fingers. "I hate that I'm angry. God, I don't want to be angry at you. I've done my best to just be angry with the tornado or the destruction, but I'm not just angry about that. I can't be the supportive wife when you refuse to be the husband who at least tries to deal with his condition. I can't hold your hand while you refuse to even consider how to make this new life work for you."

Adam's face was a strange shade of red, as if he was just as angry as she. Maybe he was. He should be. Yes, the tornado had been awful, but he was still here. Alive. He had two amazing boys who were unhurt. Parents and a twin who loved him. He had had her, right up until the moment he'd called his mother to do the laundry. Jenny knew it was a silly thing to throw her over the edge. That should have gone to his refusal to meet with the service dog company, or his lies to the doctor trying to fix his brain. She shook her head as she picked up a pair of Frankie's shorts. Carefully, she folded the garment into a square.

"I know about separating out the loads, now. It's not that big a deal." The redness had gone from his face. Adam tossed an unfolded pair of the boy's underwear atop the carefully folded shorts, then a haphazardly folded T-shirt.

Jenny had thought Adam calling his mother to do their laundry was the last straw. It wasn't. The carelessness with which he said the words and tossed the underwear made up that final straw. These things mattered. His involvement mattered.

His noninvolvement mattered even more. She was not going to go through her life desperately waiting for him to take an interest; she'd had enough of that as a child.

"I think you should move out," she said, and she hated that her voice cracked over the words. She didn't want him to go, but she couldn't bear to watch him fade away like he'd been doing for the past three months. The boys deserved better.

She deserved better.

"Jenny, come on."

She fled from the room before he could stop her, and didn't pause at the kitchen to check on the boys. She didn't slow down until her back was pressed against the closed door of their bedroom. She held a hand against her chest, felt her heart banging against her sternum, and refused to cry.

Laundry was supposed to be her first battleground, and it was killing her that it would be the only one. Fighting required two people—she couldn't do it alone.

And she was through crying for Adam, for the life they'd had before the tornado.

She might still be alone, but she didn't have to stay in the darkness.

CHAPTER FIVE

ADAM SAT IN the hallway between the laundry room and the kitchen for a long time, waiting for Jenny to come back. She always came back. Of course, she'd never spoken to him like that before. He couldn't remember a single time she'd raised her voice—not that she'd raised her voice just now—or been anything other than a younger version of his mother. Nancy followed Owen's lead. That was how marriage was supposed to work, wasn't it?

Was that even what Adam wanted? For Jenny to be some kind of clone of his mother, a woman who loved her husband and kids, but who had never made a decision that wasn't based on what was best for someone else?

He listened for footsteps in the hallway, but the house was silent except for the chattering of the boys in the kitchen.

Jenny wasn't coming back.

He wanted her to come back. Which was weird, because just yesterday he'd decided to walk away from their little family, for her benefit. Now that she was the one walking it felt…like he should maybe chase after her. Beg her to stay.

The clock in the living room chimed the quarter hour. It was better this way. She deserved more than he could give her, and at least if she was angry with him, she wouldn't cry. He didn't think he could take Jenny's tears, not on top of everything else in his world falling apart. So he'd go. This time of year there would be rooms available at the B and B near downtown. He could make it a clean break, for her and the boys.

Adam wheeled himself down the hall. Frankie and Garrett were at the kitchen table, their backpacks leaning against the island. Fall hadn't yet hit Slippery Rock, and they both wore shorts and T-shirts, with Velcro tennis shoes on their small feet. God, he was going to miss his boys.

"Morning, Dad," Frankie said.

"Where's Mom?" Garrett asked, but didn't wait for an answer. "I put Washington in my pack for show-and-tell, but now there's no room for my lunch. I think I need a bigger pack. Like Frankie's."

"My pack is full of school stuff, not stuffed animals," Frankie said, referring to the giant yellow-and-purple stuffed cat Garrett had won at the fair over the summer. Adam's younger son and the cat had been inseparable ever since. "You can just carry your lunch sack until you get to school and put it in the bin."

"But what if someone sits on it?"

"Who's going to sit on it? It's just you and me and Mom in the car, dummy."

"*Dummy* isn't a nice word." Garrett clenched his jaw and leaned forward. Adam had no idea what else the boy was about to say, but he didn't want this whatever-it-was between them to go any further.

"Okay, okay. How about the three of us walk to school, then, and you can both hook your packs on the chair so your hands are free for the lunches?" Adam wanted to pull the words back into his mouth. The last place he wanted to be was in public in the chair. He'd avoided most Slippery Rock events and businesses since the accident. Walking kids to school was one of those everyday events, and he would run into people he had known most of his life. People he'd avoided since the tornado.

Garrett stared at him, wide-eyed. Frankie looked past Adam to the empty hallway and the living room beyond, as if he expected Jenny to come rushing in at Adam's words. She didn't appear, to save him from his declaration.

"You're gonna walk with us to school?" Garrett said incredulously.

"Mom drives," Frankie added.

"Well, I can't drive, but we have time to walk

it." He motioned to the backpacks, and the boys dutifully hung them on the handles below Adam's shoulders. "Let's go."

Neither boy said anything until the three of them were down the driveway and a few houses along the street. When his grandfather left him the land and broken-down farmhouse on the edge of Slippery Rock Lake, Adam had imagined one day walking his kids to school. He'd never bothered before today, not even before the tornado. He'd always had a reason for leaving the school runs to Jenny. He couldn't remember a single one of those reasons now.

"So, it's show-and-tell day?" he asked Garrett, not wanting to delve too far into why he'd never walked his kids to school. Had to be his schedule. Running a business was time-consuming.

"No." Garrett stopped to pull a couple yellow dandelions from the grass in Mrs. Hess's yard. "Friday is show-and-tell."

Adam blinked. "Then why did you put Washington in your pack today?"

"So I won't forget him." Garrett skipped ahead, and this time pulled some purple ground cover from another neighbor's yard.

Adam looked to Frankie for help, but the older boy only shrugged. "Kindergarteners," he said, with no small amount of disgust in his voice.

"You don't have show-and-tell in third grade?"

"We have I-C-M-M days, and we have to earn them. We can't just bring toys in anytime we want."

"What's an I-C-M-M?" Adam had a feeling he should know this.

"I Can Manage Myself. It means we're doing our work and not messing around. I'm already halfway to mine and when I get it, I'm gonna bring in my Xbox."

"I don't think a gaming system is a good option for show-and-tell."

"It's not show-and-tell, it's I-C-M-M, and it's a whole afternoon. Not just five minutes. If I get ten more marks on my card, I get a whole afternoon to myself. And I'm bringing my Xbox." He crossed his arms over his chest, but kept pace with Adam's chair. Garrett was still picking wildflowers from neighbors' yards, blissfully unaware of the conversation.

"I think your iPod or DS would be a better option. For the Xbox, you'd need a TV and the system and the games. That's a lot to bring in."

"I'm bringing the Xbox," Frankie said through clenched teeth.

A few kids turned onto the street ahead of them, and Frankie took off at a run to catch up with them. Adam returned the waves of the parents. The faces were familiar, but most faces in Slippery Rock were. Ruby Kildare, who had been a couple years ahead of him in school, trailed her son, Bobby. There was Jackson Crane and his twins, Blair and Bree. The other parents watched him, but didn't say anything, and Adam was grateful. Blair and Bree started picking wildflowers with Garrett, and Jackson slowed to keep pace with Adam.

"You're looking good," he said after a moment.

"Doing fine," Adam said.

"Think the weather's going to break anytime soon? October will be here in another couple weeks."

"Won't be much longer." He watched as Garrett presented his small bouquet to Bree. Blair stomped her foot. Garrett twisted his mouth to the side, then took back the bunch of flowers, split it in two and gave half to each twin.

"He's going to be a heartbreaker, Adam," Ruby said. He hadn't noticed the woman slowing her pace, but now here he was with two people who probably wanted the intimate details of his injuries. He should have stayed home.

Blair lifted the bouquet to her nose, then sneezed all over it. Jackson hurried forward, wiped her nose with a handkerchief from his back pocket. The group turned the corner, and Slippery Rock Elementary spread out before them. The school took up most of the block, with the big gymnasium on the right side and the junior high classrooms making up the wing on the left. Playgrounds and a small nature area were in the courtyard behind the elementary classrooms, the gym and the junior high.

On the block beyond was the high school, football fields and the natatorium where they taught swimming lessons in the summer, and where the high school and junior high swim teams practiced and competed. Between the high school and the football field was the State Championship Memorial. The town commissioned it, setting Adam's, Aiden's, Collin Tyler's, James Calhoun's and Levi Walters's names in gray limestone, along with their jersey numbers the summer after their team won the state high school football championship. The five of them had been co-captains, and the only seniors on the team. Adam didn't play at all, thanks to a car accident that sidelined him, but his name was still on the monument. The damn thing looked like a tombstone, and although Adam couldn't see it, the thought sent a shiver up his spine.

He hadn't been a football player in a long time, and he might be in a wheelchair right now, but he wasn't dead.

They reached the school, and he realized he couldn't go any farther because of the steps.

"Want me to push the chair up the stairs for you?" Jackson asked.

Adam shook his head. "I've got it." Jackson shrugged and continued on, as did Ruby.

Adam called to the boys. "You guys have a good day at school, okay? Frankie, work toward that Xbox thing, and Garrett, don't let anyone sit on your lunch." The little boy giggled. Frankie rolled his eyes.

"Will you walk us back after school?" Garrett asked, his hazel eyes looking so much like Jenny's it hurt Adam's chest. His son threw his arms around him, hugging him tightly.

"Sure, I can walk you home."

"Mom drives," Frankie said, and Adam was getting tired of hearing those words.

"It's a nice day, and I'm sure your mom would like the break. I'll see you both right here at three."

"Three-oh-five," Frankie corrected, his voice quiet. The warning bell rang out.

"Three-oh-five," Adam repeated solemnly. He remembered what Jenny had said the night before about Frankie wanting to know where she was. "I'll be here," he said, and squeezed the little boy's hand.

Garrett hopped up the steps that led inside. Frankie watched Adam for a long moment.

"I'll pick you up right here," he said again. "Everything okay? Did you forget something?" What was going on here?

"I have everything," the boy said after a long moment. "You sure you can be here?"

Adam swallowed, Jenny's words of he day before ringing in his ears.

Garrett's drawing attack tornados in art class and Frankie won't let himself sleep until I promise him Buchanan's is a safe place to be.

"I'll be here, Frankie. Mom will be at work, but I'll be here."

His son nodded and started up the steps. At the top he turned and waved. Adam waited until Frankie disappeared inside the big double doors, then he turned the wheelchair and started back toward the house.

Adam blew out a breath. Yes, his wife and his kids deserved more than the shell of a man he was now, but he couldn't just vanish on any of them. He needed to figure out how to make sure they were taken care of first.

He needed coffee. Caffeine was on the list of things the doctors told him to limit, but one cup couldn't hurt anything. He texted Jenny to let her know he'd taken the kids to school, and that he'd promised to pick them up.

A few minutes later she texted back, Thank you.

Adam wheeled himself past the house and noticed the Mustang was still in the drive. He considered going inside to talk to Jenny, but he needed a plan. Their last two conversations had ended badly. She was better off without him, but he didn't want to fight with her. He could wheel himself to the backyard. Sit on the patio to think. But if she saw him, she might want to talk, and he needed a solid plan before talking to her again.

Mr. Rhodes from across the street waved and started toward Adam. He didn't want to talk to the older man, so he pushed the chair a little faster. Adam didn't want to deal with the public, but if he had to choose between Jenny and the public at large at this point, he was going public all the way.

A few minutes later, he crossed the street into the downtown area. Parking slots were filled with trucks and SUVs. Patrol cars were parked outside the Slippery Rock Sheriff's Department. He waved to a few people he knew, but didn't stop. Bud stood outside the bait shop, sweeping his section of concrete. He crossed the street when he saw Adam, and pointed to the new farmer's market.

The foundation of the old building remained, but the rest had been gutted by the tornado. Now, new picture windows fronted the structure, and new brick had been laid to reinforce the walls. Slippery Rock Farmer's Market was painted on the windows, and someone had painted a water scene on the sidewalk in front with the words Clean Water Makes the Earth Happy painted around it. Adam had heard about the storm drain art, but this was the first he'd seen. It wasn't bad.

"Headed to work?" Bud asked. Adam pushed the chair a little faster, but the man kept pace.

"Still on the disabled list," he said, and for the first time, the words actually felt a little like a joke. Like walking his kids to school meant something. "Going to the coffee shop."

"Want some company? Haven't had my fourth cup yet." Bud didn't wait for Adam to approve, just continued walking beside him. "How's that pretty wife of yours?"

"She's good." *Wants me to leave the house, but that's probably for the best*, he thought, though Adam didn't say the words. "Turning into quite the cabinetmaker, or so I hear." It was actually an assumption. He'd avoided all talk of work since the doctors told him he couldn't operate the machinery. Bud didn't know that, though.

Bud held open the door to the coffee shop so Adam could navigate the chair through. The bell over the door tinkled as it closed behind them. A teenager at the counter took his order for a caramel mocha and Bud's black coffee.

"See ya around, Adam," the older man said as he headed back to his street sweeping.

Adam waved. He put the cup in the little holder Jenny had installed on the chair when he first came home, and went to a little table in the corner.

For a long time, he sat and watched the activity on the street. A few late-season fishermen went into Bud's, and boats bobbed on the still water of the marina. In another few weeks, the boats would all be in winter storage and the downtown area would be a ghost town.

If Adam turned around, he would see part of Buchanan Cabinetry, and the warehouse where his employees built and stored the cabinets and furniture they made.

Her employees. Jenny's. As she'd said, he'd abandoned the business. And if he couldn't make things, he didn't see the point in going back. His fingers flexed at the thought of making something again. He missed the feel of wood in his hands, missed figuring out how a slab of oak or cherry could have a new life once it had been cut down.

He needed to get back to the plan. He'd screwed up his family's life enough. He wasn't going to screw it up even more by just disappearing. Jenny needed to see that he was okay, and the boys deserved a father who was present with them, not just existing in the same space. In the side pocket Jenny had put on the chair when she'd added the cup holder, he found a small notebook and a pen. Adam smiled. Jenny liked her lists. She was always making lists.

For the business. For Christmas. For vacations and groceries. It made sense she would give him a notebook, and it was another failure on his part that he hadn't noticed it before today. Adam didn't think he could have been more self-involved over the past few months—hell, few years—if he'd been actively trying to make the people around him feel unimportant.

The first thing he had to do was make sure Jenny and the boys were okay financially. That meant figuring out how to make Buchanan's work for her. The simplest thing would be to go back to the way things had been before his parents sold the firm to them a few years before. Making and installing cabinets was a solid business. Jenny was a smart woman; she could handle the invoicing and scheduling, and Duane might make a good foreman for the men on the floor. That would work.

The thought of the Adirondack chairs he'd made last winter weighed heavily on Adam's mind. They'd never sit in a yard overlooking the lake now. Hell, Jenny might not even know they were in that far corner of the warehouse.

Not that it mattered. He couldn't build anymore, so it didn't make sense to add the deck chairs or tables to the plan. And it certainly didn't make sense to add in the other expansion plans.

He stared out the window for a long time. Those plans were part of the past. This list was about moving forward. He had to let those plans go, just like he was letting Jenny go. He glanced at the paper again then tore it from the notebook and stared at it. While he'd been thinking about those chairs and his old plans, he'd drawn a laundry storage unit. Four units. He'd drawn his personal symbol for cherry wood as the links between the different bags. Jenny like cherry the best.

Adam wadded up the paper and wrote the number *1* on a clean sheet. She already knew about the invoicing and bookkeeping, and the business was on solid financial ground. Maybe he should make getting his parents out of Buchanan's the first thing on the list. He'd figure out how later.

What were some other things he could do? School runs would clear out a little more time from her day. Maybe cook a few meals. She had a shelf full of recipe books—they couldn't be that hard to follow.

He needed something bigger, though. Something that would really show her he was making good changes in his life. There was always that service dog place. Adam cringed at the thought. A service dog was permanent.

The pen hovered over the page for a long moment, and before he could talk himself out of it, Adam scribbled it down on the list. Service dog.

It was the last thing he wanted.

It was what Jenny wanted, though.

He couldn't stop staring at the wadded-up sheet.

He sat like that for a long time, staring at it and the new list. Thinking about his old life, telling himself it was time to embrace the new. Jenny. Frankie. Garrett. They deserved new.

Slowly, Adam smoothed out the wadded-up paper. He'd certainly screwed up their lives, way more than they deserved.

He read over the first thing on his list: fix things so he could let them go. That was what he had to do.

Then something on the original sheet caught his eye. Beside the hamper he'd drawn were the words *Get My Family Back.*

Adam closed his eyes. His brain kept telling him his family deserved more, deserved better. But his heart… His heart wanted them back.

"YOU'RE LEAVING? IT'S BARELY ELEVEN." Nancy sat behind a broad, built-in desk that Owen had installed when they first turned the second floor of the old warehouse into offices for the business. She'd tied her bobbed hair, streaked with silver and white, at her nape and wore an orange-and-green-striped polo with her denim capris. She held the phone in her hand and scribbled something on a notepad beside her.

"I have a lunch meeting." Self-consciously, Jenny swiped a hand at her naturally curly hair. When was the last time she'd had it trimmed? She couldn't remember. The past few months she'd taken to simply pulling it back into a ponytail. Today it hung just past her shoulders. Maybe she would stop by the house to pick up a hair tie. She didn't want to look like Little Orphan Annie or something for these meetings. The first was important to keep the business going, and the second important for future growth. For the plans Adam— No, the plans *she* had for Buchanan's. She waved the clipboard of papers. "Two, actually."

"At eleven? You don't usually eat lunch until noon."

True enough, but she wasn't technically eating now. She just needed to get through coffee with the construction company representative so that she could meet with the Springfield distributor at Rock Pizza at twelve-thirty. Her fight with Adam this morning made one thing crystal clear: she had to take her life back.

Adam didn't care about the business, which left its stability in her hands. This was one ball she was not going to drop. She had the designs that he'd come up with last winter, and the guys in the shop could put some sample pieces together from that. Adam might not want to move forward, but she still wanted to make Buchanan's more than a cabinet shop.

"I didn't have breakfast this morning," she lied.

"And I have a meeting right after, so I won't be back in the office until at least two. I'll have my cell phone if you need me." Not that Nancy would call.

"We haven't spoken since yesterday afternoon. There are things we need to discuss."

"Like you leaving me to answer phone calls so you could do the laundry for Adam?" Jenny shook her head. "There is nothing to talk about."

"Adam is sick. You can't expect him to become a housewife just because you're working now."

Jenny gripped the clipboard tighter. She skipped over the Adam-as-a-housewife bit because that would lead to more than the two minutes she had before leaving for the first meeting. "I've been working at Buchanan's since I was eighteen. First, answering phones like you've always done. When you and Owen retired, I took on a larger role. This is our company, and I'll run it the best way I know how."

"Buchanan's is fine just the way it is."

"Buchanan's could be more than a cabinet shop. Adam wanted it to be more—"

"That was before he got sick." Nancy's words were staccato, but Jenny refused to flinch.

"Adam isn't sick. He doesn't have a cold or the flu. He has epilepsy, and it may never go away. He has to learn to deal with that."

"By doing your laundry?"

"No." Jenny put her hand on Nancy's and felt a slight tremor from the older women. "By showing him that he can still do whatever he wants to do."

"He can't operate the machinery here."

"He can still design."

"He can't drive."

"He can walk." Jenny squeezed her mother-in-law's hand. "He isn't an invalid, and you running to his rescue when he calls isn't helping."

"I just…" She cut her eyes to the big window that looked out over the warehouse floor below. Owen would be down there with the employees, working on cabinet runs and packing up trucks for shipments. "We just want him to be Adam again."

A half smile slid over Jenny's mouth. "So do I, but he has to want it, too. Right now, he just wants to quit."

"And you think when I went over to fix the laundry situation, I let him quit?"

"He knows how to use Google to figure out the best bait for walleye, and to look up woodworking videos. I'm sure he could have figured out how to get those color runs out of a few shirts."

Jenny swallowed. She should tell Nancy that she'd asked Adam to move out, should tell her about the problems the boys were having. Nancy doted on her grandsons as much as she had doted on Adam and Aiden when they were little; she might understand better where Adam's mind was if she could see the impact he was having on their children.

Telling her, though, would be a betrayal of her husband. He didn't want to be seen as weak or injured. He wanted all of this to go away. Putting Nancy on his case might only serve to make him retreat even further into himself. Jenny couldn't bear to see him fade away any more. She couldn't live with him, not this way, but that didn't mean she wanted him to completely disappear from her life. So she held back the words.

"I appreciate that you tried to help him, but maybe the next time he calls, you let him figure it out for himself." She checked her watch. Fifteen minutes until coffee with the contractor. She needed to hurry. "I'll be back after two. Phone me if you need anything," she called over her shoulder as she hurried down the stairs leading to the street.

It took only a couple minutes to walk to the coffee shop, The Good Cuppa, downtown. Jenny ordered an iced coffee with extra ice before choosing a table in the corner. The contractor, a man in his midfifties, hiding a spare tire beneath his navy polo, arrived a few minutes later. He ordered black coffee, and when he got to the table, added four sugars to it.

"I thought Adam might make it," Leo McCartney said.

"He had another commitment." Funny how

easy it was to lie for her husband. Jenny pushed that thought out of her mind to focus on the contract at hand. "I worked up a few numbers on what we can provide your company. You know we do the design, and build on an individual basis, so our costs will be higher than those companies who offer prefabricated cabinetry."

McCartney flipped through the pages as he spoke. "My clients want economical, but they're will to pay for quality products. Cherry and mahogany, oak."

"We are familiar with all the best woods. Last winter, the design team tested out bamboo. We aren't quite ready with that option, but we're getting there."

McCartney sat back in his chair. "I like a prepared contact. I know about Adam's, ah, problems."

"He is still very involved." Jenny squeezed her hands together in her lap at yet another lie that slipped from her lips so easily. "Before the accident, we had divided the work. He built and designed, I handled contracts. Nothing has changed." Nothing except everything. Nothing was the same as it had been before the tornado in May, but if it took another year, she would stabilize her life. The business. The boys' outlooks.

"I'll take this to my office manager—" Leo grinned "—who also happens to be my wife. I'm sure she'll be as pleased as I am." He stuck his hand out and Jenny took it. "I'll be in touch."

When the older man had gone, Jenny sat back in her chair and closed her eyes. Step one in her plan to get the business back on track was complete. Leo McCartney was one of the best builders in their part of the state. He handled contracts for subdivisions as well as single builds. Partnering with him would lead to more contracts. A stronger profit margin. More financial stability for the boys would be important if—no, when—Adam moved out.

Now, she just needed her meeting with the Springfield distributor to go as well. She finished her coffee as she went over the proposal one more time.

ADAM'S ARMS WERE TIRED. He didn't think he'd expended this much energy since…well, since he'd been in high school. After taking the boys to school and stopping in at the coffee shop, he'd wheeled himself to the police station to see his friend James, who hadn't been in the office. So he'd continued to the new grandstand area, which had been built after the tornado decimated much of the downtown. It was impressive.

Several of his employees had worked on the project, and from what he could see from the outside, they'd done good work. The live oak that

Collin Tyler and Savannah Walters had planted soon after the dedication of the grandstand looked good, too. The two of them had placed a plaque, too, which read, "The strength to rebuild is one of the finest acts of courage."

Adam cringed as the words circled his mind. Walking away might not be courageous, but he would make sure Jenny and Frankie and Garrett would be okay before he bowed out of their lives.

He blew out a breath when he reached the corner of the street. All this wandering, which would have taken him an hour, max, before the accident, had taken closer to three, and he was starving. For a moment he considered going to Buchanan's to see if Jenny wanted to have lunch.

Not the best idea, after this morning when she'd suggested he move out. He didn't think a quick pop-in for lunch would help that situation. On the next block, Rock Pizza's sign beckoned, as did the smell of baking pizza. The growl from his stomach shocked him. It had taken a while to regain his appetite after leaving the hospital, but most of the time he still ate out of necessity, not for enjoyment.

A truck honked from the street and he raised his hand in a wave. Calvin Harris, an older gentleman who ran a dog school near Walters Ranch, stuck his arm out the truck window as he passed. A few minutes later, Adam made it to Rock Pizza, a fine sheen of sweat covering his face and rivulets running down his back. He was tempted to leave the chair, just to give his back a break from the vinyl covering. If something happened, though, it would be better to be safely sitting. He reached for the door handle and froze.

Jenny sat at a table inside with a man Adam didn't recognize. A handsome man. He forgot about food and simply stared. What about her having no time to do her job because his parents were messing things up? This didn't look like work to him. Which left one explanation: this was the real reason she had asked him to move out. Because she was ready to move on. It made much more sense than the idea of his doing laundry sending her over the edge.

His wife picked up a pizza slice from the tray on the table, took a bite, then laughed at something the man said. He looked to be solidly built, maybe five years older than Adam, with dirty blond hair that brushed his collar. Jenny tucked a wayward curl behind her ear and said something to the guy. He laughed in turn. Adam wanted to go inside, grab the guy by the collar of his shirt and drag him into the alley behind the pizza place. Or pretend he hadn't seen anything and just go home.

Except it wasn't his home, not anymore. She'd told him he should leave. Had accused him of not being present in their lives. He'd been there. She just hadn't paid attention.

She laughed with the guy at the table again. Adam couldn't sit here and watch his wife having lunch with another man. He backed away from the door before either of them noticed him. Something hot and prickly stabbed his belly, and he pushed against the wheels, wanting to get away from there as quickly as possible.

She wanted him to go.

He knew he should.

Adam rounded the corner that would lead to the pretty street where he'd been building a life with Jenny for the past three years. She wanted him to go. The house came into view, with its blue-shingled roof and blue shutters. Jenny had taken out the petunias and impatiens from the summer, replacing them with big pots overflowing with chrysanthemum blossoms. A riot of yellow and orange greeted him as he pushed the wheelchair into the driveway. She'd cut back the rose bushes, too, in preparation for the winter months.

He'd done nothing to get the house ready. Hadn't finished the backyard fence that she wanted. Hell, he hadn't even started it; the boxes of supplies still sat in the corner of the yard. He hadn't cleaned out the shed so the lawnmower and other yard tools had space. In his defense, he wasn't technically allowed any heavy work. But he could have hired a handyman to do it.

No wonder she wanted to move on. He wasn't holding up his part of the bargain. The minister had said for better or for worse, hadn't he? Adam couldn't see how things could get any worse than they were right now, and what was he doing to get through it? Nothing.

He took the ramp through the back door, and left the chair there before stripping down and tossing his sweaty clothes into the washer. He added the boys' pajamas and a few other items, then started the load. He needed a shower, then he needed to pack his things.

Adam froze. Packing meant leaving. Leaving meant more space between him and Jenny. She was already going to lunch with some dude he didn't know. If he wasn't at the house, would those lunches turn into dinners? Cold spread through his body at the thought of the other man in his house. On his couch.

In Adam's bed.

He wasn't moving to the B and B so some other guy could make Jenny laugh. If Adam was to reach his wife, he had to be here, not in some guest room at the Slippery Rock B and B. Being in the house, though, meant going against Jenny's wishes. Adam considered his options. Stay in the house even though she'd asked him to go. Move to the B and B, and put even more space between them. He didn't think Jenny would like him camping out in the backyard.

Camping out. That might work. Not in a tent.

Adam grabbed his cell phone from the counter and punched in his dad's phone number. Owen answered on the first ring.

"Hey, kid, how's it going today?"

"Fine. Dad, I was wondering if I could borrow the RV." Owen was silent on the other end of the line, so Adam kept talking. "Could you bring it by the house this afternoon? I'll explain when you get here."

"You want to borrow the RV?"

"Yeah."

"Why?" Owen asked after another long pause. Adam didn't have a good answer, at least, not one that wouldn't add even more stress to Jenny's life.

"I have to pick the boys up at three, but I'll be home until then."

"I guess I could drive it over in a little bit. But, son, the RV?"

"It's a surprise," Adam said, knowing how much his father liked surprises. "For Jenny." And that would ensure that Owen didn't say anything to Jenny until after the RV was here.

"I'll see you in a little bit, then," Owen said, and ended the call.

Adam put the phone down, then stepped into

the shower. He didn't know if he could reach Jenny, but he was going to try. First step, move out. Second step, win his wife back.

After showering, it took him only an hour to pack the few things he'd moved to the guest room. And that was just depressing, he thought. A duffel with a few clothes, and he was ready to go. He limped down the hall to the wheelchair. A horn honked in the drive, and he wheeled himself outside.

His father was backing his RV into the drive. Adam waited near the garage until his father had the camper positioned as he wanted it. He climbed down from the high seat.

"You gonna tell me what kind of RV surprise you have in mind for Jenny, son?"

"Thinking about taking a trip." He'd decided a little lie was better than telling his father he planned to live in the RV until he'd won Jenny back. Owen would tell Nancy, and Nancy would hover. Over him. Over Jenny. It would make things only worse. He wasn't sure Jenny could take any more worse, especially if it was linked to him. "Kids have a long weekend coming up, and you and Mom aren't heading back to Florida until after the holidays."

"Until you're ready to come back to work."

They would cross that bridge later. Adam wasn't sure he would ever be able to go back to

Buchanan's. Not if he couldn't do the things he used to do. It would be too hard. "We can figure that out later. You're sure this is okay?"

"Sure, it's just sitting in our side yard until we turn into snowbirds again. You kids can use it for as long as you like." Owen eyed him for a long moment and Adam cringed. His mother might be the one who hovered, but Owen was the parent who always seemed to know what was going on with his sons. "Weekend trip, hmm?"

"Yeah. Branson, maybe. Or down to Eureka Springs. We'll figure it out. I, ah, want it to be a surprise for Jenny. So don't mention it when you get back to the shop." He tried to find the right words. "This has all been really hard on her. A break will do us all some good."

"How was the doctor?"

"The same. He says this medication regimen might be the right solution." Adam wanted to be as certain as the doctor had seemed.

"He say anything more about the dog?"

"Jenny has a number to call." Adam definitely didn't want a dog. A dog would make this permanent. Wanting his wife back didn't mean he was ready to capitulate to everything. He was not going to be an epileptic for the rest of his life. Not if there was anything he could do to stop it.

"And the physical therapy?"

"Monday, Wednesday and Friday at the clinic."

Not that he'd made a single appointment yet. The lies were piling up faster than he wanted. "I, ah, need to go get the boys. I promised I'd walk them home this afternoon."

"Want me to drive you over?"

Adam shook his head. "I've got it covered. But thanks," he said.

Owen tossed the keys to Adam, who caught them one-handed. "Why don't the four of you come over for Sunday dinner this week? We can barbecue."

"I'll talk to Jenny."

Owen strode off toward downtown and the cabinetry shop. Adam waited until he was out of sight before tossing the packed duffel inside the RV. At least his father hadn't asked about the bag.

Adam started toward the school. He had a place to live; that was a good step forward. Now he just had to make sure he didn't end up living in his parents' RV for the rest of his life.

THE BOYS WANTED to go to the park after school. Then they wanted sodas. He convinced them to settle for lemonade from Bud's, and laughed with them as they told him about the school assembly that day.

The Mustang sat in the drive, looking dwarfed by the RV. Frankie's eyes widened. "Mamaw and Papaw are here?"

"Just the RV. We're borrowing it for a while. But we're going to their house for a barbecue on Sunday."

"Barbecue!" Garrett exclaimed, before grabbing his backpack from the wheelchair and rushing inside. Frankie followed, telling his younger brother to settle down. Adam had seen the excitement in his older son's eyes, though. Frankie loved visiting his grandparents, and they hadn't spent much time together since the tornado. Another misstep by Adam.

Well, he was fixing those missteps.

He started around the side yard to the back door ramp and stopped short. Jenny knelt in the garden, stabbing her spade into the rich earth over and over. Weeds landed in a bucket beside her, along with the last blooms of lazy Susan and daisies.

Her hips were covered in denim, and her legs were bare. A thin T-shirt covered her torso, and she'd pulled her wild curls into a ponytail that hid her face from him.

God, she was pretty. She had been his entire world for most of his life. And now she wanted something, *someone*, else. That prickly feeling hit his belly again.

Adam left the chair by the back door, and stepped onto the lawn for the first time in weeks. Grass tickled his feet. He'd shoved his feet into flip-flops before getting the RV keys from his father. He thought it might be the best feeling he'd had in a long time.

"Jenny," he said, and saw her shoulders stiffen at the sound of his voice. He hated that he made her uptight.

She turned, then stood quickly and started for the chair he'd left on the walk. "You aren't supposed to be—"

He reached out a hand and stopped her. His palm sizzled at the touch. She was so soft. He'd missed the feel of her skin. "I'm capable of walking in the backyard."

"But—"

"I'm not going to have a seizure, and I thought we should talk."

She studied him for a long moment. "Okay."

"I'm moving into the RV." He didn't know a better way to tell her what the plan was. Well, what part of the plan was. He didn't think she'd be receptive to the winning-her-back part, at least not right now. He stroked his hand up her arm. "I thought that might be less, ah, gossipy than moving into the B and B or with my parents."

"I think you moving anywhere other than this house is going to start a game of Telephone all over Slippery Rock."

"I told Dad we're going to take a weekend trip. Get away. No one has to know I'm actually living in there."

She raised an eyebrow at him. "You don't think the neighbors are going to notice?"

He hadn't thought of that. "I'll be careful. And this way I can still walk the boys to school and back. Take some of the burden off you."

She folded her arms across her chest. "Thank you. Adam. I…"

He couldn't stand that sad look in her eyes. Didn't want her to tell him she was glad he was moving out. He didn't want to talk about this at all. He wanted… It didn't matter what he wanted, he wasn't going to get it, not in the backyard. Not tonight.

"I went to the pizza place for lunch today."

Her eyes widened. "With your dad?"

"Before he dropped off the RV. It felt good to be out of the house, so I went downtown for coffee, and then wandered around a bit until lunch." He waited, but she didn't say anything. That feeling in his gut was back. He liked the prickliness even less than he liked that look he'd seen in Jenny's beautiful eyes a moment before.

He didn't want to talk about whoever she'd met for lunch or what that meant. He didn't want to talk at all. He just wanted to feel her mouth on his. Adam reached across the space between them and pulled her closer. Her mouth opened slightly, and her hazel eyes went dark.

"Jenny, I saw you," he said, but he didn't know what else to say.

"Saw me?" She frowned.

"At the table. With that guy."

"Mike Harrison?"

"That's his name?" Adam folded his arms across his chest. "Well, at least it isn't something stupid like Blaine."

Jenny tilted her head to the side. "Are you kidding me right now?"

"What? You ask me to move out and suddenly I'm not supposed to wonder if the stranger you're having lunch with is the reason?"

"You have got to be kidding!" Jenny mumbled the words under her breath, but she was only a few feet away from him, and Adam had no trouble understanding her. She brushed her hands together, knocking off most of the dirt from the flower beds. "You think I asked you to move out so I could move on with some random guy? A guy who takes me to our local pizza place, for lunch of all things, where we could be found out by everyone from the minister at the Methodist church to the ladies in my mother's bridge club?"

When she put it like that, no, it didn't seem plausible. Jenny didn't have a devious bone in her body. And she wasn't stupid.

"Didn't you recognize him?"

Adam blinked. Jenny kept talking.

"Mike Harrison is the distributor. From Springfield. The one who likes your outdoor designs so much he's willing to partner with our little company."

She'd been having lunch with the distributor?

"How would I recognize him? I've never met the man." The words came out more defensive than Adam intended, but he felt blindsided. More blindsided than he'd felt watching Jenny having lunch with a stranger. And this was so much worse, because that was the kind of man she deserved. Healthy, financially stable. A man who listened to her ideas. Adam hated him.

"You talked to him on the phone a hundred times. Saw his picture on his website."

So he had. But that didn't change the fact that the man on the website hadn't looked so…tall and fit as the man sitting with his wife in the pizza parlor. Adam opened his mouth to say something, anything, that would make more sense than the rest of this conversation. Words failed him. So he tilted his head and took her mouth with his.

Her lips were warm against his, soft and yielding. He'd expected hard. Wary. The softness spurred him on. He dipped his tongue inside her mouth, tasting her. Flames of attraction replaced the uneasy feeling in his belly. Adam wrapped one arm around her slender waist and cupped her jaw with his opposite hand. She trembled, but made no move to embrace him. She didn't draw away, though.

Adam pulled her body more firmly against his, catching his fingers in the belt loop of her jeans. A little squeak escaped her throat, then Jenny's arms were wrapped around his neck, holding his mouth against hers. Her tongue pushed into his mouth, as if she were as hungry for him as he was for her. Her small fingers teased his nape. He wanted more.

Wanted to feel her body under him, not just against him. Wanted to watch her head fall back against the pillows in their big bed. He'd settle for a few more minutes like this, though, in the soft grass with the sun sinking into the lake behind them.

"Jenny," he said against her mouth, and it was as if his voice broke the spell that had settled over the backyard. Jenny pulled away, putting her hands to her mouth.

"This isn't a good idea," she said, backing away from him. "For the record, I'm not having secret lunches with men I'm romantically interested in. I'm not romantically interested in anyone right now, and I'm not sure I want to be anytime soon. You're moving out. We need to set boundaries or this is going to get messy."

He didn't want boundaries, but Jenny was nearly to the sidewalk now. Her heel hit the concrete, but she caught herself midstumble. Adam stepped forward, but she held out her hands as if warding him off.

"I'm fine. I'm fine," she said, as if reassuring herself with the words. She reached behind her, grasping the doorknob. "I, ah, dinner will be ready at six," she said, and fled inside the house.

She was gone. Adam swallowed. For now, she was gone, but for a moment, she'd been right here with him.

He just had to keep her with him next time.

CHAPTER SIX

Jenny closed the door to the bedroom she'd shared with Adam for the past three years, and pressed her back against the cool wood. She put her fingers to her mouth. She could still feel his mouth on hers and, damn it, it shouldn't have felt so right.

Kissing him was…a mistake. A confusing, annoying, end-of-the-world mistake. One she wished she could repeat again right this second. In her mind, she knew she shouldn't do it again. Shouldn't go down those stairs.

God, but she wanted to. To kiss her husband until… Until what? Kissing him wouldn't change anything. Kissing Adam again would only muddy the waters between them even more. She loved the man, but she couldn't live with him anymore. Not like this. She couldn't be the devoted wife—couldn't be like his mother, who had always fallen in line with what Owen wanted. Or her own mother, who ignored her husband until he did something sweet like send her a bouquet of lilies.

Jenny kicked off her tennis shoes and picked up the bottle of water from her bedside table. Sipped.

She wasn't being fair, and she knew it. Nancy was a smart, capable woman who happened to like living out of an RV with her husband six months of every year. She liked owning a cabinet shop, and couldn't understand why her son had wanted to expand the family business, though she had still been supportive of the move. Until the tornado, anyway.

As for Margery Hastings, she was self-centered and spoiled and distant. Jenny didn't want to be any of those things, either. She wanted… Jenny sighed. She wanted to be like one of those confident, capable, professional women she watched on television. They all had careers and aspirations and went after the things they wanted. She had only ever chased Adam, had never thought about her own career. Maybe she should have listened to her father.

Doug had given his blessing when Adam proposed on Jenny's graduation night, but he'd suggested—several times—that she go on to college. Had even offered to pay for the courses. She'd thought the idea was silly. All she had wanted was Adam.

She still wanted him, but wanted more, too. Did that make her selfish like her mother? She didn't want to be selfish.

Jenny tossed her grubby jeans into a corner, and grabbed clean shorts, a T-shirt and underthings from a drawer before turning on the shower in her private bathroom. Considered briefly adding a sweater to the pile of clothes, but another layer wasn't going to stop her from wanting to kiss her husband. Neither was a hot shower, so she turned the water to cold, then stepped under the chilly spray.

She needed to get her head on straight before she saw Adam at dinner. She had a feeling she was going to need all her wits about her or she'd fall right back into those old habits.

ADAM WOKE TO a shaft of brilliant September sun, and for the first time in a long time, he wasn't mad at the sun for putting out the darkness of the night. He still didn't know what his diagnosis meant for his family, but he knew he wanted to be with them. Maybe that made him selfish.

He stretched his arms over his head and hit the soft headboard in the sleeper compartment of the RV. It was a Wednesday, not exactly the first day of the week, but he figured fresh starts didn't have to begin on a Monday. Or in January. He would start here, and he would start with breakfast.

His knee protested when he stood, but he made it into the compact shower of the RV without banging either his injured knee or his hip on the wall. Another win. Taking the narrow steps to the driveway was much harder than stepping up into the vehicle last night, but the wheelchair was only a few feet away inside the garage. He punched in the code to open the door and dropped into the chair. He rubbed his shoulders and biceps. Taking that trek around town yesterday wasn't the smartest move he'd made. What was it the doctor said? Baby steps. Wheeling himself to school with the boys and then all over downtown was more than a baby step.

Pain wasn't a bad thing, though. He could deal with sore muscles.

In the kitchen he grabbed a pan from the drawer beneath the oven, eggs from the fridge and bread from the basket. Some women liked crêpes or fancy waffles. His Jenny liked scrambled eggs on dry toast. He scrambled the eggs in a bowl while the pan heated, then poured them in to begin cooking, and put bread in the toaster oven.

The boys' pounding feet sounded on the stairs.

"Dad!" Garrett launched himself at Adam's wheelchair. He caught the boy and hugged him, taking a long moment to soak in the smell of the baby shampoo Jenny still used on the boys. "You're up. You gonna walk us to school again? So we don't have to take the mom bus?"

"It's the Mustang, dummy, not the bus." Frankie

rolled his eyes at his younger brother, and Garrett narrowed his eyes at the insult.

"Let's put that word away for a while." Adam was certain he and Aiden had called one another much worse than *dummy*, but something about the way Frankie said it made Adam's skin tighten. "How about scrambled eggs and toast for breakfast?"

"With jelly?" Garrett eyed the plates on the counter.

"Jelly on scrambled eggs? Where else would it go?" Adam teased. He put eggs on the plates, then reached for the jelly as Garrett grabbed at his arm, trying to wrest the jar from his hand.

"On the toast, Dad, on the toast."

Adam twisted his mouth as if considering the merits of toast and jelly versus scrambled eggs and jelly. He shot a glance at Garrett. "You're sure it goes on the toast?"

The little boy giggled. "I'm sure, Dad."

Frankie mumbled something under his breath. Something that sounded awfully close to *stupid*. Adam would address that later.

Once the boys were settled, he prepped a plate for Jenny, then rolled the wheelchair into the living room and eyed the stairs. This was not going to be fun.

He was halfway up the stairs, and starting to think installing a lift would be a brilliant idea, when Jenny appeared at the top. She wore jeans with a rip in the knee, and a sleeveless red blouse. She'd left her hair down around her shoulders, and Adam caught his breath.

"What are you doing?" She hurried to him and put her arm around his waist, taking some of his weight.

"Bringing you breakfast." He gestured with the covered plate in his hand. Breakfast in bed had seemed like a good idea in the RV. A way to show her he could change, could be the man he'd once been. Halfway up the steps, with his knee and hip screaming at him to stop climbing, breakfast in bed seemed more like torture.

"You didn't have to do that. Come on, let's get you back down the stairs."

He would protest, but at this point, sitting in the wheelchair for a little while sounded like a vacation from the pain. "I wanted to. You were right. I haven't been pulling my weight around here. I'm sorry," he said, as they reached the living room. "I didn't realize I was taking advantage."

"You weren't… I just…" Jenny reached for the plate. She sucked her lower lip between her white teeth. "Thank you for breakfast."

"You're welcome." He wanted to tell her things would be different now. He couldn't just tell her, though, not after the distance he'd put between them because of his injury. He had to show her.

THE SILENCE BETWEEN them was deafening. It shouldn't be this hard to talk to Adam, especially now that he knew where she stood. Especially when he was offering her apology eggs.

Seeing him on the stairs, the hard kink of his mouth showing the pain, she'd had to catch her breath. But he'd kept climbing. He wore an old Slippery Rock High T-shirt and jeans this morning, had Nikes on his feet. Normal clothes, so why were butterflies attacking her belly? And now she was staring at him.

The grandfather clock chimed eight, and she grabbed at the conversation starter. "How did you sleep?"

"Fine. The bed in the RV is remarkably comfortable."

"Your mom put one of those memory foam mattresses in when they bought it, remember? She dragged me to every mattress store in Springfield until she found one willing to deal with the space issues of the RV." That had been a fun trip. They'd shopped and had lunch, and Nancy had talked about the places she and Owen would see in retirement. Jenny had been making plans for the business expansion, filled with excitement about the future. Had that been only three years ago? It seemed like a lifetime.

Jenny sighed. Last week seemed like a lifetime ago. The doctor's appointment seemed like a year.

"Right, and Dad and I went fishing."

They'd been under contract with a construction company out of Joplin, but Owen insisted there was time, and if Nancy and Jenny were shopping, they could go fishing. Jenny had wanted to argue the point—she and Nancy taking a day off from the office and phones wasn't the same as Owen and Adam not meeting a deadline—but she hadn't. Because good wives followed their husbands' lead. Adam wanted to go fishing with his dad, and so he went. In the end, they made the contractor's deadline easily, so what had it really mattered?

It mattered because it was one more example of Adam doing what he wanted, and of her going along with him.

And today he'd made her breakfast, something he'd done only a handful of times in their married life. Because she'd given him an ultimatum? It would make sense. And it didn't matter if breakfast was his way of manipulating her or was a true symbol of his contrition. Jenny wanted more out of life than to blindly follow Adam's lead. She wanted to be her own person, have her own dreams, build a life in which she could be proud.

"I'll just go check on the boys. Thank you, again, for breakfast." Jenny turned toward the kitchen.

She was only twenty-six. There was still plenty

of time to build a good life, plenty of time to stop blindly following.

But it was nice that he'd thought of her.

CHAPTER SEVEN

ADAM DIDN'T TELL Jenny he was going to physical therapy. He didn't want her to feel obligated to take him.

More to the point, he didn't want her to see how hard things were for him now.

The PT nurse adjusted his leg, setting the ultrasound machine under his knee, where his hamstring had separated.

"So you're going to feel heat for a while, and maybe some light pulsing. You just have to lie here, relax, and let the machine and I do the work."

He'd expected something more…strenuous than an ultrasound machine under his knee. "Then what?"

"We'll work you up to the recumbent bike, maybe a slow treadmill, but that's down the line. Once we have the go-ahead for the hip surgery. You know, if you'd started on this knee a few weeks ago, the hamstring might be showing better improvement."

More ifs. Adam put his hands behind his head.

If he'd listened to the doctors. If he'd started the physical therapy.

If he'd just stayed in the storm shelter at the warehouse instead of running for the day care where the boys were.

If he hadn't made Jenny feel as though he didn't want her around.

But he had done—or not done—all those things.

Seeing Jenny with that guy the day before had been more of an eye-opener than all the doctors' appointments had been. This wasn't just affecting him. Her life had changed, too. She was carrying all the burden, while he'd been sulking. Contemplating just walking away from everything. When he saw her at that table, though, he'd realized he didn't want to walk away. He wanted to figure out how to make this life he'd been handed three months ago work for him.

"I'd like to try the recumbent bike today."

The therapist kept working the ultrasound machine under his leg. After a few minutes, she looked at him. "It would be better to have a couple more ultrasound treatments first."

"I can handle it." The sooner he got the parts of his body he could control under control, the better.

The therapist shrugged, but when the half hour with the ultrasound was over, she led him to the bikes.

JENNY SAT IN the lounge area at the local boutique. It was just after noon, and she had a million things to do at work. But when a girlfriend called about picking out her wedding dress, you dropped everything to go. When two called at the same time, participation was mandatory.

Besides, she'd needed to get out of Buchanan's before the sickly sweet scent of a dozen lilies made her ill. She hated lilies, and not just because the flower was her mother's favorite. Although, she had to admit, that was part of the problem.

Twenty minutes after the lilies arrived on her desk, a dozen red roses had showed up. The combination of lilies and roses was almost too much to deal with. A rosebush? She was all over it. A peace lily in a great planter? Definitely. But not cut in vases with baby's breath and greenery. Adam had only signed his name to the cards in the vases, which was just as well. She didn't want flowery sentiments that he didn't mean to go along with the flowers she didn't need.

Savannah Walters, who had returned to Slippery Rock just before the tornado last spring, stepped out of the dressing room door. Her light caramel skin glowed against the white dress. Pearls and rhinestones embellished the bodice, and the low-cut neck showed just enough cleavage that Jenny knew Collin would be practically salivating when Savannah walked down the aisle toward him. She'd pinned her thin braids up, but long strands still fell over her shoulders.

"Too much?"

Jenny could only shake her head. She'd barely known Savannah before she left Slippery Rock to try out for a talent show in Los Angeles, but since her return, the two women had spent a lot of time together. Collin and Adam being such good friends had pushed them together, but the friendship that blossomed between them wasn't only because their significant others were buddies.

"Exactly enough," she said, sipping the iced tea the store clerk had brought her a few minutes before.

Savannah twirled before the three-way mirror, the skirt of the dress billowing prettily around her. Her feet were bare, and Jenny had an image of her walking between the apple trees at Collin's orchard rather than down the aisle of one of the local churches. Barefoot. With flowers in her hair instead of the traditional bridal veil. Oh, it would be perfect.

"You're sure?"

Mara, Savannah's future sister-in-law, stepped from the other fitting room. "Definitely," she said.

Mara and her fiancé, James Calhoun, had scandalized the town when news of their long-term affair hit the grapevines. But they were so perfect for one another that most of the gossip had died quickly. That, and the fact that they had one of the cutest two-year-olds in the universe. Everybody loved baby Zeke. James, who was in line to become the next chief of police, was a straight-and-narrow kind of guy. Mara, who had led the prankster ring that Collin, Adam and Aiden, James, and Levi Walters had been part of in high school, added levity to the couple.

Savannah gasped when she saw Mara's dress. "Oh, yours, too."

At first glance, the plain sheath dress looked ordinary. But when Jenny focused, she saw varying hues of white and ivory that created a swirling effect. It was perfect for Mara. Both dresses were just…perfect. Pain pricked Jenny's heart. Her friends were in the throes of passionate affairs, while she was…ending something that she'd thought would last forever. It was all just too much.

"You don't think it's too—" Mara twisted to the side, putting her hand over her belly "—young looking? I know I'm not fat, but this baby bump is never going to go completely away."

"It's beautiful," Jenny said. "You're both just so beautiful." Her voice cracked on the last word.

"Sweetie, what's wrong?" Mara sat beside her on the overstuffed sofa, crumpling the beautiful dress.

"Don't ruin that gown." Jenny tried to push her

back to her feet, but Mara wouldn't budge. "I'm fine, really."

"People who are fine don't look like they're about to vomit at the sight of two women in wedding dresses," Savannah added, sitting on her other side.

"Or like they want to burn every wedding dress in this place," Mara said. The comment earned a raised eyebrow from the clerk.

"I'm not going to burn this place down, and I'm not going to throw up."

"Then what?" Savannah and Mara spoke in unison, then laughed. They had become a sisterly unit, along with Mara's teenage sister, Amanda. While Jenny had been desperately trying to hold her life together, their lives were falling into place like clockwork.

God, was she jealous? Under the anger she was trying desperately to hold on to, did she not want her friends to be happy? Sure, she and Adam had eloped, but she'd suggested it. Their parents hadn't been thrilled when they announced their plans, but they'd fallen in line. Jenny hadn't wanted her mother's version of a Slippery Rock society wedding, and at the time, she and Adam hadn't had any money. It seemed much easier to cross the Arkansas border and elope. And now, seeing her friends ready to celebrate their weddings, she couldn't even manage a supportive smile without automatically going to her own shortcomings? How pathetic could she be?

"Adam sent me flowers," she said miserably. It was more than the flowers. It was another symptom of what was wrong between the two of them.

"And that's a bad thing?" Mara cocked her head to the side.

"A dozen red roses and a lily bouquet. They're currently competing for the right to perfume the entire Buchanan warehouse and cabinet shop." Jenny sighed. "And I'm being a complete bitch about it, I know. Today is about finding the two of you the perfect dresses, not complaining about the mess my relationship is in."

Mara and Savannah exchanged a look. "We're going to need to change to get to the bottom of this," Savannah said.

"And we'll need coffee," Jenny said, feeling tired all the way to her bones.

Savannah studied Jenny for a long moment. "Nope, that expression calls for some kind of frothy, decadent, highly alcoholic beverage. Slippery Slope?" she asked, naming the local bar, where she'd been a waitress before leaving town for Los Angeles.

"Merle isn't going to be happy to see us," Mara said, mentioning the curmudgeonly but totally loveable bar owner.

"Merle is always happy to see his favorite ex-waitress." Savannah checked her watch. "We've got another ninety minutes before school releases. Plenty of time to sob into a drink and still get Frankie and Garrett from school."

Jenny sighed again. "Adam is walking them home today."

"Perfect. We'll have time for two drinks, then."

Twenty minutes later, the three of them slid into a side booth at the Slippery Slope. Juanita, the waitress, laughed when they ordered margaritas. "Merle's going to have to break out the blender. He just decided enough of the summer traffic had died down that he could go back to beers and shots."

"Girl talk requires more than tequila and Miller Lite," Mara said.

Juanita winked. "It'll do him some good to get out of the beer rut, anyway."

When she was gone, Mara focused her attention on Jenny, who tried to focus on tearing a napkin from the dispenser against the wall into tiny pieces. "And?"

"I'm just feeling sorry for myself." And she wasn't going to put her relationship issues on the shoulders of her best friends. Not when they were both so happy. Friends didn't bring friends down.

"Because Adam sent you flowers?"

"Because of a lot of things." She'd started this by not keeping it together while Savannah and

Mara were trying on their wedding dresses. Time to retreat, let them get back to being happy and in love. Except she'd made this mess by not talking about what she wanted. Maybe talking to Mara and Savannah would help her figure out what it was she did want.

"He's been so withdrawn since he came home. Since he woke up in the hospital, actually." She pulled another napkin from the dispenser, needing something to do with her hands so they wouldn't shake. "We had a fight the other day, about laundry of all things, and I told him if he was going to keep moping around the house instead of working on getting better, he could move out."

Savannah's jaw dropped. "You asked Adam to move out?"

Jenny shrugged. This was a mistake. Taking time out of her day to support Mara and Savannah was one thing. Crying on their shoulders was something else entirely. She would not cry over Adam, not now. Jenny focused on the mass of torn paper and began pushing the pieces into little piles in the middle of the table.

"But you and Adam are…you and Adam. You've always been together," said Mara.

No, they weren't together. Hadn't been since the tornado. "He's different since the accident, or maybe I am. He sits in the living room, staring out at the world most days. Doesn't do his physical therapy, lies to the doctors about his progress, won't consider options the doctors suggest. And while he's staring out the window, I'm running the business, taking care of the boys and the house, keeping his parents from turning Buchanan's back into the small cabinet shop they built before retirement. I asked him to do a load of laundry. He called his mom to clean up after the colors ran together."

Savannah blinked. Mara just stared.

"And so he sent you flowers to apologize for all of that?" Mara asked.

"I think so. I'm not really sure—the card just read 'Adam.' No note." She pushed the piles into one big heap. "The flowers are fine, but it's just another symptom of what's wrong between us."

"And what's wrong?" Savannah tapped the back of Jenny's hand. "He isn't pulling his weight, I get that. But what's really wrong, Jen?"

"Everything." She closed her eyes for a moment, and when she opened them, Savannah and Mara reached across the table, stilling her hands with theirs. She tried to smile, but couldn't. "Until the tornado and his injury, he was still high-school Adam. Hanging out, playing with the boys but not disciplining them. I did that. And I did the grocery shopping and cooking, and cleaned up after everyone." Jenny tried to slow her words, but now that she was talking, it was as if they couldn't get out fast enough. "And I worked at the shop. I didn't complain, not about any of it. I—I didn't care that he decided our vacations, and I liked helping him figure out how to turn Buchanan's into something bigger. I liked doing the boys' laundry and making their lunches. I liked our life." She took a breath. "Then he got hurt, and I had all that plus trips to the hospital, and trying to calm frightened children. And his parents swooped in and started trying to turn our life into their life. And he's home now, but nothing is the way it was. And even if it could be, I don't think I want it to be like that anymore. I don't want to be Nancy Buchanan. I want…" Jenny considered her next words carefully. She wanted the old, happy Adam back, but she didn't want him to just be the happy-go-lucky guy who played with their children and thought a road trip to a NASCAR race was the height of adventure.

"I want more," she said, "and I know that sounds heartless."

"There's nothing wrong with supporting the person you love." Savannah clasped her hands on the table. "And none of that sounds heartless."

Juanita brought their drinks. "Merle says if you want refills, find another bar. But don't worry, I know how to work the blender better than he does. Anything else?"

Mara shook her head.

"Then I'll check back in a bit. You girls have a good afternoon." The older woman returned to the bar, where she began arranging glasses. Jenny realized they were the only patrons. At least no one would overhear her.

"What if that person doesn't support me back?"

Mara shook her head. "Adam loves you. He's head over heels, always has been."

"But he never asks what I want, what I need. The flowers are proof of that."

"How? They're flowers."

"I don't like cut flowers. Give me a planter or a package of seeds. Gardening is my thing, not watching cut flowers go limp. I didn't carry cut flowers at our wedding, I've never ordered flowers for either of our mothers or for our house, and—" she sipped her drink, needing the false courage the tequila offered "—roses are his mother's favorite flowers. Lilies are my mom's. He didn't know what I'd like, so he sent me things our mothers would like."

"Jenny." Mara reached across the table. "Maybe he—"

"He doesn't know me. I've been married to him for nine years. We dated all through high school. My husband doesn't know me, and rather than attempting to get to know me, he's trying to turn me into either my mom or his. I don't want to be his mother, and I sure as hell don't want to be mine." That was the crux of the problem. Jenny knew she'd let Adam make a lot of the decisions in their marriage, but there were things he should know about her.

Like the fact that her favorite flowers were daisies, and she preferred them in planters, not vases.

"Have you tried talking to him?" Savannah picked up her drink.

"You mean before I melted down over the laundry?" Jenny grunted. "Not really." She'd yelled at him. Made a few accusations. But actually talking about their problems? It all seemed so selfish—as if her feelings of being overwhelmed were so much more significant than the brain injury he was dealing with. "And now I'm not sure I should, because I asked him to move out, which he did." Jenny wanted to pull the words back into her mouth.

Savannah set her glass down, hard. "Adam moved out?"

Jenny lifted her drink to her lips, needing a moment to decide just how to deal with the bomb she'd dropped. Hell, maybe she should go with it. Telling Savannah and Mara wasn't the same as putting more strain and stress on Adam's shoulders.

"Technically, he moved into his parents' RV. Which is now parked in our driveway. He thinks, until we decide exactly what we're doing, it will be easier this way. You know, we won't have his parents or mine asking questions. No gossip around town. Easier for the boys, who haven't even realized he's living in the trailer and not the house."

"How are his parents in the dark when it's their RV?" Mara asked. She snagged a peanut from the bowl on the table, then sipped her drink.

"He told them we were going on a vacation. It's only been a day, so no one is asking questions." She would know if their neighbor, Mrs. Hess, was suspicious about the RV in the drive. The older woman would have been on the phone with Nancy immediately, and Jenny's morning would have been spent talking about some fantasy road trip instead of finalizing the numbers for the contract with the Springfield distributor.

"Do you want him to move out? I mean, farther than the RV?" Mara finished her drink and signaled Juanita for another round.

She did. Definitely. Probably. God, why did this have to be so hard? If he'd just not kissed her, everything would be fine. Okay, maybe not *fine,* but she wouldn't be so wishy-washy about it. But he had kissed her, and that brought back a lot of those old, happy, sexy feelings. Feelings that made her want to just go back to the way things had been. Her carrying the load while Adam lived his life.

Then there were the flowers, which weren't

what she wanted, but wasn't the thought behind them the important part? So he'd gotten the format wrong; at least he'd thought about her.

"He made me breakfast this morning, and that was sweet. But he sent me flowers that are so not me it's not even funny." Jenny sighed. She pushed her glass away. She didn't need alcohol to make this decision for her. She didn't need alcohol to numb the pain that Adam not appreciating all the things she did for him caused. She needed to feel the pain, and maybe then she would be able to make the changes to her life that would really matter. Changes like asking for what she wanted. Changes like having a career that she enjoyed and was good at.

Changes like having a man in her life who enjoyed not only her body, but her mind, and who took her wants and needs into consideration, too.

"He's *trying*. I've been waiting for him to start living again since that first day he woke up in the hospital. He walked the kids to school yesterday and this morning, and I know that's great for the boys, but that's *my* job. What happens to them when he stops paying attention to them again?" And what would happen to her? God, she didn't think she could take another round of Adam's cold shoulder treatment.

"What if this is the wake-up call he's needed— you know, so that he can fully appreciate what you're bringing to the table?" Savannah asked. It was the question Jenny had been struggling with from the moment he'd kissed her the night before.

"Are you kidding me?" Mara shook her head. "No—"

"Mara," Savannah began, but she continued talking.

"Just no. Adam has been one of my best friends since we were kids. I love him like a brother. But being with James, having Zeke… Loving someone isn't only about what he or she can do for you. It's about what you do for each other, putting their needs above your own. You have to be strong, Jenny. You have to know what you want, and you have to know what you're willing to give up to get it."

Give up. Jenny swallowed. She had to give him up, no matter how sweet he was being right now. This could all be an act. Making her breakfast, sending her flowers. Walking the kids to school a couple times. That kiss in the backyard. Those could all only be ways to get her to give in one more time. And then what? She couldn't go back to doing everything for Adam, and getting nothing in return. She had to let him go, for her own peace of mind. She released the breath she'd been holding.

"Jenny?" Savannah asked, her voice quiet in the still bar.

"We're right here with you," Mara added.

Tears welled behind her eyelids, but Jenny refused to let them fall. She wouldn't cry for Adam. She wouldn't cry for herself. She had friends. Two boys depending on her. A business to save. She would be strong. "I love Adam, but I can't stay married to a man who doesn't value me. My opinion. My dreams, my plans. I just can't."

Mara put her hand over Jenny's, and then Savannah added hers to the pile. "What can we do?" they asked in unison.

Jenny offered a wan smile. "If he sends me flowers again, remind me that I like them planted and not cut." And if he tried to kiss her again, well, she just wouldn't let that happen. No more kisses from Adam Buchanan. They were too dangerous.

ADAM AND THE boys rolled into the driveway at three thirty to find a classic Corvette with California plates parked beside the RV.

"Uncle Aiden," the boys said, and raced ahead of Adam. He heard chattering and laughter from the backyard, but didn't want to be in a wheelchair the first time his twin saw him postepilepsy. Adam left the chair at the side of the house and walked around the corner.

There, sitting at Jenny's slate-and-iron patio table, was a man who looked almost exactly like him. Same hair, same stubble, although Aiden's was probably more of a fashion statement than laziness. Or not being allowed to use a razor for fear of cutting his throat if a seizure hit. There were enough differences that they weren't considered identical, though. Where Adam's eyes were green, Aiden's were more hazel. Adam had the scar on his neck from the car accident in high school, Aiden had a broken nose from going after the opposing team's defensive back without his helmet on. But the basics were all there—six foot two inches tall, muscular build, tanned skin.

"Hey," Adam said.

"Hey," Aiden returned. "No chair?"

Adam shrugged. "It's more of a guideline than a requirement." Although his knee was already protesting at the short walk around the corner. Or maybe that was from the twenty minutes he'd managed on the recumbent bike at PT.

"Either way." Aiden stood, hefting Garrett with him. The little boy giggled when he lifted him into the air, then swooped him back to ground level.

"Guys, there's string cheese in the fridge. Go grab a snack while I help Aiden unpack."

Once they had disappeared through the back door, Adam turned to Aiden. "Bags?"

His brother shook his head. "I'm staying at the B and B. You don't need me underfoot."

Actually, Adam had been thinking that the company might ease some of the strain between him and Jenny. Force them to look on the brighter side of things instead of dwelling in the past. He knew that was a chickenshit way of dealing with the problems in their marriage, but wouldn't they both be better off if they forgot all that stuff and started fresh?

"We have plenty of room."

"And I'm not used to living with anyone else. It'll be better this way. You'll be sick of me after our first day of working together, anyway. This way, we can both have our space."

The brothers stood staring at each other for a long moment. Adam considered leaving it at that, but if things were going to change in his life, he was going to have to do more than leave the past in the past. With his brother, and with his wife.

"Do you think you'll ever forgive me?"

"There's nothing to forgive. I painted Simone's phone number on the water tower after she dumped me, the same as you."

"You didn't plant the petty cash from Dad's safe in her car." Adam wanted to sit at the table, take some of the pressure off his leg. Facing Aiden, though, seemed more important. "After the accident, when they told me I couldn't play football, you'd just signed your letter of intent to play ball in California. I heard Mom and Dad talking about you deferring for a year."

"You were already working for Dad. He needed you there because he'd had to lay off a couple other guys. The doctors weren't sure yet how long you would need the halo." Aiden shrugged. "It would have been a year."

Adam didn't hear a trace of anger in his brother's voice. This time. When Aiden realized Adam had planted money on her, that she'd run away because of it, there had been rage. Fiery rage.

"It would have been your whole life. You'd have kept dating Simone because she was easy to date, and she'd have made sure you didn't take the scholarship, not even after you deferred enrollment. She'd already cheated on you—"

"And I was so mad, I went along with the plan to paint her phone number on the water tower."

"But she apologized and cried, and you took her back. I knew she had to do something that would hurt someone other than you. Otherwise, she'd have hurt you."

"And you planted the petty cash from Buchanan's in her car."

Adam picked up the water bottle from the table and turned it in his hands. "I was the one who wanted to stay. I wasn't going to be the reason you had to stay, too." Maybe that was why bad things kept happening to him. Because Fate was a cruel bitch who didn't care that he'd been a stupid teenager reeling from a near-death experience. Fate wanted to make him pay for being a callous, careless eighteen-year-old.

"It was a long time ago."

"I didn't know you were in love with her. If I had—"

Aiden shook his head. "You weren't wrong. I'd never have gone to college if Simone was in my life. If I hadn't gone, I wouldn't have the job I have now, wouldn't be living in California."

"It could have gone differently."

"You mean you could have not framed her as a burglar, and she could have not run away with a twentysomething biker with Shark tattooed across his neck?" Aiden shrugged. "Yeah, that probably wouldn't have happened."

Adam shoved his hands in his pockets. "I didn't want you to feel like you had to stay here, especially after the accident when I totaled Dad's car. I knew you needed to go." Adam had never wanted more than Slippery Rock. Aiden had always wanted more. It was the thing that most set the two of them apart. More than the slightly different eye color, more than the scar on Adam's neck or the epilepsy he now had to deal with.

Aiden had wanted a bigger life, and now here he was, back in small-town Slippery Rock.

"She and I weren't like you and Jenny, Adam."

Aiden putting it like that made him cringe. Were he and Jenny really the Adam and Jenny everyone thought they were? Because, from everything she'd been saying, their problems began long before the tornado ripped their lives apart, only he'd been too blind to notice. He couldn't say so, not yet. Aiden was his twin, but Adam had torn their relationship apart a long time ago.

"Do you know where Simone is?"

Aiden shook his head. "It was ages ago. Who marries the girl he dated in high school, anyway?"

Adam pasted a smile on his face. If Aiden could play this down, he would follow suit. "You mean other than your miles-more-attractive twin?" Marrying Jenny had been the best thing he'd ever done in his life, and he'd nearly thrown her and their marriage away. He still wasn't sure he could fix that, but he wanted to try.

Breakfast and the flowers were a good start. Nothing made his mom happier than when Owen surprised her with flowers. Showing Jenny he could take on more of the household chores was a good step, too. One breakfast wouldn't make up for the years she had done most of the cooking, but it was a beginning. Plus, he was actually going to physical therapy now. That was another good thing, although that benefited him more than it would Jenny.

He eyed his brother. "You up for manning the grill tonight? We should surprise Jenny with dinner."

"Sure. Steaks?"

Adam nodded and started for the house. "It's good to have you home, at least for now."

Aiden was quiet for a long moment. Once they were inside, he said, "It's good to be home." He looked around the room, taking in the refinished floors and renovated kitchen. "You've done a lot of work here."

Discarded string cheese wrappers were strewn across the kitchen table. Adam gathered them and threw them in the trash. The boys were nowhere to be seen. Probably upstairs watching afternoon cartoons or something. He'd check on them in a little while.

"Renovated everything. Turned Grandpa's den into a guest room." Their grandfather had been the superintendent of Slippery Rock schools.

Adam pulled steaks from the freezer and set them on the countertop to begin thawing. "I'm glad you're here, Aiden." His brother grabbed a beer from the fridge. He offered Adam another, but Adam shook his head. "Can't. Not with the medications I'm on. I'll take a Coke, though."

Aiden tossed a cold can and Adam caught it one-handed. "I'm here as long as you need me." Adam started to speak, but his brother stopped him. "And if you don't, I'm here anyway. I didn't leave only because of Simone, and I didn't stay away because of her or you. I just had to figure out who I was, away from you. Away from Buchanan Cabinetry."

Adam sat at the table, and Aiden joined him. "Did you figure it out?"

"I did."

Adam considered his next words for a long moment. "Did you figure out women? Because you could let me in on the secret. If you know it."

"Everything okay with Jenny?"

Adam waved a hand. "Sure. Fine. I've just been thinking, you know, about what women want. Like, Mom always talked about going to Paris, but Dad won't travel outside the States, so she's never gone. You think she actually wants to go?"

"I don't think you can base a healthy relationship on our parents, A. They love each other, don't get me wrong, but Dad is the one in charge of that relationship, and that's the way Mom wants it."

Then what was Jenny so mad about? She'd never so much as suggested a vacation destination for him to shoot down, but she was acting as if he'd treated her as an afterthought.

"Why's the RV in the driveway?"

"Thinking about taking Jenny and the boys on a weekend trip." It was amazing how easy it was to lie to everyone lately. "Dad offered the RV." What was one more lie on top of the thousands he'd already told?

"You know, Jenny doesn't seem like the camping type."

"RVing isn't like camping." Adam finished his soda and crumpled the can in his hand.

"It's also not Paris. You should ask her where she wants to go." Aiden stood, put his empty beer bottle and Adam's soda can in the recycling bin. "In my experience, what women want is to be asked, and not just about vacations."

"Yeah." Adam stood in turn. "Yeah, that makes sense."

Asking. That was going to be hard to do without also admitting he didn't already know the answer. But if asking Jenny a few things would show her he was willing to change, he'd ask. Everything.

CHAPTER EIGHT

THE NEXT MORNING, Jenny woke with a new sense of purpose. She was not going to let her failing marriage diminish the happiness of either Savannah or Mara. If yesterday showed her one thing, it was that she wasn't alone. Good friends couldn't take the place of her husband, but it was nice to know she had support. There was more right in her life than she had allowed herself to see in the past few months.

She had a job she was good at, sons who surprised her every day and friends who listened while she talked herself around to the most important realization she'd had in her life: she would never have what she wanted if she didn't ask for it. Having a husband who sent flowers? That was a nice thing. Having a husband who didn't know the type of flowers she liked? Wasn't. She deserved more than to be an afterthought.

If Adam truly wanted to change, she would support him in whatever ways she could, starting with helping him to be less self-absorbed. A man should know the kind of flowers his wife liked. That was a basic thing.

She glanced out the window, saw the RV parked in the driveway and sighed. Only about fifty feet separated the back of the RV and her window, but the gap seemed enormous.

She showered and dressed before poking her head into the boys' room. For a long moment, she stared at them. Frankie and Garrett. She'd had no idea she could love two people as much as she loved her sons. They were the reason for the RV. If it weren't for them, she might not have gotten up the courage to tell Adam things had to change.

They both deserved better than she and Adam had given them. They knew they were loved, but did either of them know how to give love to another person? How to listen to another person? How to be emotionally available? Those were skills she wanted to teach them.

She didn't want them to be lonely the way she'd been lonely—either as a child or as an adult.

She didn't want them to be so overprotected they were completely self-absorbed and unable to see beyond their own wants and needs.

She wanted them to grow into strong, empathetic men, so she had to start teaching them how to be those things now. With their father living in an RV in the driveway.

She flipped on the light, then crossed the room to open the blinds.

"Rise and shine, boys."

Frankie grunted into his pillow. Garrett sat up, wiped his hands over his eyes and stared blearily at her for a long moment. "Isn't it Saturday yet?"

"Nope. Thursday, and you have school." She put jeans and T-shirts on their beds. "Get dressed, and come downstairs for breakfast. Any requests?"

"McDonald's," Frankie said, his voice still muffled by the pillow.

"We don't have McDonald's, goofball. How about cereal?"

"Syrup, syrup," Garrett began chanting, his little body practically vibrating at the thought of all that sugar. She usually saved pancakes and waffles for weekend days but—she checked her watch—there was time, if the boys hurried.

"If you're downstairs in five minutes, we can do pancakes."

Garrett vibrated his body off the bed, then took off at a run for the bathroom, shouting, "Give me five minutes!"

Frankie sat up. "Pancakes are Saturday food."

"We have time."

"Pancakes are for special days. School days have a plan."

Jenny's heart hurt for the little boy. She'd been so busy making sure Adam had everything he needed, she'd missed that her boys needed something, too. "Sometimes, it's okay not to do things according to a plan. It doesn't mean something bad is going to happen."

"We were late."

"We have time. If you hurry." Jenny ruffled his hair, but Frankie just watched her solemnly. Jenny sat, taking in his words. He'd said *were*, not *are*. "When were we late?"

"The tornado day." His little hands twisted the edge of the blanket. "Garrett didn't want to get dressed, and Dad wanted to start working on the new chairs, and I didn't want cereal, so I wouldn't eat. And we were late."

Pain radiated in Jenny's chest. Her sweet little boy thought the tornado was his fault, for not eating his cereal, for running late. "Oh, sweetheart, the tornado didn't happen because we were late that day or because you didn't want cereal for breakfast. It just happened. There was nothing any of us could do to stop it."

"This is just Thursday."

Jenny stilled his little hands, then put her finger under his chin so he had to look at her. "The tornado wasn't your fault or mine or Garrett's or Daddy's. It just was. Things are different now, but that's okay. You're okay, and so is Garrett. I'm okay. Daddy's sick, but he's getting better every day. We all love you, and we're all here."

"Pancakes are for special celebration days," he said, his voice barely a whisper. Jenny hugged him tightly and caressed his hair.

"Today we are celebrating the ordinary days."

Finally, his arms came around her neck, and he held on for a long moment. "You're okay?"

"I'm okay. I love you."

"Love you, too, Mom."

Jenny unwrapped Frankie's arms and sat back. "Any time you want to talk about this, you can. Okay?" He nodded. Part of her wanted to keep talking to him, but she didn't want to put too much emphasis on the tornado. *Little steps*, she told herself. "Now hurry up or you won't have time to eat."

In the kitchen, she gathered the ingredients for pancakes and began mixing. "Two more minutes," she called up the stairs. The only response was the stomping of feet as the boys ran between their bedroom and the bathroom.

"Good morning." Adam stood in the doorway, wearing jeans and a gray T-shirt. His eyes looked a little sleepy and a half smile played over his face. Jenny told herself to ignore the little zing of pleasure at seeing him.

"Morning."

"Breaking out the weekend specials on a Thursday?"

She shrugged. "Anything to get them moving on a school day, right?"

"I can take them again this morning." He shifted and Jenny realized he must have walked inside, because the wheelchair was nowhere to be seen.

"Is there something wrong with the chair?"

He shook his head. "Just trying to build up the strength in my knee and hip. The physical therapist mentioned that a little walking would be good for the muscle—"

"Physical therapist?" She blinked. Had she just hallucinated?

"I went to the appointment yesterday afternoon."

"You did?"

He nodded. "I decided I don't want to lie to the doctors. And I may never be a candidate for surgery, but if the therapy will help with the knee, at least maybe I can get rid of some of the pain."

Joy at his words hit Jenny hard. She forgot to stir for a second, and just stared. Scar on the neck, check. Eyes green not hazel, double-check. This was definitely Adam standing before her, but it was a different Adam than she was used to seeing. Gone was the wheelchair. Gone was the sullen, angry man. This guy might not be the Adam who had proposed or who was so excited about expanding the business that he'd practically vibrated—like their son—but this was a man she could—

Jenny stopped herself.

Having a couple good days didn't change what had happened between them during the past three months. He couldn't erase that neglect with a few flowers she didn't even like, and a trip to physical therapy.

Adam leaned a shoulder against the door jamb, and the move reminded her of how he used to wait for her in the doorway after school. Jenny swallowed, trying push thoughts of the past from her mind.

The past wouldn't solve the problems of the present, as sweet as it was to look back there.

"I'm glad you went. How was it?"

He shrugged. "Different. I thought physical therapy would be a bunch of useless stretches or maybe Pilates, but they used this ultrasound machine and heat pulses. The therapist said the best treatment was to get the blood flowing again through the hamstring, and heat does that."

"Are you going back?"

"Tomorrow afternoon." He stepped into the kitchen, took the bowl from her and began stirring. Trying to focus on anything other than how adorably sexy Adam looked holding a bowl of pancake batter, Jenny turned on the stove element and dropped a pat of butter into the pan. When it was sizzling, she took the bowl and dropped dollar-sized dollops of batter onto the skillet to cook.

"I was wondering what your day is like today. If you're busy."

"Working on the books, and I need to finalize a contract. Why?"

"I can get myself to physical therapy, but I was thinking, if you could spare an hour or two, maybe you could drive me to that service dog place?"

Jenny's breath caught in her throat. Slowly, she turned to face him. He'd shoved his hands in his pockets, but that haunted look was gone from his eyes. Maybe the flowers weren't just a throw-away *I'm sorry*. "You're willing to go?"

"I'm still not sure about adding a dog to the house, even a service dog with extensive training. But I don't want to be stuck in that chair for the rest of my life. If a dog will show the doctors that I'm serious about recovery, I'll check it out."

"Adam." She wanted to reach out to him. To touch his cheek and let him know she was still here for him. She couldn't love him out of this depression, and she didn't want to be the crutch that made it okay to slip away from life again. But how could support and encouragement be a crutch?

Jenny reached out, and the stubble on his cheek felt rough against her palm. "I think that's wonderful," she said.

He stared into her eyes for a long moment, then his hand encircled her wrist and he leaned forward. Jenny stepped back quickly. Loving support didn't, couldn't, equal kissing. Or holding. She turned away. "Don't want the pancakes to burn," she said, flipping the cakes in the pan to finish cooking. She glanced at him from the corner of her eye. He was still watching her, but he didn't crowd into her space or reach out.

"We'll see how it goes. It's only a first meeting. The dogs might not even like me."

Jenny didn't see how anyone wouldn't like Adam Buchanan. The man was handsome, loving, strong. He'd gotten lost, but seemed to be finding himself. "I'm sure the dogs will like you just fine."

"So you'll take me? I can ask my dad, or Aiden if you're too busy."

"I can clear my afternoon." The sound of the boys' clattering feet filled the house. Her husband had gone to a physical therapy appointment, all on his own. Jenny ordered herself not to read too much into the changes in Adam. This could all be an act, a way to get out of the RV and back into the house. Back into the wheelchair. Back in front of that damned window, where he could watch the world go by and wait to die.

She put the boys' plates on the table, then offered a third to Adam. He sat with their sons, talking to them about school. Jenny filled her own plate before joining her family at the strong oak table Adam had built for her before they'd started renovating this house.

Their conversation about the strength of water balloons versus regular balloons was a bit non-sensical, but it made her smile. It had been a long time since she'd smiled. She didn't know how long this change in Adam would last, but as inconvenient as it would be to rearrange her afternoon, she would do it. Because if he were willing to make this concession, she was darned sure going to meet him halfway.

ADAM LOOKED OUT the window of the Mustang, watching closely as a man close to his father's age exited the white farmhouse with black shutters. The dog trainer lived just outside Springfield, and Adam was already regretting asking Jenny to bring him here. Of doing this at all. On the one hand, he knew the dog would give Jenny another reason to believe he wanted to change—a definite bonus. On the other hand, getting a service dog was so…permanent. As if by even considering it, he was giving up his hopes of ever being a normal person again.

Adam wanted to be normal. So badly.

"Ready?"

He wanted to offer a clever quip, but his mouth was too dry. What if the dog didn't like him? What if it did? What if getting a service dog somehow signaled his brain to go crazy again? What if he'd already had the last seizure he would have, and this dog was meant to go to someone who really needed it?

"Sure." He got out of the car, pain shooting through his knee and hip when he forgot how low the Mustang was to the ground. He held out a hand to the handler. "Adam Buchanan."

"Dave Wheeler. Nice to meet you. And this is Sheba."

The dog was a golden Lab, with soft yellow fur and curious eyes. She sat patiently beside Dave, as if waiting for permission to do something. Adam waited, but Dave didn't say anything more.

"Am I supposed to ask it to shake or something? Introduce myself?"

The trainer laughed, and his eyes crinkled at the corners. Somehow, his amusement with the questions wasn't reassuring. "Why don't I take you through some of the things Sheba can do? Then you can get a feel for her yourself."

For the next half hour, Dave and Sheba went through a series of instructions, everything from typical sitting and walking, to how the dog would behave if Adam had a seizure. It was fascinating, and a little scary. Jenny stood beside him as they watched the dog go through its paces.

"It's different than I expected," she said at last.

"I wasn't sure what to expect," he admitted. "I

know it isn't a pet, but doesn't some of this look like pet stuff?"

"It's probably meant to. Less scary that way," she whispered. Her shoulder brushed his and Adam felt that familiar zing of attraction. It was funny—before she'd asked him to move out of the house, he couldn't remember the last time he'd allowed these little zings of attraction for his wife free rein. This time he was going to enjoy it, to feel it from his shoulder all the way to his toes. If he could, he would bathe in it, and hope that maybe, if he changed enough, she'd allow herself to feel it, too.

He wanted to hold her hand again. To kiss her and not have her draw away from him. Make love with her. Hell, he wanted to sit with her at the kitchen table and just *be*. Wanted to walk with her along the lakeshore or downtown to get a cup of coffee. He hadn't allowed any of those little moments into their lives in…too long. Maybe since before the tornado, even.

Adam squeezed his eyes shut, trying to remember the last time they'd gotten a babysitter for the boys so they could have time together as a couple. Maybe Christmas? Was it a date if he took his wife Christmas shopping for their sons? Adam had a feeling Jenny wouldn't think so. Hell, *he* didn't think so. Eating at the mall food court in Springfield wasn't a sunset sail on the lake. It wasn't even a quick dinner-and-a-movie evening.

He needed to add "take Jenny on a date" to his to-do list.

The dog handler headed in their direction.

"Do you think there is a trial period with these dogs?" Adam asked her. "Or once we take it home, it is ours, regardless?"

"It's a she," Jenny corrected, but there was a hint of amusement in her voice, not annoyance. "She seems like such a sweetie, I doubt there is anything to worry about."

Adam frowned. "Being nice with the trainer might not be the same as getting along with an eight- and a five-year-old."

"And it might be just that easy."

Was she trying to come up with the simplest answers? Or was he being deliberately opposed to the possibility that he needed a service dog? He'd finally read all the literature last night, after he'd gone to bed, alone, in the borrowed RV. He'd been sleeping in there only a couple days and already he was sick of it, despite the creature comforts his mother had made sure it held.

Jenny stood so close to him he could feel her heat. He wanted to take her hand in his, but didn't want to overstep the boundaries she'd put up. Winning her back would have to be a slow process.

"How does this work?" Adam asked Dave, once

he and Sheba came to a stop. "Do I need to take classes so I know what to do with it?"

"With her," the trainer correctly mildly. "You don't need classes. The basic commands are simple. The most important thing is to make the dog a part of your life. Take her to the store, on walks. Let her know she is a member of your family, not just an employee, for lack of a better word. She'll do the rest."

Adam looked at Jenny. She nodded, almost imperceptibly. If the dog made her feel more secure, maybe he should just go ahead. He watched the animal closely for a long moment. It stared right back at him with big, chocolate-brown eyes. No barking, no slobbering. No antsy pacing. It just sat, waiting. The way he'd done so many times since the tornado struck Slippery Rock. They waited for different things. The dog for her next order. Adam for…oblivion.

He didn't want to wait any longer—it would only make things harder. "When can we pick her up?"

"Give us a week, just to make sure Sheba is fully prepped. We'll do some owner-specific training, anything you want her to learn that will be helpful in your situation. I have the basics of what you're facing, but not every detail."

"I—well, we—just want to make sure she'll be

okay with our boys. They're eight and five, and they've never had a pet."

"It's important to remember Sheba isn't a pet, not the way most people think of it. Although she likes a long walk, she doesn't play fetch, and you should keep her to a schedule. Whatever you do, wherever you go, she does and she goes."

They talked a bit more with the trainer, then scheduled a time to return to pick up the dog the following week. In the car, Adam considered what he wanted to learn from the dog, or teach her. Or how to just deal with her.

"For what it's worth, I think this is a good decision." Jenny began speaking once they were on the highway leading back to Slippery Rock. Adam didn't want her reasoning for getting the dog. He wanted to show her that, dog or no dog, he was the same man she had married.

Maybe it would be better, though, to show her that he could be the man she wanted now. He needed to figure out what that was, but in the meantime, it couldn't hurt to remind her how things had been before.

"When I saw you at lunch the other day, at the pizza place—"

"During your jaunt around town?" she said, a smile on her face. She looked so happy, he almost convinced himself not to say anything more. But if he were to show her he had changed, that he was changing, he had to be honest. She needed to know how he felt, and maybe that would give him a clue how *she* felt. About him.

"I didn't like it." Her hands were at the perfect ten and two positions; he thought she was the only person he knew who drove with their hands at the precise positioning taught in driver's education courses. It was kind of cute.

She shot him a questioning look.

"It made me feel like…" He waved his hand between them, as if she might understand what he was trying to say through the motions, but Jenny only glanced at him, then back at the road. "Like I wanted to march in there and drag him out by his perfect hair."

Slowly, she turned her head to look at him. "It was a business lunch," she said after a long moment.

"I know. Seeing you there, happy and laughing, after you'd been so unhappy and sad with me… I don't want to make you unhappy, Jenny. I think I've been making you unhappy for a lot longer than these past three months, though."

Jenny swallowed. Her knuckles were white with tension. Adam didn't think she was going to answer, then she pulled the car off the road and parked on the shoulder.

Despite the early afternoon hour, the road wasn't busy, only a few cars whizzing past. When

Jenny finally looked at him, there was pain in her gaze, and Adam wanted to do something, anything, to make that pain go away. He didn't know how.

"I wasn't," she began, but then shook her head. "You didn't make me unhappy. The tornado didn't make me unhappy. *I* made me unhappy."

Adam didn't understand. She said he wasn't the same, and he knew he'd been withdrawn since the tornado. Just how far back was this going to go? "How did you make yourself unhappy?"

"I don't know. I think by not paying attention to what I want for myself all these years."

"The business? You can have it." He would sign all the papers over to her today, if that was what would make her happy. He couldn't work there anymore, anyway. The thought of never going back to Buchanan's, though, stabbed at his heart a little bit.

"It isn't the business. Or the kids or your parents or mine. It isn't even you, at least not entirely. It's me, Adam." She put her hands to her chest. "It's me. I went from living with parents who never allowed me to have an opinion on anything, to living with you, who never asked my opinion on anything. And that doesn't mean I didn't want the things we built together. I did want those things, and I did like my job."

"You planned our wedding." And she'd done it

perfectly, getting them out of town and married before either set of parents knew totally what was going on. She'd avoided dealing with her mother's pretentious wedding plans, while also not hurting his mother's feelings. Nancy had always wanted a girl she could spoil. Their wedding would have been some kind of cross between bad chick flicks and *The Beverly Hillbillies*.

"Elopement," she corrected, and she smiled. A real smile that eased the panicky feeling in Adam's chest. Having good memories about their past had to mean something, didn't it? "What I'm trying to say, and doing a bad job of, is that as much as I like the responsibilities of work and at the house, I don't want to be the only responsible adult."

"I can be responsible." Adam wanted those four idiotic words back as soon as he said them. He sounded like Frankie trying to get fifteen extra minutes at bedtime. "What I meant was that we can work out responsibilities for the house, the kids, work."

"I'd like that," she said. "You know, that lunch? I pitched him our plan. The one we were working on before..." She trailed off.

Before. Before the tornado. Before she realized she wanted more than Adam in her life. Before he decided she was better off without him. Before everything went crazy.

"Before," she said, and this time there was a note of defiance in her voice. "He liked the plans, and he's presenting them to his partners in the next week. If he wants to move forward, we're going to need a designer. Or two. I already told him to call my cell and not the office line, because if you mother keeps telling him Buchanan's is only a cabinet shop, he might believe her."

"A cabinet shop is a good living, especially with Buchanan's reputation." If she didn't want him back, and since he couldn't work there in his condition, going back to cabinetmaking was the safe bet. Duane in the warehouse was as good a cabinetmaker as Adam had been.

"Yes, it is. But furniture making could be so much more. If this partnership happens, it could be that last support that makes the cabinet part of Buchanan's the small end of the revenue line." *Revenue line? Support? Partnering?* She sounded serious. Like she'd put a lot of thought into the business. Adam was both awed and humbled.

She pulled back onto the road. "I know your parents aren't thrilled with the changes we were making to the business, but that doesn't make the changes bad decisions. They've been really helpful, in their own way. Your dad still runs a tight ship in the warehouse, and people love talking to your mom on the phone. It would be good, though, if you reminded them the business is ours now. Yours and mine. Nothing stays the same forever."

Jenny kept talking as she drove, about returns on investment, pricing structures, delivery models. All the arguments he'd used to convince her to consider this expansion months ago. The more she talked, the more queasy Adam felt. She really was moving on. Without him. Adam's head swam with the information she shared in the hour it took to finish the drive from the dog trainer to Slippery Rock.

"Is this expansion what you want?" he asked.

Jenny nodded as she pulled the Mustang into their driveway. "It's exciting and scary. It's what we talked about."

"You said earlier that your parents didn't let you have an opinion, and that I never asked for your opinion. I'm asking now. Is this expansion what you want? Not because it was something I dreamed up a couple years ago when I was making our kitchen table or the bed, but because you want it?"

Jenny put the car in Park, then shifted in the seat to look at him. He wondered what she saw. The broken man she'd brought home from the hospital? A guy she used to love? "It's what I want for the business, yes. I just have to figure out how to make it work, now that things are different between us. For you."

Adam watched her for a long moment, trying to merge the image he'd held on to, of his sweet, small-town love, with the savvy, smart woman who had just spent forty minutes talking in business terms about the plans he'd tried to convince himself were no longer possible. She made those plans seem possible, though, and he realized he still wanted the plan, too. He wasn't ready for it. He couldn't work with his tools. He couldn't build a three-tiered shelf, much less a set of patio furniture, but the thought of his furniture in homes around the state made that hot lick of ambition he hadn't felt in months fire back to life.

He wasn't ready for this kind of life, but apparently life wasn't waiting for him any longer.

"Would you mind sharing those profit margins with me?"

She nodded. "Of course. It's your business, too."

He'd wanted to take her hand at the dog farm, for reassurance. As a reminder of who he was, who they were together. He hadn't then because he didn't want her to think getting a service dog was him faking to get in her good graces or something. Now, Adam reached across the car and took her hand in his. Not to reassure himself that she was here with him, but to show her that he was here with her.

"I think it sounds like an amazing plan, and I

don't know how I can help, but I'd like to learn more about it. If you wouldn't mind sharing."

He needed to add one more thing to his to-do list: figure out how to be part of their business again.

LEGO FIGURES RAN across the TV screen, fighting with one another as they offered up sarcastic jibes. Jenny shook her head, seeing the rapt faces of her boys as they took in the cartoon movie. Frankie and Garrett had seen this film at least a dozen times, and yet every time President Business appeared on the screen, it was as if they'd never seen him before. She curled into the corner of the sectional, pulled her legs up under her and rested her head on her palm.

Adam returned from the kitchen, holding a bowl of freshly salted and buttered popcorn. Instead of the recliner that he usually chose, he sat next to her in the corner, with only the cup console between them.

"This is my favorite part," he whispered, nodding to the screen as President Business made his first appearance on the screen. The boys shushed him, making Jenny grin. Adam shrugged, an exaggerated what-did-I-do expression on his face. He pushed the bowl of popcorn in her direction and Jenny shook her head and patted her stomach.

Between the hamburgers and potato salad and

the first round of popcorn, she didn't think she would eat again for at least a week. Adam took a handful, then put the bowl between the boys on the floor. Neither seemed to notice.

This was nice. The four of them used to watch movies together every weekend. It was one of the family events that Adam always made time for, although he was usually with the boys on the floor or in his recliner and not on the sofa with her. He ate the last of his popcorn. Jenny's hand started to tingle so she shifted, settling her back into the corner of the sectional and stretching her legs along the side.

"Comfortable?" he asked, the words barely a whisper. The fighting on the screen had revved up, and the boys didn't notice. Jenny nodded and shook her hand from side to side to get the blood flowing again.

Adam didn't say anything more, just settled his arm across the back of the couch. She could feel it behind her, but didn't ask him to move. Didn't shift her position. It was just an arm on the back of the sofa; something he'd done a thousand times in their marriage. Just as she had taken up the long side of the sofa a thousand times. Old habits were hard to stop, even when one of them no longer technically lived here.

She didn't want to think about that. She only wanted to enjoy this evening. Tomorrow was Saturday; the boys would have football practice in the morning. Then grocery shopping and meal planning for next week. She should probably mow the lawn one last time, make sure the grass was low so that any falling leaves would blow away and not get caught up in their yard. Which reminded her, she should make sure the batteries were charged for the leaf blower. Summer was bound to break one of these days, bringing fall to Slippery Rock.

A wave of exhaustion hit her, the combination of too much food, too little sleep lately and an often-watched movie too much to combat. The last thing she remembered was the character on the screen vowing to save the world, then it was like she was floating. Jenny could hear the characters, could feel Adam's heat near her on the sofa, but her eyes were too heavy to open, and there was the most delicious gentle massaging feeling at her scalp. Like she'd gone all in at Helena's Boutique, getting the full treatment instead of the quick cut she'd opted for in the past.

Tension left her body. Thoughts about work floated away. Worries about Adam's health, how the service dog would fit into their family. What was going to happen to their four-person unit now that Adam was living in the RV. Everything flowed away, and all she could do was lie there contentedly listening to Morgan Freeman's voice tell the other LEGO characters that they had to fight.

Fight for what? She couldn't imagine. Everything seemed fine. She was here; the boys were adjusting. Garrett hadn't brought an attack tornado drawing home in several days. Frankie still asked for her schedule, but he didn't seem so rigid since they'd talked about pancakes and schedule changes. And Adam... God, it felt good to be here on the sofa with him. Watching a silly movie. His hands playing with her hair, like so many times in the past. Like nothing had ever happened to him. To them.

Only things had happened. Things had changed. No matter how comfortable she was right this second, this movie would end. What happened when the movie ended?

Jenny sat up, needing to put space between herself and Adam. The boys were still focused on the movie, but this wasn't a movie. Things between her and Adam weren't settled just because he'd started walking the boys to school. He couldn't live in the RV forever, and she didn't trust that if she asked him to move back into the house, any of the changes he'd begun making would continue.

She put her hand to her chest and squeezed her eyes closed. She wanted him to get better. She wanted Adam back. As frustrating as it had been to be married to him from time to time, she wanted him back. Adam put his hand on her arm, but she shook him off.

"I just need a minute," she said, and slipped out of the living room.

Morgan Freeman's voice echoed in her mind. *You only have to believe. You only have to believe.*

Yeah, life wasn't a kid's movie about self-confidence. She wiped the counter and put the rest of the dinner dishes in the dishwasher. Then, because she couldn't think of another reason not to go back to finish watching the movie—and that wouldn't accomplish anything—she went out to the patio.

She had to figure out what she wanted, without Adam's hands in her hair, making her wish for things that just weren't true. She had been frustrated before the accident. She wanted more than to take the kids to school and pick them up. To cook the meals and clean the house. She wanted to go on dates with her husband. There had to be more to life than being a mom and a housekeeper. She wanted the business to expand, but she didn't want to be the only one working for those changes, either. There had to be some way to be the mom and the businesswoman and the wife.

Didn't there?

"Hey." Adam's voice came from behind her. "Mind if I join you?"

"The boys will notice you're gone."

"They wouldn't notice if a carnival broke out on the street out front."

Jenny motioned to the chair across from her.

"Everything okay?" he asked.

"Why would anything be wrong?" She didn't want to talk about this with him, not right now. Not until she was clear about everything first.

"Because you were relaxed for the first time in ages, and then all that tension came back and you ran out of the room."

God, had she been that transparent? "I just wanted to get the kitchen cleaned up."

"You wiped the counters after dinner."

"But then you made popcorn. Plus the grill stuff needed to be prepped for the dishwasher." And she had needed to get off that couch. Away from Adam's hands. Away from his presence.

"Those things could have waited until after the movie."

"Not everything can wait until you feel like doing them, Adam." Jenny winced. This wasn't about him. She had to stop pushing everything off on him. This was her mess. She'd been the one to ignore what she wanted. Sure, he'd been the one going out and having fun, but she was the one who insisted on staying home. The situation they were in now was as much her fault as it was his.

Wasn't it? What if she fell back into that old routine? Where would they be in five more years?

She didn't want to hate Adam, but if she didn't start saying the things that were on her mind, she might. "Sorry, you didn't deserve that."

He was quiet for a long moment, tapping his index finger against the tempered glass of the tabletop. "I probably do. I know I haven't been a good husband to you since the tornado. I'm trying to do better."

"I know. I appreciate that."

"This isn't only about the tornado, though, is it?"

She didn't want to have this conversation. Not now. Not when Adam was finally coming out of the shell he'd been hiding in since he woke up in the hospital. Morgan Freeman's voice echoed in her mind again. "Shut up," she muttered. A cartoon lecture about being the best Jenny she could be was so out of place at this moment. She needed to support Adam right now. What *she* needed could come later.

"What?"

She shook her head. "Nothing. Just…losing what's left of my mind."

"Jen, I'm sorry," he said. His index finger tapped even faster against the glass of the table, and she wanted to scream. Every tap made the muscles in her shoulders tighten, made her feel how close he was to her on the patio, and underlined how far he really was from her.

"I don't care." Jenny swallowed. She couldn't

even wish the words back. "I don't care that you're sorry. I care that you don't *know* what it is that caused all of this. I get it—you're trying to change. You're walking the boys to school, and you're not totally against the expansion at work anymore. But none of that is about me. I want it to be about me, damn it. For once in my life, I want something to be about *me.*"

"This is all about you."

"No, it's not. It's about you. You haven't done one thing for me."

"I sent you flowers to apologize."

"I hate cut flowers. I've never once asked for cut flowers. I didn't carry them when we eloped. I don't keep them in vases around the house."

"You work in the garden all the time."

"Because I like plants," she exclaimed, unable to keep the annoyance from her voice. "Rose-bushes and flowering hedges and those annoyingly time-consuming bonsai trees. I like *plants,* Adam, not cut flowers. We've been together since high school—that's ten years—and you don't know the simplest thing about me."

And she was ruining this moment. When she should be calm and collected, she was angry and almost yelling at him. About freaking flowers. Jenny took a breath and willed herself to calm down. "I needed five minutes to myself, just five freaking minutes when the boys aren't asking me for something, when you don't need anything, and you had to follow me out here. I don't want this, Adam. I don't want any of it. I don't want to be angry and I don't want to be alone and I don't want you to be sick and I don't want the boys to be sad." Jenny stood, held her hands out to her sides and shook her head. "I just want to be left alone for five damn minutes."

Jenny fled. Out the back gate and down the street. She didn't care where she was going; she just had to get out of there. Away from Adam. Away from the words she hadn't meant to fling at him. Away from the mess she was making of this. Because he was trying. He'd gone to the dog trainer, was going to physical therapy. He hadn't come back to work, but he'd been interested in their plans for the first time in months. And she'd yelled at him. When she should have accepted his apology so he would know he was doing what she wanted, she'd been angry and obnoxious and probably ruined any progress the two of them had made over the past week.

She looked around, saw the playground at Frankie and Garrett's school. She'd made things worse when she could have made them better, and now she had no idea what to do next.

ADAM WATCHED THE backyard gate for a long moment, but Jenny didn't come back. Just like she hadn't come back after their fight about laundry. Through the open windows, he heard the boys laugh at something on the movie. He couldn't just sit here and believe Jenny would return. He had to fight to make her come back.

He grabbed his phone from his pocket and dialed Aiden's number. "How do you feel about babysitting?" he asked.

Ten minutes later, Adam walked down the street toward the school. He didn't know where Jenny had gone, but doubted she'd have headed downtown, not when she wanted to be alone. He rounded the corner and saw her sitting on the little bench on the sidewalk near the front doors. In the twilight, she didn't look angry. She looked sad.

Maybe this wasn't such a good idea. Maybe he should give her more than the five minutes she'd asked for.

Maybe he should grow a pair and stop hoping all this would go away. He had to face the fact that Jenny might not want him back, that she might not be able to admit that, even to herself. So he continued up the walk and sat beside her on the bench.

She blinked, as if seeing him for the first time. "What are you doing here? Without the wheelchair?"

As painful as it had been to walk the distance from the house to the school, Adam had been determined to do it on his own. He swung the handle of the walking stick he'd found in the RV. Well, mostly on his own. "I did ten minutes on the recumbent bike today at PT. Figured I'd try walking, and before you get mad about that, the walking stick will at least slow the fall if...you know."

"You shouldn't have taken that risk." She clenched her hands in her lap.

Adam reached out, tucking an errant curl behind her ear. "I've decided that I've been hiding behind the wheelchair and the epilepsy long enough."

She sighed. "It isn't about hiding. It's about protecting yourself."

"I know that." He shrugged. "Maybe I was tempting fate. This isn't your fault, at least not entirely. It's mine, too."

"Oh, Adam." Jenny shook her head, but he kept talking, hoping she would hear him.

"From where I'm sitting, you've done everything in your power to hold us together, while I did everything I could to make you walk away. You didn't walk away, and I'm grateful for that because I love you, Jenny. Saying I'm sorry isn't enough, and I know that. And you don't have to love me back, although I kind of hope you can. Some day."

"Loving you has never been the problem. Loving you has always been the easy part."

She didn't say she loved him, but that had

probably been too much to hope for. "What's the hard part?"

"Talking. It's embarrassing, being so needy."

"I don't think you're needy." She was the strongest person he'd ever known. He'd crumbled after waking up in that hospital room. Jenny, on the other hand, had taken all that hurt and fear and stood up to it. Was still standing up to it.

She made a little snorting sound. "I just screamed at you for giving me the wrong kind of flowers. I'm not sure what you'd call it, but I call that being needy."

He was still in shock that he'd never realized something so simple about the woman he'd loved for ten years. She loved tending plants. She didn't like watching their blooms die. And he'd never bothered to notice because, in his parents' relationship, roses were the expected gift for any occasion. "I call it being honest. What else do you want to be honest about?"

She shook her head. "Nothing."

Adam bumped his shoulder against hers. "Come on, it's nearly dark. I can barely see you in the dark. Pretend I'm not here and be honest with yourself."

Jenny was quiet for so long, Adam thought maybe he'd pushed too far, too fast.

"I resented it every time you went off to the

Wednesday dart game with Levi, Collin and James without asking if I wanted to come along."

"Did you?"

"I don't think I even realized it at first. Levi had gotten hurt and couldn't play professional football anymore, and if I'd been there, he wouldn't have talked all that through with you guys. But then you kept playing."

"And you resented that I went?"

"I resented that you never asked." She scooted away from him, putting a couple inches between them on the bench. "Okay, honesty. Here we go. Do you know the last time you asked me out on a date?"

Adam considered the question. "Last Christmas?" he asked, and even he heard the hopeful lilt to his voice.

"August 23. A month before Frankie was born."

The night came crashing back to him in a rush. The hot, muggy afternoon. Jenny so pregnant and miserable she'd taken about five cold showers every day. "It was a Friday night."

"And about a hundred degrees out, and all I wanted was to stay in that little apartment and sit in front of the air conditioner. You took me out on Bud's fishing boat, remember?"

"You kept saying you wanted a vat of ice cream that you could swim in," he said, chuckling. "No one we knew had so much as a wading pool to fill up, so I thought the lake might make help you cool off."

"You kept diving over the side, trying to coax me into the water, but I was positive I'd never make it back into the boat. I was so miserable." Jenny tucked a lock of hair behind her ear. "Did you stop asking me out because I made you so miserable that night?"

Adam blinked at her. "No, I just…kind of thought with Frankie around that spontaneity was out of the question. Then Garrett came along. You were tired, and I was tired. Then Mom and Dad retired and we had the business to think of, too." He reached across the table, taking her hand in his. Jenny shivered at the light touch. "Is that what you want? You want to date me?"

IF SHE'D KNOWN that night would be their last spontaneous date, she'd have tried a little harder to enjoy it. And she shouldn't want him to take her hand now, but she did. Not fifteen minutes ago, she'd yelled at him to leave her alone, and now all she could think about was touching him. She had to be some kind of lunatic to be ping-ponging her way through life like this.

"Do you?" he asked again, his voice quiet in the still night.

No. Yes. God, she wanted more of her husband's attention. Was it so much to ask?

"I want—" She blew out a breath. "This isn't all your fault, Adam, it's me, too. There were things you did that annoyed me before all of this—" she waved her hand between them "—and there are probably things I do that annoy you. But you disappeared on me. I didn't complain, not even when you shut me out. I kept going to work, and raising the boys, and trying to get you well, but you weren't there. You disappeared on me."

"I'll fix it, Jen."

"You can't. Before, it was me, letting you do whatever it was you wanted to do while I had diapers and cooking and groceries and work. I wanted to be part of the fun bits, not just the work bits." She shook her head. "But you can't follow me around all the time, asking what I want or what I need or if I'm okay, because sooner or later you're going to resent the fact that you're only taking what I want into account."

"So what do we do?"

She had to figure out how to ask for the things she wanted, and she had to learn to trust that when he said he wanted to change he actually would change. She couldn't do that sitting on this bench with him.

"I took you for granted before. I won't do that again," he said.

"And I didn't share what I needed with you. I'll try to stop doing that."

"I hate living in the RV."

"I like it when you play with my hair."

He smiled at her, and for the first time, Jenny thought maybe there was a chance the two of them could straighten this out. She'd loved him since she was a kid. She could give them both a little more time to grow up.

"It has to be both of us this time, or it's not going to work."

"I'm in if you are," he said.

"Okay."

Adam began walking toward their house. "Let's go see if the boys—"

"Oh, my God, the boys. We left them alone at the house." Jenny nearly tripped over her feet as she realized they'd left the boys alone, but Adam's hand was steady on her arm.

"I called Aiden. He's babysitting. The boys are fine."

Jenny put her hand to her chest. "You called Aiden?"

"I figured eight might be old enough to be home alone for a half hour or so, but five was definitely too young. And I didn't know if you had babysitter information anywhere, so I called for reinforcements." Adam squeezed her hand in his. "Let's see if Emmett and the crew have saved LEGO City from President Business yet."

"You don't have to stay in the RV," she said.

"Yeah, I do." He smoothed his hand over her hair, and when his thumb caressed her cheek, Jenny leaned into his palm. "For now, I think the RV is the best option for all of us."

CHAPTER NINE

A WEEK AFTER going to the trainer's home with
Adam, Jenny was still trying to figure out if he
was serious about changing his life, of taking his
life back, or if this was just his way of getting her
to do things for him again.

If this wasn't a serious effort, he deserved a spot
in the next Hollywood blockbuster.

If he wasn't serious, the little fantasy bubble
she'd been building since that night in the school-
yard might burst and destroy her whole life. She
sat in their office, watching out the big window
as Adam wheeled himself around the warehouse
floor with Aiden. Jenny didn't understand why it
had taken Aiden three months to come to Slippery
Rock, but since his arrival, he had dived right into
work here, and he'd brought Adam with him. It
was good to see Adam enjoying work again. Good
to see him at breakfast every morning, to have
lunch with him and to make dinner with him. To
see him playing with the boys again.

This morning, Adam and Aiden were poring
over designs of some kind, and pointing to dif-

ferent areas of the production floor. Owen had tried to join in, but angrily walked away when his sons continued doing whatever it was they were doing. Jenny had the feeling, since Owen wasn't involved, they were discussing the furniture. She doodled on the draft of the contract with the Springfield firm.

Before the tornado, Adam would have been down there with the other guys, protective glasses shoved up on his head until a machine was going, laughing away. This morning he had on the protective glasses, had the plans for a cabinet or something in his hands, and wasn't even grinning. There was determination in the set of his jaw, in the straightness of his shoulders. Determined Adam was sexy. More sexy than Fun Adam had ever been. And that was dangerous.

Fun Adam had overwhelmed her with day trips to Springfield or Little Rock, had built her things like the kitchen table and had made her smile when, instead of disciplining the boys, he played with them. She hadn't been able to resist Fun Adam's charms. Watching him now, from several hundred feet away, she had the feeling Determined Adam would be just as hard to resist. She should stay in her office, but after two hours of pretending to go over the contract when she was actually watching him, she decided she had to do something different.

The back stairs were empty this morning. Nancy sat at the front desk talking on the phone with one of her friends, and Owen had been on the floor, supervising the guys loading a truck.

"I was thinking different woods," Aiden said when she joined him and Adam near the table holding pieces of an Adirondack-style chair. "To give it a little more character."

Adam arranged the pieces and stepped back to study it. He'd left the wheelchair on the other side of the table, and Jenny's first instinct was to tell him to sit down. There was mechanical equipment around here. But he wasn't near it, and as she'd told him more than a week ago, he had to start taking responsibility for himself. So she didn't say anything.

Adam rearranged what would be chair legs, brought more of the mismatched wood that could be used for the chair backs. Studied them some more.

"You know, if we cut down the back, so there's more space between the strips, it might work." He fiddled with the arrangement of the woods. "Add in a varnish that makes the different types really stand out, and it's a showpiece for a lake home."

It was only a rough mock-up of what one of the chairs might look like, but Jenny liked it. Not just because it had been too long since she'd seen this focused, intent expression on Adam's face. And it had been too long. A shiver of awareness ran down her spine and her mouth went dry. Intent Adam was a whole other level of sexiness. One she had nearly forgotten.

Keep your mind on the work, Jen, on the life you want to build. Focusing on the amount of sex appeal he's putting out right now isn't going to do anything for your plans.

It might do something for her libido, which had lain dormant since the tornado. She couldn't remember the last time Adam had touched her. Well, not counting that kiss in the backyard last week. Before that it had been… She thought back. Too long.

Aiden caught Jenny's eye from across the table and winked. This was what she'd hoped, and it was happening so much faster than she expected. Aiden had been in town for only a week, and Adam was back at Buchanan's. True, coming to work for a few days wasn't the same as committing to life again, but at least he had come. And for the second time in a week, he'd been the one to make breakfast for the boys. Since that first morning, when he'd met her on the stairs with breakfast, she had made sure she got to the kitchen ahead of him. Let him cook if he wanted to, but she didn't need Adam delivering breakfast in bed.

It was just too weird.

He lived in an RV in the driveway. Accepting

breakfast in bed from him felt like the two of them were up to something…sketchy. There was nothing sketchy about separating from her husband. Heartbreaking, yes. Sketchy, no. At least, that was what she told herself. And now here she was, practically beaming because he'd taken a little interest in something that used to consume all his days.

At this point, she was confusing herself about what she wanted. Adam back at home. Adam in the RV. Adam working, showing signs of life.

Just what did she want out of all this? A real change for her life or to get back into those old, familiar ways? God, it had to make her some kind of idiot not to know which direction she wanted for her life.

Okay, one step at a time. Jenny stood back, letting the guys work. What did she want?

She wanted Adam to come back to work, but she knew if he didn't, she'd be okay. The business would be okay. She wanted a real marriage partnership, one where she wasn't the only one doing adult tasks like raking the leaves and grocery shopping.

"What do you think?" Adam stood back. The piece wasn't finished, but he'd rigged it so that it looked more like an actual chair than a few random sticks of wood. The highlights and grain patterning, the fanciful look of it, fascinated her.

Jenny stepped forward to run her fingers over

the smooth strips and pieces. Not a single splinter. The wood felt like satin under her hands. She could see this chair, and another just like it, in their backyard, overlooking Slippery Rock Lake. Sun setting behind the forest of trees on the opposite side, the water turning fiery red, then orange as the sun faded into the western sky. And in the chair beside her, the Adam she remembered. The sweet, funny, charming man she'd married.

The image pricked at her heart. She wanted that Adam, and she wanted to be sitting beside him, making more plans. For the business. For their life.

Her opinion on the chair was that it was perfect.

Her opinion on her marriage was that it could be.

"I think it's beautiful. It needs a matching chair, maybe a little table to set between them for drinks. One of those sudoku magazines we see on the racks at Mallard's."

"That is really specific." Aiden grinned and put his hands in his back pockets.

"I have opinions. Thoughts on things. For example, my thought is that you shouldn't just be here on vacation. Building boats is probably a lot more challenging than building cabinets and lawn furniture, but you have a talent." She held her clipboard to her chest, watching her brother-in-law closely for a long moment.

"Funny, I was just thinking you don't really need me here at all," he said flippantly.

"She doesn't. Jenny has a vision for this place, one I shared until a few months ago, and she'll make that vision happen with or with you." Adam's voice was quiet, but despite the noise from the warehouse, Jenny heard him clearly. "I'm the one who needs you here. I can design, but I can't build, and I've never designed anything like this chair. We could make a good team. If you stayed."

Aiden and Adam watched one another for a long moment. "I could stay a little longer," Aiden said eventually. "But I can't say that I'll stay forever."

"We'd love to have you here for as long as you want," Jenny said, emotion clogging her throat.

"I'm going to grab a Coke from the vending machine," Aiden said, and slipped away from them.

Adam gazed at Jenny. "I don't think I've ever asked your opinion on a chair. I didn't even ask you about the kitchen table," he murmured.

"You didn't have to ask. Our tastes were always evenly matched in that department." Jenny kept her hand on the arm of what would eventually be a chair. She couldn't touch him. They needed this talk, and if she touched him, she would stop talking. She would assume that he understood what the touch meant, like she had done so many times before. Having an opinion, at this moment, meant sharing that opinion.

"I loved the table. Round and solid, and you finished it in my favorite honey oak tones. It was perfect for the kitchen. It's still perfect for the kitchen."

"But I didn't ask. I never asked, I just did."

"And I never objected. I just went along because I thought… I didn't want to be the stringent harpy, always demanding. Never getting or having enough. I love my mother, but that's how she is with my dad."

"You could never be a harpy." Adam tucked a curl behind her ear. "It isn't in you."

"It's possible you'll change your mind about that. I made a vow to myself after our fight over the laundry that I'd tell people what I thought. What I wanted. What I need. I don't want to be so bottled up and angry that a messed-up load of laundry sends me over the edge." The words were like a release. When she'd told Mara and Savannah about the fight, about the flowers, it had been like a small valve had opened, letting her thoughts trickle out. Telling Adam was like opening that valve to maximum capacity. She wasn't angry. She wanted to move forward.

"What other opinions do you have?"

"That you don't have to try to make up to me by making me breakfast. That walking the boys to and from school is so helpful, but I miss those few minutes when it's just the three of us. That I really want this contract with the Springfield distributor, and I think we can handle it and the new contract with the builder out of Joplin by adding about eight more employees."

Adam blinked. "You want to hire more staff? We already have more employees on the books than Buchanan's has ever had."

"I know, but it can work, Adam. It's what you'd planned, before—" Jenny blew out a breath. "Before the tornado. You wondered how we would find enough workers because Slippery Rock is such a small town. But there are still people out of work because of the damage done, and a few people have moved into town because they hoped there would be more construction work. It'll be tight, but we can make it work."

Adam looked around the busy warehouse and shop floor. She wondered if he saw what she did: busy workers, guys swiping at one another good-naturedly after they finished loading the truck. The satisfied expression on Owen's face. The woodworkers so intent on shaping straight boards into spindles, and chair backs, and cabinet fronts. Buchanan's was still alive. It could still grow.

"I can't build anything." His words were quiet. "I want to build something."

"You're wrong, you know. You can't work with

the machinery, at least not yet. But you can still design." She paused to consider her words, then said, "You can still build this business. Buchanan's can be more than a local shop. We had plans, and we'll have to adjust, but…" Jenny stopped talking. She couldn't make him want this any more than she could make him want her, want life in general. He had to want those things.

He watched her for a long moment. "We?"

He wasn't hung up on the business plans. He was hung up because, without thinking, she'd used the word *we*.

Jenny tried to cover. "We both signed the papers to buy the place. I put these contracts in motion, but you would have to approve. You. Me. We." The explanation felt weak, as weak as she was for insisting she wanted more out of her life, but falling right back into old habits.

Her gaze met his, and it didn't matter that she'd asked him to move out. That their marriage might be over. What mattered was the look in his eyes. The green darkened to nearly emerald, and seemed to cut right through the confusion she felt at what she wanted, professionally and personally. All that mattered was that, for this moment, the two of them were together. He'd come out of the shell she had begged him to exit.

Adam was back. Jenny swallowed.

"And if I approve?"

"I have drafts of the contracts in my office. All you have to do is sign."

"I'll sign anything you want me to."

Jenny couldn't breathe, and not because she was afraid or worried. This was Adam. Her Adam. The man she'd loved since she was a teenager. The man she'd seen herself growing old with.

Adam was back, and she wasn't going to let him go.

JENNY WAS UP in her office, studiously going over some kind of paperwork. Adam couldn't take his eyes off her. All she needed was to put all that crazy, curly hair into a bun, maybe get a pair of reading glasses at the drugstore, and she would be the sexiest executive Slippery Rock had ever seen. He could be the printer repair guy, sneak into her office after everyone left for the day. Flick those blinds closed and—

"So when are you taking this trip?" Owen asked, startling Adam.

The pencil in his hand snapped, and he nearly fell off the three-legged stool he'd brought over to the drafting table. Instead of a few chair designs on the paper before him, Adam saw the sketch of a face with long, curly hair, a straight nose. High cheekbones.

He had to figure out a way to work with his wife without his hormones going into overdrive every time he caught a glimpse of her. That wasn't the way to win her back.

After their conversation at the school a few nights before, he had a better idea of what Jenny wanted. All the things he'd promised her but never delivered on. He'd sworn to love her, to support her, and what he'd done was leave her alone with two babies and a lot of housework. Like she was some 1950s housewife who had no ambitions other than a perfectly vacuumed carpet.

"Well?" his father asked. He wore old work jeans, a flannel shirt over a striped T-shirt and a leather tool belt strapped around his waist.

"Well, what?" Adam racked his mind for the question Owen had asked, but the only question he could come up with was how he could make up the last nine years to Jenny.

"When are you going on that Branson trip?"

"Branson trip?" Jenny didn't hate Branson, but it wasn't on her list of dream destinations. Was he having another seizure? Only this time instead of his body shaking uncontrollably, was his brain just cutting out portions of the conversations going on around him?

"You said you were taking her and the boys on a camping trip. That's why you wanted the RV. I was just wondering when you were leaving."

Right. His reason for borrowing the RV. Not

because she'd asked him to move out, but because he wanted to take her on a trip.

"Maybe in a week or two. The boys don't have any days off from school for a while—"

Owen waved a hand. "Third grade and kindergarten. What are they going to miss? A couple of art projects? Take your family on a vacation. God knows you could use the time away."

Actually, taking Jenny on a vacation wasn't a terrible idea. Now that Aiden was in town, his dad would have help at the warehouse. Adam caught a glimpse of her in the upstairs window. She'd pulled her hair into a makeshift bun atop her head and stuck a pencil through it to hold it in place. His hands itched to caress her graceful neck.

"We, ah, we're figuring it out, Dad." There, that wasn't a complete lie. What he and Jenny were figuring out was a bit more serious than vacation plans, but Owen didn't need to know that. Not right now.

His dad pulled another stool up to the table, examined Adam's sketch as if were a Louis XIV chair instead of part of his wife's face. "Always so much on her mind, our Jenny," he said after a moment.

Adam wasn't sure what emotion Owen had taken from the pencil lines of curly hair or the shadowing of a high cheekbone, but his father wasn't wrong. Jenny kept a lot inside. Adam had never taken the time to figure out what those things were, not until she'd blown up at him over the laundry a few weeks ago. He'd been too comfortable going about life as he always had, a bit effortlessly.

More like carelessly.

He glanced up at the office window again, but Jenny wasn't there. Probably on the phone or getting a cup of coffee. Silly for her absence from a window to make his heart clench like this. Adam shook himself.

"Yeah. She has big plans for this place."

"From what I've seen, you both have big plans for this place." Owen knocked his shoulder against Adam's. "When you were still sick, I thought those plans might be too much. I was used to how I ran the shop, I guess."

"You were a good boss."

"You're a better one. You delegate. I always had to be in the middle of things, especially things I didn't have any business in."

"Well, Jenny has us both beat in that respect. She takes a rough idea and makes a plan."

"She's a detail girl, that's for sure." Owen picked the broken pencil off the drafting table and held it out to Adam. "You're pretty good with details yourself. I fiddled with those chair pieces all day yesterday, knowing they might be something. Took you five minutes to have the design worked out. It's going to be a pretty chair. Might look nice with a low table, just big enough for a couple cups of coffee. On a beach somewhere."

Yeah, he could see two chairs, mismatched wood, low table, just as Jenny had said. Sun setting over water, making the wood warm in the twilight.

"I miss doing the actual work. Cutting down the rails, sanding out the rough edges."

"Design might not make you sweat like woodworking does, but it's still work, Adam. It's hard work. It's challenging."

Sitting at a drafting table wasn't how Adam had envisioned his working life, though.

"You're figuring out it's more of a challenge than you imagined, but that doesn't mean you should give up."

Something in his dad's voice caught Adam's attention. He focused on his father, but the older Buchanan was staring at the empty window upstairs.

"Some things are too important to give up on so easily," Owen said.

"What things are too important to give up on easily?" Nancy, wearing jeans and a lightweight sweater, joined them. She held a steaming coffee mug in her hands. She sipped.

"Vacation plans. They borrowed our RV, remember?"

"Adam, sweetheart, I love that camper, but the

last thing you need is an RV vacation. Pick a hotel, go to a beach. RVs are hard work. You should relax."

"But they'll have more time with the boys if they drive."

Nancy rolled her eyes. "The boys have school. If Adam needs some time away, he should go to a hotel."

"Jenny wants an RV trip," Owen argued, as if he had inside knowledge of what she preferred in a vacation.

"Jenny wants, huh?" Nancy rolled her eyes again. "Jenny should know that Adam needs his rest." She put down her mug, then placed her hands on either side of her son's head. "What are you doing on the warehouse floor? You should be home. Resting."

"I'm not tired, Mom, but thanks."

"I'm just saying—"

"I know what you're saying." She was saying he was too hurt to work, too damaged to offer anything to the business. "I have some work to do, if the two of you don't mind."

Owen hooked Nancy's arm through his, then grabbed her coffee mug. "Too much sugar," he said, after tasting it.

"Just enough sugar, thanks. Some of us like to enjoy our coffee, not squeal in pain when it passes our lips."

"I only squealed once, and that was thirty years ago, and it was because I didn't know it was so hot."

"Well, of course it was hot. It's coffee, dear," Nancy said, and their conversation faded into the warehouse noises as they walked away.

Adam glanced at the office window. Jenny was back, and he couldn't stop the smile that spread over his face. Some things were too important to give up on easily. Which was why he wasn't giving up. Not today.

Not ever.

He went upstairs to talk to her, but Jenny wasn't there. The contracts with the new distributor were on the desk, and he didn't think she would mind, so he sat down to wait for her and read them. Adam skimmed through the papers for both the home builder and the distributor.

She'd done good work. But then, when did Jenny ever do anything that wasn't good? She'd raised their sons, and the boys were amazing. Held the business together and it was thriving. She'd gotten these two contracts past his parents, whom he loved, but with whom he was going to have to lay down some ground rules. They'd sold Buchanan's to Jenny and him; that was where their vision had ended and where his and Jenny's vision had begun.

When Owen, then Adam, used this office,

it had been dusty. An old desk Adam's grandfather built had dominated the room. The desk was still here, but Jenny had refinished it—Adam wasn't sure when—so that it glimmered in the sunlight coming through the windows. Instead of the utility blinds that had shaded the space, she'd hung gauzy drapes. Added plants on a table. Not flowers like he'd sent, but a small fern and a couple pots with daisies.

A drawing Frankie brought home from school last spring hung on the bulletin board, along with a sketch of the bed Adam had designed for them. He'd given it to her when they still lived in the apartment over the coffee shop, telling her that someday they would have room for not only a bigger bed, but a family. He'd made sure that promise came true.

His grandfather had given him the house and land, but Jenny had turned the place into a home. Adam had built the bed, but Jenny had softened the hard lines of cherry with a cozy comforter, pillows.

His ideas. Her execution.

God, he loved her. And he'd almost thrown her away. Thrown their family away. Adam tapped the walking stick in his hand against the floor. It had taken a tornado and epilepsy to make him see what he had in his life, and now that he'd seen it, he wouldn't give it away like so much trash.

She returned a few minutes later, a file folder in her hand.

"Do you want to have lunch?" he asked.

She blinked at him. "It's barely eleven."

"I know. I thought we might go someplace special." When she only stared at him, Adam balked. "You know, we're signing the contracts. We should celebrate."

A look he couldn't quite describe crossed her face. "Oh. Okay. Sure," she said, but her voice was flat, not excited. He hadn't expected cartwheels or anything, but a little enthusiasm wouldn't hurt. Still, it was lunch. With Jenny. It was an opening.

After they got in the car, he directed her out of town. This would be better if he could drive, but he still wasn't cleared for driving. Might never be. He didn't want to think about that. When he instructed her to turn on the road that would take them to the west side of the lake, she shot him a curious glance. But when she switched on the signal to turn into the fancy restaurant that over-looked Slippery Rock Lake, Adam shook his head. "Just keep driving."

"There's nothing else out here."

"It's a nice day for a drive."

"Adam, I have work."

"And *we* have contracts to celebrate. It's just lunch, Jen." She inhaled once, a long, slow breath.

She didn't turn the car around, and Adam took that as a good sign. Jenny always liked surprises.

"So, where are we going?"

"You'll see," he said, and was rewarded with a smile. They drove for a while along the south side of the lake. At the crossroad that would take them back around the lake toward town and then to Tyler Orchard, a local favorite and his friend, Collin's, business, Adam told her to take a left. She complied, but shot him another look.

Adam turned on the radio, to find Tim McGraw singing about being humble. Adam hadn't had much humility in his life. He had expected certain things, and for the most part, he had gotten what he wanted, from football to Jenny. He was learning more about humility now. Letting other people take the lead, listening to what they said.

It started with the doctors. Now he needed to add listening to Jenny to the list. In the car, where she couldn't find something else to do, where he couldn't chicken out, seemed like a good place to start.

"I haven't said thank you yet." Adam started with the apology he had yet to offer. He'd made her breakfast, had begun spending more time with the boys. He'd sent her flowers, but had just signed his name. "I didn't realize how much I was leaving to you, and I'm sorry."

"It isn't as if you didn't have your reasons." Her

knuckles went white as she gripped the steering wheel of the old Mustang more tightly. "It scared me," she said after a long moment. "I felt like I was watching you fade away, and there was nothing I could do to stop it. When you weren't fading out, you were so angry. I didn't know what to do with the anger any more than I knew how to... Well, you know."

He did know. He'd felt as if he were fading away. As if the life he'd been living had betrayed him. As if the tornado had come for him, specifically, as if to punish him for something. He hadn't realized how much what he was going through was affecting Jenny, though, and for that he couldn't forgive himself. Not yet.

"You held things together, and for that I am thankful. I know it isn't enough, I know signing the contracts can't erase all the things I haven't done since May, but I want you to know I don't want to fade away. I want my life back. Turn here," he directed.

Jenny squinted her eyes, but turned onto the road that would lead them to a small town near the Arkansas state line. She had to know where they were going by now, but she didn't say anything, just kept driving.

And now for the harder part. "It occurs to me that while I want my old life back, you don't." Her knuckles paled even more. "I never asked if you wanted to work at Buchanan's. If you wanted to expand the business. Not now, but before."

She nibbled her lower lip.

"I never asked you what you wanted."

She didn't say anything.

The small roadside diner appeared around a curve, and Jenny slowed. Turned in and parked beneath an old maple.

"Why are we here, Adam?" She looked straight ahead, at the faded roof, at the window sign that read Pete's Diner—Food You Eat.

"What is it that you want, Jenny? Not from me. Not from the boys or my parents or yours. What is it that *you* want?"

"Why are we here, Adam?" she asked again, and the note of panic in her voice made him feel like a jerk. She'd asked him to leave. Maybe she'd really meant it, and not just as a wake-up call.

"This is where we started." He forced the words to pass his lips. He wanted his life back. He wanted her, too. A little groveling wouldn't kill him. Being honest with her wouldn't, either. "I thought maybe this could be where we start over."

Jenny turned off the car, put the keys in her bag. Slowly, she turned to face him. "I want more," she said.

Adam didn't know how to interpret those three words.

"Let's see what Pete has for lunch." She didn't

wait. Jenny slung her bag over her shoulder and got out of the car. Strode with purpose to the swinging glass door.

Adam followed.

There were a few locals in the roadside diner. An older couple eating club sandwiches in silence, a couple farmers. Adam and Jenny took a table near the front window, under the Food You Eat sign. The waitress, a woman with gray-streaked brown hair, brought glasses of water and took their order. When she was gone, Adam waited, but Jenny didn't say a word. She stared out the window as if there was more to see in the parking lot than a few farm trucks.

Adam studied the area, trying to figure out what Jenny found so fascinating. One of the trucks had a weird rust patch over the wheel well that look a little like the shape of Arkansas, but other than that, it was just a parking lot. Farm vehicles, a few scrubby patches of grass. That big maple tree shading the Mustang.

"All I ever wanted was you," she said finally. "Your parents were so involved in your life, when mine were so involved in their own. I wanted to be a part of that. I wanted to have children of my own who would experience that. I never realized how lonely it could be to be part of a big, involved family."

Adam wasn't sure what to say to that. They'd

never been alone long enough to be lonely, had they? They'd got married as soon as Jenny graduated, had Frankie a year later, then Garrett. Sunday dinners with his parents or hers. They lived and worked together.

"How were you lonely?"

Jenny sipped her water before answering. "It maybe wasn't lonely so much as feeling alone. We both work and make money, but I pay the bills. I do the grocery shopping, I figure out our meals, I clean the house. I love doing all those things—I don't expect or want you do to them. But sometimes it's like you don't even know what I do. You go to the Slope with the guys—and I think that's great—while I clean up the house and make sure the kids' homework is done and get them bathed and ready for bed. I get up the next day to make breakfast and get them to school. Then I work, and pick them up from school, and start the homework cycle or take them to karate, and you go play in the softball league. It's like you have this life with friends and your family, and you get all the good stuff with the kids. You're the T-ball coach, and you take them bowling or swimming. I clean up after them and make them dinner. I clean up after you and make you dinner. Who cleans up after me? Who takes care of me?"

Adam had never thought of it that way, which had to prove he was an inconsiderate bastard.

But he could be different, better, for her this time around. "I will. Anytime you want, anything you need."

A half smile crossed her mouth, but didn't quite reach her eyes. "Until all the rest of it fell on my shoulders, I didn't realize how separated we'd become. When I was keeping the business going, when I was trying to get you well. I love the boys, and I miss taking them to and from school. I like homework, and I like it when we all go watch you play softball. When you were hurt, all I did was work—at Buchanan's, with the kids, on the house. And I worried for you, and I tried to keep a positive attitude, not only for you, but for your parents. For myself. I don't want to be alone in this anymore."

Adam wasn't sure how to respond. He'd thought he was the only one who had to adjust to his condition. That he was the only one directly affected. But he'd drawn them all down into the darkness with him. He clenched his fists. Damn, he wished he hadn't dragged them into this, but at least now he could get them out of it. He could take Jenny to the Slope. He couldn't wrestle with the boys, but he could referee when they wrestled around. He couldn't play softball, at least not now, but he could still instruct the boys in the backyard. He was living in the RV, but there were ways he could show Jenny that she meant the world to him. Like adding to her table of potted plants.

"I don't want you to be alone, either. And I don't want to be alone." He reached for her hand, but Jenny drew it away before he could touch her, making his heart stutter. Unless…unless this was where she said she didn't want to be alone, but she didn't want him, either.

He finished his sandwich, pondering what the right move was for this moment. Drive directly through her defenses, like he did on the football field? Or juke to the side, throw her off balance so she couldn't be sure what was happening next?

Adam was never the biggest guy on the football field, so juking had always gained him more yardage. He hoped it would work now.

"What is it that you want from me?"

An annoyed expression flickered over her face, bringing out the brown flecks in her eyes. Adam backtracked, fast.

"That wasn't an accusation. I'm sure you showed me a thousand times what you wanted from me, and I missed every time. I'm asking now—what can I do to show you that I'm in this, too?"

Jenny forked up a bite of salad and chewed. She sipped her iced tea. "I want you to know what I want, and I know that doesn't sound fair. I'm asking you to have ESP or something. That isn't it.

But if I tell you to do something, it isn't the same as if you just do it."

"Like the flowers?" It had been eye-opening to learn she didn't like cut flowers. He was reminded how he needed to pay more attention to what she said, to what she did. And he had to stop to question if something he was about to do would really please her, or if it was something that would please his mom. They were two very different women. And Jenny deserved to have a husband who recognized that.

"Like I said before, I do like flowers, but I would prefer them in plant form, so I can keep them forever." She had finished her salad and pushed the bowl away.

"So, daisies and roses, right?" She shot him a surprised glance. "I saw the daisies in your office this morning. I made a mental note."

Adam paid the bill and walked with Jenny to the Mustang. Since he'd been going to the physical therapist, his knee didn't throb as much when he walked. Most of the pain in his hip happened when he sat or stood for a long period of time. He got into the sports car, wincing a little as he folded his legs inside. Jenny headed the car toward Slippery Rock.

While they hadn't made any huge strides, he thought the lunch was progress. He was getting a better sense of what she wanted; of course, it helped that she'd been giving him the same message. She wanted to be included in his decisions, or at least given the option to participate in the things he did. She wanted choices. She wanted to be remembered and thought of…and she didn't want to have to guide his actions. He had to think of her on his own, treat her like she mattered to him.

They drove in silence until hitting the Slippery Rock city limits. Jenny slowed the car. "I haven't asked lately. How's physical therapy going?"

"Good, I think. It's hard to tell. The knee seems better, but the hip is still painful."

She nodded as she negotiated the turn to the house.

"You're picking up the kids at school?" she asked.

Adam nodded, then remembered what she had said at Pete's. "Unless you want to today."

"Who are they expecting?"

"Me. Frankie asked a couple times."

"Then they get you."

"How about we trade off tomorrow? I'll take them, you can pick them up?"

"Sure. I, ah, need to get some groceries."

She stopped the car in the drive and Adam got out. Jenny pulled the wheelchair from the trunk as if the small space was made for the large chair. When she had driven away, Adam pushed the chair into the garage. He needed to make an official list, now that he was figuring out more of what Jenny needed.

He pulled the little notebook from the pocket in the wheelchair and limped toward the backyard. He sat at the patio table and wrote "What Does Jenny Want?" He knew she wanted to be considered, to have her wants attended to. His gaze landed on the boards from the fence project stacked in the backyard.

Building Jenny a fence wasn't exactly a grand romantic gesture, but she had already said she didn't want flowers. Maybe romance wasn't the best way to reach out to his wife.

He pulled his cell phone from his pocket and made a call. Maybe building a fence would be the next step in bridging the gap between them.

JENNY GRABBED A multipack of macaroni and cheese off the shelf at Mallard's Grocery, tossing it into her cart and reaching for a box of rice. She was tired of sandwiches for lunch, breakfast-for-dinner or the boys' favorite: hot dogs and home fries. If she was going to get out of the rut her relationship had been in, she might as well also get the family out of the food rut they had been in.

She'd enjoyed playing around with slow-cooker recipes before the tornado because it made things simpler after work. Chicken and rice was a good option. In the butcher department, she saw the makings for a pot roast and added that to the cart, as well.

"Hey, sweetheart." Her father's voice caught her attention, and Jenny turned.

Doug must have come to the grocery store straight from the bank he managed because he still wore his usual khaki pants, polo shirt and wingtip shoes. When she was a little girl, she'd thought it was strange that her dad wore wingtips with khakis, but he'd always insisted they were the most comfortable shoes.

"Hi, Dad. What are you doing here?"

"Your mother has bridge club tonight. I'm escaping the madness."

"At the grocery store?"

He grinned sheepishly and motioned to his cart, which held five different kinds of cookies, a loaf of wheat bread and a package of deli ham. "Your mother is on one of her kicks again. She keeps ordering all our food from one of those box companies. You know, the ones with step-by-step directions on how to create a fabulous meal from a couple chicken breasts, some chickpeas and zucchini squash? Only she never adds desserts to the box. I've started hoarding a few of my favorites."

"I think the point of those subscription boxes is to eat more healthily." Still, it was typical of her mother to think about only what she wanted.

Margery wanted to watch her weight, so she subscribed to a healthy cooking box, but didn't think that her husband might also want a dessert occasionally.

Jenny stopped short. Just like Adam had never considered the kind of flowers she liked or if she wanted to go with him to the Slope. Just like she had never said she wanted to go, had only gone along with what he was already doing.

She was her father.

Adam was her mother.

Jenny didn't like where this conversation was taking her, not even a little bit. Her dad didn't seem to notice her distraction, and continued talking.

"Man cannot live by chicken breast and zucchini noodles alone." Doug hugged her. "You're looking better. How's Adam?"

"The last doctor's appointment was positive. They may have hit on the right medication combo. And he's doing the physical therapy."

"That's great, sweetheart."

"How's the banking business?" She leaned a hip against the cart handle.

"Interesting," he said, that familiar grin crossing his face at the lame joke. "It's fine. Keeps me busy and your mom happy. How's it going with Nancy and Owen back at the cabinet shop?"

Jenny considered. As frustrated as she still was

with her in-laws' interference in the business, Buchanan's was on track. The new contracts were signed. Nancy still clucked about the furniture side of things, but Owen seemed supportive. And he'd been right about shipping the granite countertops with the lowers instead of parsing it into two shipments. "Not bad. We had dinner with them Sunday. They're talking about going to Florida after the holidays."

The thought of them leaving sent a jolt of apprehension down her spine. Nancy and Owen had meddled, but they'd been here to help her. While her own parents, who lived across town, hadn't changed anything about their interactions with Jenny, Adam, Frankie or Garrett. What if, when Nancy and Owen left, Adam went downhill?

Jenny clenched her hands on the cart handle. She would manage it. The two of them were talking now in ways they never had before. She wouldn't let things slide this time. She wouldn't be reduced to sneaking dessert into her house because her husband was on a diet.

They started down the aisle, and Doug added a bunch of grapes to his cart. "Just so you won't worry about my sugar addiction," he said.

Jenny grinned at him. She could keep this light, joke with him about grapes and dessert. Or she could ask a hard question. "Dad?"

Doug grabbed a box of Pop-Tarts off another

shelf. At this rate, his entire shopping cart would be a carboholic's dream. "Yeah?"

"When I was talking to Mom a couple weeks ago, she, ah…" No, scratch asking him a hard question. When Margery had expressed her disappointment with Jenny's choice of husband, she'd been blowing off steam, annoyed that what she wanted wasn't high on Jenny's priority list. "Never mind."

Doug stopped his cart and took hold of her arm. "Your mom, what?" he asked, in what she'd always considered his Bank Loan Revocation voice.

"Aiden's back in town. We're having a barbecue on Sunday. You and Mom should come." Because if she hadn't had a normal relationship with her parents to this point in her life, maybe she could, moving forward. Jenny was making things work with Adam. He was listening to what she needed. She could do the same with her parents. She could make their relationship better, too, but not if she undermined Margery about something her mother likely hadn't meant.

"We don't have any other plans."

"Noon."

Her father nodded. "Now what did your mother do or say that's making this frown line so deep?" he asked, and rubbed his finger along the bridge of her nose between her eyebrows, as if he could wipe her worries away just that easily.

"It's nothing."

Doug watched her for a long moment and Jenny squirmed. As if she was back in elementary school and had forgotten her homework. Again. "She kind of said I should leave Adam. That he wasn't—"

Doug folded his arms across his chest. "Nonsense. Sweetheart, your mother has always had… ideas about what your life should be like. I was busy with work so I didn't interfere. But you chose Adam. What she wants or wanted for you stopped at that point. You need to do what is right for you, not for your mom."

Hearing the words shored up Jenny's confidence. "You don't agree with her?"

"I've never known Adam to be anything but kind, loyal and caring. I might have wanted the two of you to wait to get married, but I've never been sorry that you did."

Jenny heaved a sigh of relief. Hearing those words from her father reassured her on a basic level, especially after realizing she and Adam had some of the same traits that her parents showed to one another.

"You're doing okay? Really okay?"

She smiled and squeezed his hand. She might not have the call-twice-a-day relationship with her parents, but it was nice to know her father cared about her.

"I'm doing okay, Dad. Really." She wanted to tell him more about Adam, but she hadn't even shared her worries about him with his parents. It seemed like a betrayal, especially after the turnaround he'd had in the past couple weeks. Adam deserved her first loyalty.

"I need to get home," she said instead. "And oh, I saw there's a special on bratwurst in the meat department." Her father loved bratwurst, and Jenny was positive that particular favorite would not make it into any of her mother's food subscription boxes.

Doug's eyes brightened and he pressed a kiss to her cheek. "I love you, sweetheart. We'll see you Sunday."

"See you Sunday," she said, and started for the checkout, still thinking about the parallels between her parents' relationship and the path she'd fallen into with Adam.

As much as she didn't want him to take her for granted, she didn't want to take him for granted, either. She wanted more for both of them than a tepid friendship or sharing a house. One person sneaking in junk food while the other made unilateral decisions about everything from television shows to meals.

The two of them were on the right track now. She would keep them on it.

CHAPTER TEN

JENNY HEAVED A deep sigh as she saw not one, but two, sets of parents slam their car doors on the street before her home.

Nancy, wearing cropped pants and a cardigan twinset, carried a plate of cookies in her hands. Owen had on a pair of cargo shorts and a T-shirt in deference to the still-warm October sun. Her parents, by comparison, looked like they might be headed to a formal garden party in Tulsa or Saint Louis, not a backyard barbecue with children. Her mother wore wedge-heeled, peep-toe slides and a sheath dress in royal blue, with a wrap of some sort that was bound to have grass stains on it by the end of the day. Her father wore the familiar wingtips, pressed pants in a dove gray and a pearl-buttoned oxford shirt.

"Sweet Lord, this might have been a disastrous idea," she muttered before pasting a smile on her face as she opened the front door. Their parents had never been the best of friends, but her mother's attitude had significantly cooled since Adam's accident. "Moms, Dads," she said, "come in. Everyone is in the backyard."

Nancy pressed a quick kiss to her cheek. "I'll just leave the cookies in the kitchen on my way through. Don't you look lovely today?"

Jenny glanced at her outfit: denim capris with little birdhouses embroidered along the hem, and a striped T-shirt. Nothing to write home about, but then again, at least she wasn't in danger of ruining a garden-party-fabulous dress like her mother.

Owen and Doug followed Nancy through the house, but Margery hung back. She shot a disgusted look over her shoulder toward the RV. "What is the world is that…that thing doing here?"

Jenny wasn't about to tell her mother that Adam was living in the camper, at least for now. Margery might stage an actual offensive in the hopes this separation would become permanent. Jenny might not trust that they could save their relationship, but inviting her mother's criticism would only make things worse.

"We're thinking about taking the boys on a trip," she said, deciding that if the lie was good enough for Adam's parents, it was good enough for her own.

"In that?" Margery wrinkled her nose as if the RV might hold some awful disease.

Jenny had never been overly interested in camping—not even in an RV—but her mother's instant dislike of the possibility rubbed her the wrong way. She knew it was childish, but going on a vacation in an RV wasn't the end of the world. There were RVs worth millions of dollars that had better amenities than the best five-star hotel might have.

"Yes, in that. Probably to Branson." Her mother's least favorite place. That Jenny wasn't overly fond of it herself was beside the point. This was her life, not her mother's, and Jenny would live it the way she wanted to.

"God, dear, why would you want to go there?"

"The music? The food? The golf?"

Margery shook her head and continued through the house.

Adam had set up several small tables and chairs around the patio. His parents settled with Aiden at one, watching Frankie and Garrett tussle over a football in the yard. Doug stood near Adam at the grill, as if inspecting the cooking going on. Margery sat at a table by herself, hands folded in her lap, a benign expression on her face. Jenny made a beeline to the grill.

"Anything you need from the kitchen?"

Adam shook his head. "Chicken will be ready in about ten. How are the potatoes and salad coming along?"

"Ready when the chicken is." There was nothing left to do except take a seat. Jenny sat with her mother at the second table.

"Lunch will be ready in a few minutes."

"It's awfully sunny out here," Margery said.

"Well, yes, it's the middle of the day."

"You could have put up umbrellas or a tent or something."

Jenny hadn't thought of that. The four of them rarely used the umbrella stand that folded out to cover nearly the entire patio area. Besides, it was October. The sun was high in the sky, but it wasn't exactly sweltering. In fact, Jenny thought it was perfect, just sitting in the warm sunshine on a beautiful fall day. Still, she didn't want to be rude.

"I'll get an umbrella out of the garage."

She hurried around the side of the house. The umbrella was in a corner behind a pristine trash can Adam used to hold rakes and hoes and other lawn equipment. She pulled on it, but it didn't budge. Jenny pulled again and lost her balance. Strong arms came around her middle, holding her against a strong chest. Heart beating hard, she struggled to regain her footing.

"Whoa, there, champ, what did that umbrella ever do to you?" Adam chuckled.

"Nothing," she said. "My mother is playing Scarlett O'Hara and needs to shade herself from this unbecoming sun." Jenny could feel his heat through their clothing. Little jolts of electricity seemed to pulse between them, and her mouth went dry. She stepped away from Adam's side and brushed her hands over her capris. "I'm fine. Should have just moved the barrel first."

"I'll get it for you," he said, reaching for the heavy container.

Jenny reached around him. Heavy lifting was among the no-no's on the list from his doctor. "I've got it."

"I can move a trash can and an umbrella, Jen."

"I know." But he wasn't supposed to. Things were going so well for him, so well between them. She didn't want a freaking umbrella to bring everything crashing down around them again. Jenny grabbed the handle of the can and pulled it out of the way before Adam could. "She's my mother," she said, hoping Adam would let it go if she made this about her mom instead of his injury. "Is the chicken ready?"

"I left your dad in charge."

With the oversize can out of the way, Jenny grabbed the umbrella from the corner. "I'll just take this around," she said, and turned.

"Oof!" Adam staggered back. The umbrella clattered to the floor, and he doubled over.

"Oh, my God," Jenny said, rushing to him. She put her arms around his shoulders. "Are you okay? I'm so sorry."

He took in a long, slow breath. "I'm…fine," he

said, still breathing heavily. "You pack a punch with that umbrella." He chuckled.

"Well, you were kind of in the wrong place at the wrong time."

"I should have remembered that from other times your parents came over for a Sunday barbecue." He straightened, and she saw that his clear gaze was filled with laughter, not pain. The squeezing in her chest lightened. He was okay.

"I should have been paying more attention," she admitted.

"I should have ducked. My reflexes are a little slower than I remember." But he didn't seem upset by that fact. A few weeks ago, slower reflexes might have sent him into a days-long funk. He put his arm around her shoulders. "I'm okay, Jenny."

"I know."

"If a tornado can't break me by collapsing a building on my head, you're not going to do it with an umbrella."

It was the first time he'd ever made a joke about what had happened to him. That had to mean something. Didn't it?

"I guess not." Jenny wrapped her arms around his waist and buried her face in his chest. He was still Adam. His body felt the same. That smile looked the same. She inhaled. He still used the same soap that made her nose tickle. "You're still here," she said, meaning the words to be a whisper.

His arms came around her waist. "I'm still here, Jen." They stood like that for a long moment. Finally, Adam stepped away. "I should go make sure your dad isn't burning my chicken."

"And I need to make sure my mom isn't melting in the seventy-degree sunlight."

Together, they walked toward the backyard.

"It's *my* ball."

"Well, you're not throwing it right." Frankie raised his voice, and Jenny tensed as she walked through the gate with Adam and the umbrella. Her older son held a foam football in one hand high above his head, while her younger son jumped up and down trying to reach it. "I'm teaching you how to throw it."

"I know how to throw it."

"Do not."

"Do, too." Garrett leaped again, and Jenny started toward him, ready to referee the boys. Adam's hand on her arm stopped her. She shot him a glance.

"Boys fight over balls. It's nature."

"But Frankie's so much bigger."

"So Garrett will have to work that much harder. Besides, Frankie isn't tackling him. He's holding a ball over his head."

Aiden walked up behind them. "I see the games are in full swing," he said, taking in the argument between the boys.

"Frankie's torturing Garrett about his throwing arm," Adam replied, making way for his brother, who deftly slid the large umbrella from Jenny's arm.

"Looks like you could use some shade." Aiden headed toward the tables where Nancy and Margery sat. "Hey, Mom," he said, pressing a quick kiss to Nancy's cheek once he'd set the umbrella in the stand.

"Hello, sweetheart. How are things going at the B and B?"

"Clean sheets and towels every day, and it turns out the steaks at the Slippery Rock Grill are just as good as what I could get in San Diego."

Garrett crowed, bringing Jenny's attention back to the boys. He'd managed to knock the ball from Frankie's hand, and was scrambling across the grass to pick it up. Frankie put out his foot, tripping his younger brother, then pushing his face into the grass.

"Now, we go in," Adam said, striding across the yard. Jenny reached Garrett first, set him on his feet. The little boy's lower lip trembled, but his hands were in fists at his sides. Clearly, he was as mad as he was hurt.

Adam grabbed Frankie by the shoulder. "Inside, buddy. March."

Frankie pursed his lips and scowled at his

younger brother. "He's such a baby," he said as he started toward the sliding glass door.

"You're okay?"

"I can, too, throw," Garrett hollered after his older brother. "I'm not a baby."

Aiden crossed the lawn and ruffled his hand over Garrett's head. "Nope, no babies here. What do you say we work on your throwing arm?" he asked, and he reminded her so much of how Adam used to deal with the boys that Jenny had to take a second look. But, no, Adam was marching Frankie toward the house, a tense set to his shoulders.

Aiden tossed the football to Garrett. The little boy tossed it back, no longer looking like he wanted to tear after his older brother to push him to the ground.

"I'll be right back," Jenny said, and didn't wait for either set of parents to say anything. All four of them were looking from her to the door where Adam and Frankie had disappeared.

"He's just a baby." Frankie's voice carried down the hall from the kitchen. When Jenny reached the doorway, she saw him sitting across the table from Adam, arms crossed over his chest. "I was gonna teach him to throw, but he was being a baby."

"How were you going to teach him to throw by holding the ball over your head?" Adam asked.

Jenny joined the two of them at the table. Frankie shrugged. "And the tripping?"

Frankie kicked his feet but didn't say anything.

"You're bigger than he is. That means you look out for him. You don't push him down, and you don't use words like *stupid* or *dummy*, no matter how you're feeling inside." Frankie twisted his mouth, and Adam continued, "How *do* you feel inside?"

"Frankie?" Jenny reached across the table, pushing a lock of hair off his forehead. She wanted to ask Adam how he knew what to say to their son. He'd never shown an interest in discipline, had been content to be the fun dad. Where had this come from?

A wave of tenderness swelled in her chest for him. Because he could have let the boys actually fight. Or he could have started throwing the ball with Garrett instead of dealing with Frankie, but he hadn't. He was here, at this table, and he was talking.

"Mad. Because he can't throw the ball right," the boy said after a long moment. But he didn't look at either Jenny or Adam. He looked past them, toward the window over the sink.

"I don't think you're mad about the ball, Frankie," she said, needing him to know that she saw through whatever this facade was, too.

"I don't, either," Adam said, and he slid his hand across the table to touch Frankie's shoulder.

"I just wanted him to do what I wanted him to do."

Control, Jenny realized. Like needing to know her schedule and Adam's. Frankie still wanted to control everything around him.

"We can't make people do what they don't want to do, Frankie," she told him. She looked at Adam, who twisted his mouth to the side, much like Frankie had done. Only there was no anger in the set of Adam's shoulders, only sadness.

Adam's gaze caught hers and she smiled at him. "We can only treat them how we'd like to be treated." She didn't think the little boy would understand the subtle differences between asking someone to treat you with respect and demanding they behave in a certain way.

"It isn't fair. I'm the oldest. I have to teach him how to play, but he won't listen to me." Frankie's little fists clenched again, and he wrinkled his forehead.

"Who said you have to teach him?" Jenny asked.

He shrugged. "Dad was gonna, but he can't play football anymore. I'm the oldest, so I have to teach Garrett."

"And when he doesn't listen, it makes you mad," Adam said, and Frankie nodded. "I can't play football with you guys, that's true. We can still toss the ball around, though. I can teach Garrett how to throw a spiral, and we can work on your catching."

"Really?" the boy said, considering the possibility that his dad might still play with him. It was as if a tight fist locked on Jenny's chest, making it hard to breathe.

"Really. Why don't you sit here and think about apologizing to Garrett while your mom and I get the drinks ready for lunch?"

Adam and Jenny moved through the kitchen, readying glasses, drinks and side dishes as if they'd done it a thousand times. Funny, it was getting harder and harder to remember Adam not helping, not being part of their lives. She knew the thought should make her antsy, but it didn't.

"Did I hurt him?" Frankie asked, when the rest of the barbecue things were on trays ready to take outside.

"You bruised his pride a little," Adam said.

"I'll go tell him I'm sorry." Frankie got up and turned toward the door, then swung back around. "If I'm allowed."

"Go ahead, sweetie. We'll be right behind you," Jenny said. She listened as his footsteps faded down the hallway. "Thanks. You knew just what to say to him."

"I'm pretty sure Aiden and I had at least ten

versions of that same fight through the years. Maybe not for the same reasons. That was about the tornado as much as it was about learning to throw a pass, right?"

Jenny sighed. "Yeah. I think he'll be angry about it all for a while. Your walking with them, us keeping to a schedule, talking through the rough points instead of spanking or yelling... We'll get him through it."

"What about Garrett?"

"Him, too. I haven't wanted to bring up his art-work with him, not directly, but he drew another attack tornado this week." She reached into the drawer and showed Adam the drawing, one with dark black clouds hovering over a white house. There were no people this time, and she wondered if that was an improvement. Whether it was or not, they couldn't put off talking to Garrett—or to Frankie—about what had happened. "What do you think about sitting down with both of them after everyone leaves?"

Adam nodded. "What do we say?"

"That they're safe, and that the danger is over, and that we love them."

"How do you know this stuff?"

Jenny tilted her head to the side. "How did you know what to say to Frankie just now? You're not a bad father, Adam. You were never a bad father. You have to follow your instincts."

And so did she. She had to stop reminding herself of what life was like before the tornado, or between the tornado and the laundry incident. Adam was trying to change. She had to trust that together they could both change.

"THANK YOU FOR a wonderful afternoon." Margery stood stiffly near the back gate. Doug, Owen and Nancy were playing tag with the boys in the yard, but Margery hadn't joined in. Adam wondered what his mother-in-law was afraid of. Running after a couple kids was the fun part of being a parent or grandparent. He'd like nothing more than to be taking part.

There was no pang of sorrow at the thought that, for now, Adam still couldn't run around after his boys. They could do other things. Watch movies. Toss the foam ball around, like they'd done after lunch. They could just be together.

"We enjoyed having you here. The boys have missed you."

Margery sniffed. "We didn't want to intrude."

"You wouldn't have." Was it his imagination, or did her shoulders relax a little at his words? Was she as nervous to be talking to him as he was to her? The two of them had never had a close relationship, but since the tornado, it had been especially strained.

The boys squealed, and Adam grinned when

he saw Owen pretend to fold under Garrett's flying tackle. The way he'd done a thousand times when Adam was a boy.

Aiden and Jenny returned from inside. Aiden had volunteered for cleanup, but since he didn't know his way around her kitchen, Jenny had joined him.

"Thank you for lunch," Margery said, and the stiffness was back in her voice. Maybe he'd imagined that whole shoulder sagging thing.

Doug came over, and Jenny's parents said their goodbyes. Margery hugged the boys tightly, but didn't seem to know what to do with Jenny. Finally, she offered an air kiss, then retreated through the gate.

"You're looking well, Adam," Doug said.

"Thank you. I'm feeling well." God, was it this hard for the millions of other married men to talk to their in-laws?

"Well, take care." Doug waved to the boys and followed his wife's path through the gate.

"We should get home, too. Thank you for the barbecue," Nancy said, hugging first Jenny, then Adam. "It was so nice to all be together for an afternoon." She shot a stern glance at Aiden. "Especially since one of you hasn't been home in almost a year."

Aiden grinned and threw his arm around Nancy's shoulders. "If I let you do my laundry, will you forgive me?"

"Just how many loads do you have?" she asked suspiciously. "I am not a laundry service."

"That's not what I hear," Aiden teased, as they began walking toward the front of the house. Owen hugged the boys, then followed them.

When everyone was gone, Adam turned to Jenny. "Alone at last."

"That actually went way smoother than I expected. You know, after I nearly decapitated you with the umbrella, and Frankie tried to plant Garrett like a tree."

"Speaking of. Should we?"

She nodded, and called the boys to come inside with them. When the four of them were seated around the table, Jenny turned several of Garrett's drawings over and spread them on the table. The boy traced his fingers around the lines on the page.

"Dad and I wanted to talk to you guys. About the tornado."

"The tornado hurt Dad," Garrett said, not taking his gaze off the coloring page.

"Yeah, it did, but it also hurt Mommy and it hurt you and it hurt Frankie," Adam said.

"I didn't get cut." Garrett's gaze snapped to his.

Frankie scooted his chair closer to the table, then said, "I didn't hit my head."

"It hurt your feelings," Jenny explained, when Adam could only watch his boys watching him. "It might have made you feel scared or alone, but you aren't alone. Dad and I are right here, and we aren't going anywhere."

"You go to work," Garrett reminded her.

Adam motioned helplessly to Jenny, unsure what to say. He was here at the table with them, he walked them to school, but he was living in the RV. Even when he'd been in the guest room, he'd shut himself off from the three of them. Saying differently seemed like a lie.

"Yes, I do. And you go to school. But there are people at work and there are people at school who help keep us safe. Like your teachers."

"Dad goes to work with you now," Frankie offered. "And Mamaw and Papaw are there. And Uncle Aiden."

"They're all there. And when you're at school, you and Garrett can look out for each other, but you can't be mean to each other. You can't fight just because you're mad or scared about the tornado. It's gone. There's nothing to be afraid of anymore."

"Really?" Garrett asked.

"Really."

"Promise?" This time Frankie asked the question, and it made Adam's heart hurt.

"Promise," he said, his voice sounding rough to his ears.

Frankie threw his arms around Adam's neck, then Garrett followed suit. Adam hugged the boys tightly.

I promise. I promise. I promise.

Adam repeated the words over and over in his head until Frankie's grip around his neck loosened and Garrett slid off his lap.

"Want to watch TV?" Frankie asked, directing his question to Garrett. The little boy nodded, but they looked to Jenny for approval. She nodded in turn, and the boys went into the living room. A moment later, Adam heard the television come to life.

Jenny took his hand in hers. And it really did seem like a fresh start.

A WEEK AFTER the barbecue, Jenny ran her finger over the velvety leaf of a potted African violet. The plant had been delivered that morning, and once again the card simply read "Adam." He'd sent her a plant, for no reason at all. The knowledge made her heart stutter a little in her chest. He wanted her back. She was getting what she wanted.

Everything she'd asked for.

This past week was the happiest she could remember being in…longer than she cared to admit.

So why did she feel as if there was still something missing? Like another shoe might still drop?

He was here, all the time. It was what she'd wanted—for him to be present in their life, to take an active role. So why did she sometimes feel as if he were hovering over her? As if she couldn't breathe when he was around, and not in that exciting, he's-going-to-kiss-me way. In a why-is-he-in-my-space way.

He was part of her, down to her very soul. When she woke in the morning, her first thought was still of Adam. He entered her thoughts a million times throughout the day. She saw him in Frankie's determination to master third-grade math and in the excitement Garrett had for every new thing he encountered. Adam was here—he was downstairs right now, and he'd be in the kitchen tonight—but he wasn't really there. Not fully. Because the determination and excitement she remembered were missing. God, she missed him. Missed his enthusiasm, his passion for life.

She wanted him not just living in the RV in her driveway and not in the guest room downstairs. She wanted her husband back. All of him.

"Jenny."

She'd changed over the past few months. It was as if by getting what she wanted, she wasn't getting what she needed.

The thought made her head hurt.

"Jen?" Aiden's voice brought her back to the office she'd spent so much time making her own. She focused on him in her doorway, his shaggy hair and board shorts making him look way too California for a small town in Missouri. In October.

"Sorry, I just spaced out for a minute there. What did you need?"

Aiden crossed the room and put a couple papers on her desk. He watched her closely for a long moment. "Are you okay?"

"Sure. Why wouldn't I be okay?" She stacked the papers on her desk, sliding them into a folder. Then she clasped her hands together. "Everything is fine."

"If everything is so *fine* why did you just put my notes for the next batch of cabinets into your folder for the distributorship?"

"Oh." Jenny blinked. She pulled the pages of notes from the folder. Aiden's bold penmanship covered the page, along with a few notated drawings. "Sorry. I, ah…" She had no idea how to finish the sentence without letting Aiden know just how conflicted she was about the situation, not only at work but at home. He was Adam's brother—she didn't want to bring him into their marital problems.

"He seems to be getting his legs back under him. Figuring things out."

"Yeah. Yeah, he does." Jenny glanced out the window that overlooked the warehouse and saw Adam bent over a drafting table. "I appreciate you coming out, Aiden. I know Adam does, too."

He sat down across from her. "I was thinking, you guys don't really need me. You've got the office part covered, Mom is answering phones like she never retired and Dad is keeping the truck crews on time. Adam's back on the floor, designing."

The thought of Aiden leaving made Jenny's stomach drop. No, his return hadn't been the thing that put their world back in balance, but that first day had been the turning point for Adam. What would happen if Aiden left?

"They're already talking about heading to Florida after Thanksgiving."

"Jen," he began, but Jenny talked over him. Because if this was Aiden's way of bowing out of Slippery Rock again, she had to stop him.

"He needs you here, Aiden. You're the one who got him to come back to work—"

"You did that, Jenny. You pushed and you prodded and you made him move into the RV. You woke him up. You got him back here."

Jenny blinked, choosing to focus on the RV part and not the she'd-saved-Adam part. If she'd saved him, if she'd brought him back, why didn't things feel settled? "You know about the RV?"

"Adam hates camping out, even in an RV, more than your mother probably would. The only reason for it to still be in your driveway is as a place for him to stay." He shook his head, then pushed a lock of hair behind his ear. "I saw what you saw, Jenny. That hollowed-out look in his eyes. The anger. Maybe not as much as you saw it, but it was there. I'm sorry I didn't come back sooner. There were…just some things I wasn't quite ready to face."

She didn't know how to respond to that. A football hero, just like Collin Tyler, Levi Walters and James Calhoun, Aiden had had the run of this town, or so it had seemed to her at the time. Still, California versus Slippery Rock was a big difference. He had to be bored silly, working on cabinets and furniture when he'd been building custom sailboats in California.

"I guess you'll be wanting to go back soon."

He shrugged. "Maybe. I was actually thinking I'd like to be one of the first hires here, once everything is finalized with the distributorship, and the contractor in Joplin. If you think Adam would go for it."

"But what about what you just said? About us not needing you?"

"I guess you could say I was testing the waters."

"So, you don't want to leave?"

Aiden shook his head.

"But you build boats. We build cabinets." He'd flip-flopped before her very eyes just moments ago, so she had to be certain he really wanted to stay.

"And outdoor furnishings."

"Still, it can't be much of a challenge."

"Maybe I'm not looking for a challenge."

She studied him for a moment. Was that sadness she saw in his clear gaze? The kind of sadness she'd been so focused on in Adam, but hadn't been able to see in Aiden? "Is there a reason you don't want to go back?"

"I'm not on the run from the law or anything," he said, and chuckled. "California has been good to me, but I've been missing home the past couple years."

If he'd missed Slippery Rock so much, why had it taken three months for him to get here after she'd called with the news of Adam's accident? But Jenny didn't want to fight with Aiden. He had come home when Adam needed him. That was enough.

"If you're sure this is what you want, I won't even wait to finalize the contracts. You're hired."

Aiden left the office and Jenny frowned. She and Adam made hiring decisions together, and she'd bypassed his opinion altogether. She sat back in her chair, considering what that meant.

That she was confident enough to make her own decisions?

Then the other shoe, a shoe she hadn't even realized she'd been holding, dropped.

She didn't trust Adam. Not his renewed interest in the business. Not his willingness to walk the boys to school.

She didn't trust that he was interested in her, at all. Not the way she needed him to be interested.

She'd been afraid the stress of running the business might set off the epilepsy, so she hadn't asked him to take part in it at first. Then, when the stresses of the business and the house and his health and the boys and his parents got to be too much, it was easier to start blaming his inattentiveness instead of her own fear. She'd pulled her life together, set things up to be financially stable, given everything she had to the boys. If Adam disappeared on her again, if he returned to that dark place...she didn't think she could pull all that together again.

Jenny didn't want to be angry at Adam. She didn't want to be afraid that every little thing might set off the next seizure. She wanted to be like Aiden: realize something was off or missing in life, and do something to correct it. And in doing that, Aiden had returned to Slippery Rock.

Maybe it was time for Jenny to put her trust in the work she and Adam had done. The honest feelings they'd shared over the past few weeks. Let go of the previous three months, and start living in the present.

She picked up her phone and texted Adam.

How about dinner tonight? Just the two of us?

A few minutes later, her text alert sounded.
Definitely, Adam responded.

I'll get a sitter.

"Why didn't you order the steak?"

Adam sat across from Jenny in a corner booth at the Slippery Rock Grill. On a Wednesday evening, outside tourist season, the Grill wasn't busy. Five or six other tables were filled with people he recognized—the minister from the Methodist church, the mayor and his wife.

White cloths covered the tables, and faux suede covered the bench seats of the booths as well as the chairs. Low music played over the speakers. He recognized several country love songs, all in instrumental versions.

"Felt like a burger," he answered, and the lie slid off his tongue as if he lied every day. Hell, for the past few months, it seemed as if lying had been the only thing getting him through the day.

Lying about how he felt, what he wanted to do, why he didn't get out of the wheelchair.

Actually, that wasn't entirely true. Not anymore. He realized that he hadn't been telling as many lies, not since he and Jenny had shared their talks. So maybe it was time to stop lying entirely.

"I didn't want you to feel as if you had to cut my steak into tiny bites," he confessed. "A burger makes it easier. No serrated knives involved, just in case, because you can't cut a steak with a butter knife like you can a chicken breast." Jenny didn't say anything to that. Adam wasn't sure what to say so he grabbed the first topic of conversation that came to him. "No seizures in more than a month… I thought Dr. Lambert seemed happy at the checkup last week."

"Me, too." Jenny fiddled with the edge of the tablecloth. "Have I been treating you like a child that much?"

"Only because you had to. I wasn't much help to you in the beginning. We didn't know what would set off the next seizure." He still didn't know what would set one off, but he didn't want to fight about it. He just wanted to enjoy this night with his wife. Make her remember how good things had been not so long ago. Wanted to make things better now than they had ever been.

"I'm sorry."

"Me, too. For all of it, Jen, and I'm going to

do my best to make these past three months up to you."

The waitress, a girl who'd graduated in Adam's class, brought their salads, then disappeared into the kitchen. He thought her name might be Anna, but hadn't been paying attention when she introduced herself, and now couldn't quite place her. Just one more sign that he'd been oblivious to other people throughout his life.

He would do better.

"You don't have to make anything up to me," Jenny said, but Adam disagreed, and not just because of the things she'd said after the laundry incident. Jenny deserved so much better than he had given her.

She cleared her throat. "The dog trainer called again."

He heard the unspoken question in her voice. Adam still wasn't sold on the idea of a service dog, but Dr. Lambert had suggested it again at his last checkup.

"I like being back at work," he said thoughtfully. "I wasn't sure how it would go, not being able to use the equipment. I like it, though. Now that the physical therapy is going well, and being on the warehouse floor so much, I guess it makes more sense to have a service dog than when I was just at the house and in the wheelchair."

"If that's what you want, you should do it." He

hated the stilted tone in her voice, and the words seemed to hang in the air between them. Jenny fiddled with her fork, then set it down next to her plate. "Why do you want the dog? Why now and not a month ago or six weeks ago?"

Adam fiddled with his own fork, weighing his words carefully. If anything was going to make her walk away, it would be this. He didn't want her to. "Because six weeks ago, hell, a month ago, I was considering walking away from all of you."

Jenny blinked. Her body went still and she seemed to struggle to breathe.

"You didn't do anything wrong. It was me—it was all me." He stabbed a piece of calamari off the appetizer tray but didn't eat it. "I thought you and the boys would be better off without me. Without the uncertainty of the epilepsy, without my medical bills being a drain on our finances—"

"Well, that is one of the most selfish things I've ever heard," she said, indignation lacing her voice. "As if getting past your death would be easier on the boys, on me, than learning to live with the epilepsy. Adam, don't you know how important you are? To all of us?"

"I wasn't going to kill myself." He'd been in a dark place, but it hadn't been completely black. "I was simply going to leave. I didn't see walking away as being selfish. You've told me how lost I was, how I left you alone."

Adam bit back his next words, but the accusation in her gaze was too much. He'd been an ass. He'd shut her out so that it wouldn't hurt so much when he had to let her walk away. But—Lord, it hurt to think this, which was why he rarely had—she'd been just as gone as he. There was a part of Jenny that had been missing from the moment he'd woken up in the hospital, a piece of herself she'd held back from him. And it was killing him.

"When I woke up in that hospital bed, all I wanted was to see your face. But you looked at me as if you were seeing a ghost. I was still there, and you looked at me like I'd betrayed you somehow. From that first moment in the hospital, the blame was there." He shook his head. "I made things worse, so much worse, by not talking to you. By cutting myself off from you, from the boys, but I didn't know any other way to…to make things all right for you. I didn't want to hurt you again."

Jenny pushed her plate away and twisted the napkin in her lap around her hand. "I thought you were dead when they found you in the rubble. When you woke up I was so afraid. Afraid you would go back to sleep and never wake up again. Afraid of the seizures, afraid of what this all meant for us, for the boys."

"And I was afraid you wouldn't want a man with a broken head."

Jenny was quiet for a long moment. "Adam?"

"Yeah?"

"I don't know where we go from here."

He was quiet for a long moment in turn. "Me, either."

"Do you still want me?"

"Every single day." He said the words without hesitation, as if he couldn't speak them fast enough or with enough emphasis. "Do you still want *me*?"

Jenny nodded. "I think it's time for us to go home."

THEY DROVE HOME, and Jenny went inside to check on the boys. She came out the back door a couple moments later.

"Homework done, and they're playing LEGO Dimensions with Sadie," she reported. "She's going to put them down in a couple minutes, and said she can stay until ten."

It was just after seven. Three more hours with Jenny sounded like heaven. "Let's walk, then," he said, pleased when she passed the wheelchair without even pausing. Adam grabbed the walking stick from inside the garage door. It wouldn't do much if a seizure hit, but it made him feel steadier on his feet.

"I never thought I'd be married to a man who uses a cane like those secret agents in the old black-and-white movies."

"Walking stick. Canes are curved and short. This is long and manly."

She shook her head and looked at him from under her lashes. "That sounds like a bit of compensation. If you ask me, anyway."

It was the first sarcastic comment he'd heard from her in too long, and the words made him smile. They used to tease one another mercilessly; even before the tornado, though, he couldn't remember the last time they'd done it. Hell, he couldn't remember the last time they'd taken a walk on a random Tuesday evening.

They followed the narrow road west toward downtown and the marina, and when the docks came into view, he led her along one of them. Probably not the safest route, but he wanted to walk with her in the darkness there. Enjoy the lapping of the water against the docks and pilings. Take in some of the stars. Not specifically for seduction purposes, but he wouldn't turn down another kiss like the one they'd shared in the backyard.

Her hand found his in the darkness, and Adam twined their fingers together. He pointed. "Hercules is bright tonight."

"And Orion's Belt." They came to a bench and sat together, watching the sky above them. "Adam?"

"Yeah."

"You asked me the other day what I wanted."

He didn't say anything, just waited. Whatever Jenny had to say, he didn't want to influence her.

"I don't want to watch the stars, and I don't want to talk about the past, or worry about what might happen in the future."

That didn't leave a lot of options. "I'll take you home."

"I don't want to go home, not yet."

That left even fewer options. "We could wander over to the Slope." She'd mentioned the other night that his not asking her to go with him was a bit of a sticking point.

"I don't want to drink, not without you."

"Then we could just walk." He stood, held out his hand, and when she took it, a warm feeling spread from the point of contact through his body. He didn't want to walk with Jenny, but he'd do whatever it was she wanted. Until she decided she wanted more. Or less. God, he hoped she didn't want less.

"Why don't you walk me home, and we'll see where things go from there."

Her words turned the warm comfort of her touch into something hotter. Still, Adam didn't want to push, didn't want to scare her away, or make her change her mind before he even knew what was on it.

They walked in silence for the few blocks between the marina and their home. A few cars passed in the darkness, but Slippery Rock was a quiet town outside tourist season. As they turned onto their street, Jenny squeezed his hand.

"I don't want you to take me home just yet."

"We can keep walking." Around the block as many times as she wanted. He just wanted to be with her.

"Why don't you show me around the RV?"

Adam swallowed, hard. "You're sure?"

"Why waste a babysitter?" She said the words with a lighthearted lilt to her voice, but Adam didn't want this to be a joke. He wanted to make love to his wife, and he wanted her to know why they were doing this.

"It isn't that I don't want to sleep with you," he began, but Jenny stopped his words with a kiss. She reached up, put her arms around his neck and pressed her mouth to his, taking his breath away for a moment. Adam's arms stole around her waist as he deepened the kiss.

"I want to sleep with you," she said, between nips of her teeth against his mouth. "I want to touch you, and feel you against me."

"Jen…" The word was more groan than endearment, but she didn't seem to mind.

"I want you, Adam Buchanan."

He pressed his forehead against hers, trying to catch his breath. Trying to talk himself out of sleeping with his wife before either of them had decided how to move forward with their lives—either together or apart.

"Please," she said, and the single word overpowered him.

Adam knew it was weak, that sleeping with Jenny when she couldn't really know what she wanted was dishonest, but he didn't care. He wanted his wife. He'd always wanted her, even when he thought it was better for her if he simply wasn't there. So, for tonight, he was going to pretend the tornado and everything else hadn't happened.

In the RV, Adam walked her back to the sleeping area with the double bed. This wasn't what he'd envisioned when he pictured making love with Jenny again, but it would have to do. This time.

He slipped his tongue between her lips, tasting her. Her mouth was sweet, with a little sugar from the sweet tea she'd had with dinner. She was Jenny, and she was where she was supposed to be.

With him.

She tightened her arms around his neck, pressing up against him so that Adam could feel her breasts beneath the layers of fabric between them. The softness of her shirt teased at his hands; he knew her skin would be softer, but liked the slow build of what was happening between them. He slipped one hand beneath the fabric, running the back of his fingers against the sensitive skin of her belly. Her muscles trembled at the light touch.

It wasn't enough. Adam pushed both his hands beneath the handkerchief hem of her top, spanning her waist. She trembled again as one thumb dipped into her belly button. He let his fingers reacquaint themselves with the soft skin of her abdomen, her ribs, while his mouth took its fill of her sweet lips. God, he'd missed her. Missed touching her, missed feeling her heat through her clothes. Missed talking to her over dinner, taking a walk along a quiet street. The sun had already set by the time they got home from the Grill, but he wanted to walk with her as it set across the lake, to feel the heat of the sun kissing his skin as her mouth did the same.

Adam's fingers bumped up against the lace of her bra, and he knew even though he hadn't seen the garment that it would be either stark white or a light pink. He groaned into her mouth. He knew what she felt like, but it had been so long that he could almost pretend this was the first time his palms had touched the soft mounds of her breasts. That he didn't know she liked to be kissed in the valley between her breasts. Her hips were fuller now than when they'd been teenagers, but she was still the most beautiful woman in the world to him.

The fuller hips didn't make Jenny fat, they made her the mother of his children.

How had he gotten so lucky?

Adam lifted the green top from her body, enjoying the quick rise and fall of her breasts in the pink lace. Her gaze met his, and there was no question that this was affecting her just as it was him. Her pupils had darkened, her breathing was off balance and she clenched and unclenched her fists at her sides while he took in the body that was so familiar and yet so new to him.

Jenny reached out, her finger tracing the lines of his abdomen through the cotton of his shirt. His muscles trembled, and his length hardened. She pulled his shirt over his head and tossed it somewhere over her shoulder.

He wanted more than to look at her. He wanted her in his arms. In their big bed in the house, but he would settle for this one in the RV. Adam pulled her down on the mattress, rolling so that she lay atop him. Their mouths seemed almost fused together, and it was the best feeling he'd had in a long time. He pressed a kiss to her cheek, her jaw then found the pulse pounding in her neck and focused his attention there for a long moment, while his hands stroked her back then pushed into the rear pockets of her jeans to pull her hips more firmly against his.

"I've missed you." The words slipped from his

mouth, and for a split second Adam wanted to recall them. To unsay the words that might send Jenny running straight into the house, up to their bedroom. Out of his life, or worse, back to being a virtual stranger to him. "I didn't know it until I saw you at that meeting."

She didn't run.

Jenny opened her eyes, watching him for a long moment. She buried her hands in his hair, as if studying him. Slowly, she slid to the side and insinuated her leg between his. The pressure against his length was almost unbearable, but he waited. Jenny leaned forward, taking his bottom lip between her teeth and gently nipping.

"Me, too." She licked her lips as she drew back from him. "I've missed you, too. I don't know what that means. There are still things we need to work out. Work on," she said. "But I want to be here. With you."

"And I want to be here. With *you*." He nibbled her lower lip as she had nipped at his. "I want to be anywhere with you."

She nipped his lip. "Then don't make us miss one another any longer."

The words pushed his control to the edge. He'd been without Jenny for too long. Three months, five days. He didn't care that several of those weeks he'd been either comatose, in a hospital, basically bedridden or so pissed off at life that he couldn't see straight. With the amount of medication he'd been on in the beginning, he didn't think he'd have done either of them any favors in the sex department. Even after he'd come home, he'd kept his distance. Afraid he couldn't be what she needed. Afraid his body would betray him.

He was still afraid of those things, but he was more afraid of being without her.

Adam undid the snap of her jeans and more pink lace peeked out from under the blue denim. He pulled the jeans from her long, shapely legs. He unsnapped the front closure of her bra, and pink lace made way for pale breasts and dusky aureoles.

Jenny unsnapped his jeans, reaching past the cotton of his boxer briefs to his hard length. Her touch was gentle, her hands feeling like silk sliding against him. Squeezing gently. Making him forget what he'd been doing. Adam focused on the feel of her hand surrounding him, imagining how much better it would feel to be inside her. Then he snapped back to the bed, because this wasn't only about how she could make him feel, it was about how he could make her feel.

He captured her nipple with his mouth, flicking his tongue against her pebbled skin, nipping with his teeth until she sighed with pleasure. Jenny nipped his shoulder, and kept working her hand over his hard length.

"Jenny." Her name felt right on his lips. Adam knew, in the back of his mind, that the timing was all wrong for them. He knew there were things to work out between them that were more important than sex. He didn't care. Maybe sex would help heal some of those scars left by the tornado, and if it didn't, he would figure out another way to show her that he could still be the man she'd loved before the tornado changed him.

Adam slipped his jeans and boxers over his hips, drew a condom from his wallet and sheathed himself quickly. Then he pulled her panties from her body and just looked at her for a long moment. Jenny's breasts heaved as she tried to catch her breath. Her eyes, nearly emerald in the dim light of the RV, drew him in to her magic. She reached out to him, her fingers lightly tracing the taut skin of his ribs, playing along the ridges of muscle there. He pressed her onto her back and smoothed his hand over the crazy curls he'd been obsessed with for as long as he could remember.

With one smooth stroke he was inside her warmth, and everything else faded into the background. There was only Jenny. Only him. Only this bed that was a little too short and a little too narrow, but that seemed to fit them perfectly for tonight. She smiled, a soft turning of her lips, and closed her eyes as he began to move.

Adam caught her mouth with his, their tongues

mimicking the moves he made inside her. Fast, furious. Wanting more, more. He always wanted more with her. She mewled beneath him, her hips pumping as their rhythm increased.

"Adam!" she cried. And then, softer, "Adam."

He reached between them, pressing his finger against the bundle of nerves, and watched as Jenny flew over the edge, felt her body spasming against his from her shoulders to her toes.

Then he followed her into the darkness.

A long time later, Jenny whispered, "Thank you."

"For what?"

"For not leaving. For coming to dinner. For walking the boys to school."

They were such ordinary things, but before she'd demanded that he take stock of their lives, they had seemed impossible to tackle. Now that he had, Adam couldn't imagine not taking part in their lives. Couldn't imagine ever walking away from Jenny, their boys or this life. He'd nearly thrown all this away. He'd been a fool.

"Thank you for asking me to move out."

Jenny chuckled. "That's seems like a funny thing to be thankful for."

"It made me wake up. Made me realize that I was hurting more than myself by refusing to accept the things that have changed in my life."

"And have you accepted them now?"

Acceptance. It was a hard word. "I'm not sure. I know that my life will never be what it was before the tornado, but I'm not sure I would want it to be. I know I want it to be different than it is now." He felt her stiffen beside him. "Not that I want to leave, and not that I'm asking you to let me move back in. I just want to know that, at some point, moving back into the house is a possibility."

"All I really know right now is that I'm here and you're here. Can we leave it at that?"

Adam kissed Jenny's head in the darkness. It wasn't quite the answer he wanted, but it was more than he had been hoping for, despite their having made love tonight. Besides, it was definitely a step forward. He'd take it.

"You'd better go relieve Sadie," he said, pulling her body closer to him in the narrow bed. "I'll see you for kitchen duty in the morning."

JENNY PUSHED SCRAMBLED eggs around in the hot pan, watching them change from unstructured goo to more-or-less structured chunks of food. Food the boys loved. Estimating she had about two minutes of cook time left, she walked to the base of the stairs and called up, "Boys, breakfast in one minute. Get moving."

She'd heard them rustling around earlier this morning, had poked her head inside their room to make sure Garrett was dressing in the lightweight hoodie and jeans she'd laid out the night before, and that Frankie's clothes weren't stained beyond recognition. Where Garrett was steadfast that his clothes should be immaculate—which she found odd for a little boy as active and messy as her youngest—Frankie would wear the same clothes for a week if she let him.

"Coming, Mom," they called in unison, and a moment later she heard them jostling in the hallway. Jenny returned to the kitchen and absently stirred the eggs while her mind returned to last night in the RV with Adam.

It really shouldn't be this hard to not think about having sex with a man she'd been with a thousand times over the past nine years. She'd never had this much trouble focusing on the task at hand, at least, not since that first time they'd had sex in the cramped back seat of the Mustang.

It had still been up on blocks, the top still unattached, and there had been rips in the old vinyl seats. She'd cut her knees as she sat atop Adam, learning his body.

Last night, it had been as if that night in the Mustang and all the nights since had never happened. When he'd looked at her in that cramped bedroom inside the camper, her knees had turned to jelly and the fire inside her had made it seem as if the outside temperature was over the ninety-degree mark.

Which was ridiculous. For the first time this fall, the temperatures were acting somewhat normally, topping out in the midsixties instead of the late summer lower eighties they'd been having.

And now, instead of figuring out what had changed between her and Adam, she was getting distracted by the weather. That wouldn't help anything. She had to make a decision about how to move forward with him. Good sex with Adam didn't mean the problems between them were magically solved, it only meant they still had physical chemistry.

The boys pounded down the stairs, talking about the upcoming homecoming week in Slippery Rock. The local team was doing well this season, and the week before the big game would be filled with lots of school activities. Dress-up days, bonfires, even a pancake breakfast one morning.

"I'm going to be a firefighter," Garrett said. "Firefighters rescue hurt people, like the Avengers, so that makes them heroes."

Jenny dished up their breakfasts, then joined the boys at the table. "I think that's a good choice, G. What about you, Frankie? How do you want to dress up for Hero Day?"

Frankie shrugged. "I don't know," he said, shoving in a mouthful of egg. "Probably Iron Man or something." His gaze didn't meet hers and that made Jenny uneasy. Since the day of the barbecue, when she and Adam finally came together to talk to the boys, things in their little lives seemed better. On a more even keel. Frankie not meeting her gaze was too reminiscent of those first few days after the tornado.

"I think Iron Man is a good choice, too. I'll get your costume from last Halloween out of the garage, see if it still fits." She turned to Garrett. "And I'll bet we can find a firefighter hat or something at the general store this weekend."

Frankie scuffed his foot against the floor, making it squeak in protest. Jenny hated that sound, not just because it meant extra time on floor duty to fix the mark left behind.

"I want a hat and the boots and a badge," Garrett said, forking up the last of his eggs. He slurped some milk after swallowing the food nearly whole.

"Firefighters don't have badges, dummy," Frankie said.

"Hey," she said, her voice sharp. "What did we say about those words?"

Frankie hung his head. "Sorry, Garrett. I meant, firefighters don't have badges, dude."

Jenny gave Frankie a stern look.

Garrett stuck his tongue out at his brother. "They do if they're the firefighters in charge. I saw it on TV."

"You can't be a firefighter in charge, you're only in kindergarten."

"Can, too."

"Can not."

Garrett squinted at Frankie. "Can. Too."

"Not," Frankie said, and he seemed to be enjoying the banter. Still, Garrett looked like he was about to blow, so Jenny stepped in. The last thing she needed this morning was to clean egg off her kitchen ceiling.

"How about we look up the proper uniform after school today?" she suggested.

Frankie's head swiveled to her. "You're picking us up?"

"Sure. Dad will take you, and that way I can leave Buchanan's a little early to pick you up and help with your homework." She gathered the plates. "Now get upstairs and brush your teeth or you're going to be late."

When their footsteps had receded, she turned on the water to rinse the plates, and began stacking them in the dishwasher. The back door opened and Adam walked in, that cane-slash-walking-stick at his side. He looked way too sexy carrying that thing around. Which was weird, wasn't it? Shouldn't it just make him look old or something?

Her stomach did a flip as he leaned a shoulder against the door jamb. "Good morning."

His blue eyes glittered in the early morning light.

"Hey," she said. And couldn't think of anything else to say. She stared at him for a long moment, taking in the form-fitting jeans, the faded Buchanan's T-shirt stretched taut over his shoulders. And that sexy cane. What was with her? She needed to get a grip on herself.

"The boys just went up to brush their teeth. They'll be down in a minute."

He crossed the room, and her chest tightened, making it hard to breathe. It really shouldn't be hard to breathe, Jenny told herself. This was just Adam. The man she'd been certain couldn't be part of her future just a couple weeks ago.

The man she'd been in love with for as long as she could remember. She really shouldn't have had sex with him last night. Not without knowing where this was going. Telling him she wanted to build a future was the truth, but it wasn't as if they had a plan in place to actually build that future.

He tucked a lock of hair behind her ear, sending a shiver of awareness along her nerve endings.

"Good morning," he said again, and he was so close she could feel the heat emanating from his body. "You look great."

"Th-thank you," she said, and tried to step back. But there was nowhere to go. The sink was at her back, the granite countertop already pressing hard against her spine. Jenny kept her hands firmly clenched around the edge of the smooth granite.

She shouldn't touch him. Couldn't touch him. If she did, she would lose the tenuous hold she had on the reality of her life.

She had two growing boys to care for, a business to run. Employees counting on her. She couldn't afford to get lost in Adam Buchanan, not even if his name was right there beside hers on the business loan. On their marriage certificate.

She couldn't go back to that dark place where she desperately needed a man who didn't take her wants and needs into consideration. She wouldn't go back to merely going along with the plans that man had, instead of speaking up about what she wanted, too.

Adam kissed her, his lips soft against her own. His hand cupped her neck, his fingers tangling in her hair, and Jenny nearly forgot all the plans she had begun making when the tornado changed the man she loved into a stranger. It was so easy to just be with him. To let his nearness push away all her doubts and misgivings, to make her forget that, at some point in the past three months, making Buchanan's a success had become what she wanted for herself, and not just for Adam.

She had never been a math whiz, never the star of any sports team. Her goal in life, all through school, had been to marry Adam Buchanan. To build a family with him. She still wanted those things, wanted to sit with him in their backyard and watch the sun set across the lake. But she also wanted to see the business his father had started as a small cabinet shop grow into more. She could help it grow. She'd become good at reading contracts, at figuring out profits and losses, and in determining how their small business could provide more. Giving that up, going back to the way things had been… She couldn't do it.

And it didn't matter that Adam hadn't technically asked her to go back to the way things had been. Jenny knew herself. She knew it would be so easy to focus all her energy and attention on her husband, on her sons.

And when the bottom fell out again, she would once more be alone in the darkness.

CHAPTER ELEVEN

ADAM SAT IN the backyard, watching the small construction crew use posthole diggers around the perimeter. It would take a couple more days, but the fence would be in. Just like Jenny had wanted. It was the first in the list of things he wanted to do for her—not to make her life easier so he could leave, but to show her that she mattered to him.

He didn't want to leave. The thought still hit him like one of the two-by-fours the construction crew was using. Maybe because he'd gotten himself so close to walking away. He didn't want to live alone in a borrowed RV or a hotel. He didn't want to be without Jenny in his life, period.

He hated that she thought she didn't matter or, maybe worse, that he'd taken her for granted. Even though he had. Adam could see that now. Hopefully, the fence would help to show her that he was making serious changes in his life. If it didn't, he had a few more ideas that would.

Aiden came around the corner of the house, sat beside him in one of the chairs Adam had made last winter, but didn't say anything for a long moment.

"Looks good."

"It will when it's done."

"You're going to have to resod or replant around the postholes to get rid of all that dirt." Aiden reached into the cooler sitting beside Adam's chair and pulled out a bottle of water. He wrinkled his nose. "I remember when this cooler was always filled only with beer," he said, then twisted off the cap and swallowed half the bottle in one gulp.

So did Adam. He missed the taste of a cold beer on his lips. The smell of the hops and barley. Beer and the medications he was on, though, didn't mix. He wasn't going to take any chances in that area. Adam finished his own water.

"What brings you over here today?"

"Wanted to run something by you. About Buchanan's."

Talking about work was a dicey subject, mostly because Adam still wasn't sure where he fit at the company. Jenny had a handle on the distributorship, and she'd pushed through that new contract with the builder out of Joplin. All he'd done was put some random pieces of wood together in the general shape of a chair. Okay, that and come up with some new design ideas. But would it be enough?

Figuring out his place at the company, now

that he couldn't build things, was harder than he'd expected.

"What about Buchanan's?"

"I'd like to come back, on a permanent basis."

Adam blinked. He had to be hearing things. Aiden had left Slippery Rock after a bad breakup, but even before that, all he'd talked about was moving to California. Building boats. He'd hated those summers the two of them had spent building and installing cabinets for their father.

"You hate cabinetry." Adam was the Buchanan twin who liked making cabinets, tables. Aiden the one who wanted to build bigger objects, things that would take him away from Slippery Rock. Adam had enjoyed having him back in town, but for the first time ever, it felt like Aiden was taking something from him.

Like, his life.

Adam clenched his jaw. Twin or not, Aiden wasn't going to get what was his. Buchanan's was Adam's, and he didn't care if he sounded more like an eight-year-old than a twenty-eight-year-old.

Aiden rolled the now empty water bottle between his hands. "Cabinetry may not be all that innovative, but it's a solid profession. Involves woodworking. I'm good at woodworking."

"So are most of the people who've had a year or so in a high-school shop class." And then Adam realized what Aiden was doing. This wasn't about his brother wanting to take something from Adam. It was about Aiden filling the gap Adam had left at Buchanan's. This was more of the pity he'd grown to hate over the past few months, only in a different form. "I don't need you taking on Buchanan's because you feel sorry for me."

"I'm not."

"I don't need your pity. Is this because Dad and Mom will be heading to Florida soon?"

"It has nothing to do with our parents, and before you bring her into it, it isn't about Jenny, either. And it's not about your..." he paused "...diagnosis. I want a change. Buchanan's will be a change from building sailboats."

"Because cabinets are so challenging when you're coming from the world of custom-built boats."

"Those chairs aren't as simple as they look. And the work you did on that table in the guest room? It's top of the line."

He'd given up on the furniture aspect after the tornado, because Fate seemed obsessed with taking life away from him. He'd survived a car accident and he hadn't complained. Not when it took football from him. He'd laughed and joked until it wasn't hard to come up with something fun to say or do.

Aiden had walked away from the wreck without a scratch. The tornado didn't follow Aiden into that church or bury him in the rubble.

Adam had thanked God every day that he wasn't paralyzed from that wreck, but another twist of Fate had wrenched the life he'd built with Jenny out of his grasp. Had taken away his control of his body. If he tried to make another place for himself at Buchanan's, if he could really make things work with Jenny, what else would Fate take from him?

Jenny took the fuzzy dream he had about furniture making and turned it into a reality. Just like she'd helped him with his homework after he'd wrecked his dad's car. Although he didn't know how he could fit into Buchanan's now, it gave Adam a sense of pride knowing those were his designs that had caught the Springfield distributor's eye in the first place.

He'd have liked to work on one of those boats with Aiden, just once. Leaving Slippery Rock had never been part of Adam's plans, though.

Building a life with Jenny, raising a family, taking the small cabinetry shop to the next level. Those had been Adam's goals. He didn't consider building furniture until Jenny described the bed she wanted, and he hadn't been able to find anything similar. Once he'd put those designs together, other ideas came to him, and he'd begun to use the slower winter months to come up with other designs.

"I want to come home." Aiden's voice was quiet in the backyard, so quiet Adam thought he had to have heard his brother wrong. That the hammers and shovels had caused some kind of sound vortex. "I was angry at you, for a long time, after Simone. But she isn't why I left or why I didn't visit more often. I just used her, used what happened as a way to break away from Dad's business. See if I could build something of my own."

"So why come back now?"

"Catering to the whims of the wealthy isn't all it's cracked up to be, I guess." Aiden fished another bottle of water from the cooler. He glanced at Adam. "I'd been considering coming back before the tornado. Then you were diagnosed, and I couldn't. You were my best friend until the wreck and Simone. I didn't want those last words between us to be our last words. And I was afraid that if I did come back, you'd think it was because I was trying to take your place or something."

Adam had thought that, somewhere in a jealous corner of his mind. The corner of his mind that hated that things came so easily to Aiden.

"I always wondered why things happened so easily for you. How you could latch on to a calculus theory or a new woodworking technique so easily when I had to struggle to understand it."

"I always wondered how you could know, at twelve, that a life in Slippery Rock was all you wanted."

"Because Slippery Rock made sense to me. The gossip, the pace, the work. Going into Springfield to shop or to the gulf for vacation. My favorite part of every trip was seeing the Welcome to Slippery Rock sign at the edge of town."

"My favorite part was watching it disappear out the back window."

When they were in that accident in high school, Adam had never wondered why he'd been the one injured. When he woke up in that hospital after the tornado, though, he'd wondered why it had been him. Again. Why bad things happened to him, while Aiden lived a charmed life.

Childish. Aiden had his own problems, at least one of which had been brought on by Adam.

"If I could find Simone, I'd apologize to her."

"So would I," Aiden said. When Adam stared at him, he went on. "I could have followed her, brought her back to town. Simone was a cheater and a liar, but she wasn't a thief. I didn't follow her, not even after the money from Buchanan's reappeared."

"I am sorry, Aiden."

"Me, too."

"I love this town." The people, the relationships. The steady rhythm of life here. He'd nearly lost it, and still might. Adam couldn't imagine living in Slippery Rock without Jenny. If things didn't work out between them, he would have to pick up his life in some other place. The thought of that sent a quick hit of panic through his system. He inhaled once, twice, counting to ten between the breaths.

"So do I. I just had to figure out where I might fit outside of it to realize how much."

"You think you can step into my place at the business?" The thought filled Adam with sadness. He didn't want anyone taking his place, not at Buchanan's, not with Jenny, not in his town. More than that, he didn't want Aiden to think he had to somehow become someone he wasn't because a tornado had wreaked havoc not only on their town, but on Adam's health.

"Why don't we just say I think I could do a good job? I like building things. I've designed a few things on my own. Smaller scale, because boats aren't as big as houses, but I think some of the elements I've worked in could be used in home construction."

"Jenny does the hiring."

"I know. Already talked to her, told her I'd like to stay on."

"And she wanted you to run this by me first?" He exhaled a sigh of relief. Jenny wanted his opinion, trusted him to make a business decision. That felt good.

Aiden shook his head. "She said the job was mine. Running it by you, that's just on me. I don't want to step on your toes."

And just like that, the stress of the unknown was back. Jenny didn't need his approval or his input to run the business. Maybe she never had. Maybe she never would. Where did that leave him?

Working with his brother. They'd made a good team as kids, both on the football field and working for their father during summer breaks. Adam had made a mess of things for Aiden before, and regretted it. Having him around now would give him the chance to make things right between them.

"You're not stepping on any toes. Buchanan's is a family business. Always has been, always will be." As long as he was turning over this new, it's-not-all-about-me leaf, he might as well do it fully. He held his hand out. "Welcome home, brother."

Aiden took his hand and shook.

"Have any suggestions for the business? Maybe we can incorporate some California cool into Buchanan's."

Aiden chuckled. "I feel like my first suggestion is that you not finish the back wall of the fence. It's going to kill your view."

Adam considered the materials stacked up in the backyard, at the guys finishing the last of the postholes. He took another swig of water. "It'll be a short fence, more decorative than compound-like. Besides, Jenny wants it."

"And Jenny gets what Jenny wants?"

Adam smiled. "Something like that."

JENNY WATCHED OUT the window, anxiously waiting to see the truck with the dog trainer's logo on the side. She'd been prepared to drive Adam to the trainer's, but the man insisted it would be better if he delivered the dog to them.

Something about handing off, letting the dog know Adam was her new master.

How bringing the dog here rather than them picking it up would clarify the whole master thing didn't make sense to Jenny. At least, though, the dog would be here for a couple hours before the boys were home from school. And the fence would soon be completed.

When the crew showed up the day before, she'd been shocked. Pleased. She loved living with the lake as part of their backyard, but it made her nervous not to have some kind of barrier between the boys and the water. The four-foot-high fence would have a gate, and the boys knew how to open gates, but she hoped the symbolism of it would at least slow them down when they played outside next summer.

If not, at least the symbolism might work for her.

The sound of saws and hammers and shovels in the backyard rang out through the quiet afternoon. And now that they would have a dog, that fence would be even more important. Service dogs were well-trained, but she had yet to meet any dog that didn't run straight to the water at the first opportunity.

Aiden walked into the living room, Adam close on his heels. She'd never had trouble telling the two apart, but the differences between them were so striking now that it was unsettling. Adam was still regaining his strength, and his shoulders were a bit stooped. There was the walking stick, of course. New lines around his eyes and mouth that hadn't been there before the tornado and his injuries.

She wished the lines on his face were from a lifetime of laughing, but although she knew the cause was more likely pain and stress, she still found them sexy.

Which just went to show what a warped individual she was. Finding a cane and wrinkles on her twenty-eight-year-old husband sexy had to mean she was seriously deranged.

"How's the construction going?"

"They'll be finished in another couple hours," Adam said. He leaned on the cane and tilted his head toward Aiden. "He tells me he's staying."

"We could use the help."

"Trying to get rid of me already?"

A week ago, those words from Adam would have made her mad. Or scared. Now, she heard the teasing note in his voice. Remembered how he'd been with her in the RV a couple nights before.

"You've been a little hard to work with lately," she returned.

"I can see the two of you have some weird thing going on right now. I'll see you at work tomorrow, Jen," Aiden said, and disappeared through the front door.

"We scared him," Adam said, and she thought she detected a note of pride in his voice. She had no idea why the thought of Aiden being afraid would make Adam proud, though.

"Your parents leave for Florida after Thanksgiving. We could use the help, and not just with the building."

"I know. I'm glad you hired him."

Jenny nodded, unsure what else to say. She folded her arms over her chest and turned to watch out the window again.

"It's Wednesday."

"I know. The trainer should be here with the dog anytime."

"I was thinking, if Sadie could watch the boys, you could come with me."

"Come with you where?" Adam didn't have

any appointments; she would have known if he did. Calendars were part of her job description.

"It's Wednesday."

"We've been over that. You don't have to be anywhere."

"Darts. Collin, Levi, James. Aiden's back. The gang will all be there."

And Adam had avoided Wednesday night darts since his release from the hospital. She'd forced him to go, once, and that had been a disaster. They'd fought in the middle of the Slope, in front of his friends and what felt like the entire town.

Now he wanted to go? The change made her heart stutter in her chest. Adam had never asked her to darts before the accident. He'd gone and she'd stayed home with the boys. She had no idea if Sadie was available, but there was no chance Jenny would pass up this opportunity.

She'd offered the first olive branch when she asked Adam to dinner. The olive branch he was now offering her was so much bigger because it involved not just the two of them, but friends. An actual gathering, a social occasion. A couple's occasion.

Dinner led to sex, and you're still not sure sex is the best idea, Jenny reminded herself.

"I'll text Sadie to see if she's available." *And this time, we won't have sex*, Jenny vowed.

This time, she would keep her physical attraction to him to herself.

IT FELT WEIRD to be walking with a dog beside him. The cane hadn't seemed as awkward, maybe because Adam immediately felt some pain relief in his hip. The dog, however, didn't offer pain relief. The dog was a reminder of all the things that were now wrong with him. Like the wheelchair had been.

Sheba was a nice dog, though. She didn't bark, didn't growl at the kids. Hadn't tried to run around the backyard with them when they arrived home with Jenny a few minutes before.

"You've got the basic commands, and I'll leave a pamphlet for you in the house," the trainer was saying. He wore jeans, a Kansas City Royals T-shirt and hat, along with a denim jacket. "And if you want additional training, I can come to you or you and your wife can come up to the house. Anytime," he said.

"What about the boys?"

The man had already explained that Sheba was trained not to expect playtime. As a working dog, her focus had to be on Adam at all times. "In my experience, kids want to play, especially with bigger dogs like Sheba. She won't unless you give her permission, so don't give her permission. You're the one in control here."

Yeah. He was in such control that he needed a service dog to tell him when a seizure was coming. Adam shook off the gloomy thought. It wasn't the trainer's fault, and having the dog would give him a bit more freedom. Sheba couldn't stop a seizure, but she might detect one so that Adam could ready himself. That returned a measure of control the epilepsy had taken from him. That was what he would focus on.

"Work, home, restaurants. She goes where I go?"

"That's the objective. People will ask questions at first, but they'll get used to her quicker than you might imagine." The trainer took a pamphlet from his back pocket. "I'd like to get back before dark. I'll just leave this on the table."

"Sure, through the door, straight down the hallway."

When the trainer had gone inside, Adam turned to the yellow lab sitting beside him. "Hello," he said. The dog didn't reply. "I'm Adam. You're Sheba."

Talking to an animal that couldn't return the gesture was just awkward. Adam didn't know of a better way to get acquainted, though.

"You want a beer? We're going to the Slope tonight. I'll bet Merle would give you one."

Sheba tilted her head to the side, as if curious what a beer or a Merle might be. Laughter from the yard caught Adam's attention, and he turned. Jenny was running around with the boys, whooping and hollering as they chased her. He'd played this game with them before, and he missed not being able to capture them. He sat in the chair on the patio, and Sheba joined him.

"That's Frankie and Garrett. And Jenny is the silly one pretending to be a moose. At least, I think she's being a moose. It's kind of hard to tell." Sheba focused her attention on the yard. Adam sat back in his chair, resting his forearms on the smooth wood.

Hand dangling over the side, he watched his family playing a version of capture the flag he'd never before witnessed. He grinned when Jenny cornered Frankie at the fence. Their older son beetled his eyebrows and crossed his arms over his chest.

"No fair! I can't get around the fence."

Jenny took a step back, giving him a little space, and Adam could practically see his son's mind going over the possibilities for escape. So he wasn't out there with them. At least he could watch them. Maybe, one day soon, he would be the one capturing them.

Sheba moved closer, fitting her head against his palm. Adam rubbed the dog's ears. "No offense to you, Sheba, and you're welcome to stay as long as you like it here, but I really hope I never have to put your particular skills to work."

"BUT I THOUGHT we were just going to the Slope."

"We are, just a quick stop first."

Jenny shook her head, but got into the Mustang and turned on the ignition. Adam moved the passenger seat so Sheba could jump into the back, then settled in himself.

"Fine. Where are we going?"

"Make a left at the stop sign."

Jenny blew out a breath. "I don't need turn-by-turn directions, thank you. This is Slippery Rock, not Springfield. Just tell me where we're going."

"You'll see."

She cut her gaze to him. Adam sat in the passenger seat looking like the proverbial cat that ate the canary, and she couldn't read anything past that I-know-something-you-don't-know expression. She had no idea what he was up to now, but the possibilities sent excitement pulsing through her veins. He'd asked her to go with him to the Slope this evening. They'd had an actual date a few nights ago. This was the Adam she remembered from long before the tornado. The one who wanted to spend time with her. This Adam was dangerously close to making her ignore all the reasons she had for asking him to move out.

Since the flower incident, he'd taken care in his

attentions to her. He'd made her favorite break-fast, sent her an African violet for her office and he'd finally built the fence. Well, hired someone to do it, but still, the idea had come from him. And without any kind of a suggestion from her.

The idea that Adam was finally realizing what she needed from him made her insides feel warm and gooey. Like they'd felt that first time coming out of American literature class when she saw him watching her so closely.

But Adam flirting and paying attention when things were going well was too familiar. She didn't know what would happen if things went sideways again. Which Adam would she see then? The Adam who bought her African violets and built a fence or the man who shut her out and left her alone?

Sheba panted in the backseat. Jenny caught the dog's gaze and smiled, and she swore the dog smiled back. Like they had some kind of insider understanding, which was ridiculous. She barely knew the dog, though she seemed like a sweet thing.

Was Jenny falling back in love with her hus-band? She'd never truly stopped loving him; she knew that. And it wasn't that she just selfishly wanted him to do things for her. She wanted him to know her, the way that she knew him. To value her opinions and ideas the way that she valued his.

He'd been her life, and she felt as if she'd been only a small piece of his.

When he woke up in the hospital, she'd been so relieved. But instead of the tornado bonding them more closely together, it had torn them apart like it had the church. As rewarding as it was to see him regain his footing, why did he have to lose it at all? Why wasn't she enough for him? Adam was the one who had nearly died in the tornado, but her dreams for them had died, too.

No matter how hard he tried, no matter how much she loved him, Adam would never be the man she had known before tragedy struck.

"Left again, and then a right on the next block."

Jenny cocked her head to the side, trying to figure out where Adam wanted her to go. From the directions, they would be just off downtown. Near Mallard's Grocery and the old train station. He obviously wasn't going to tell her, though, so Jenny simply drove.

"Pull in here," he said as they drew abreast of the only car lot in Slippery Rock.

Gleaming minivans, sedans and giant trucks shone in the lot. A few of the hoods were raised, with large cardboard letters placed in them that spelled out New Year's Sale. Since New Year's was still three months away, Jenny wondered what kind of new year they were about to set foot in.

"What are we doing here?"

"Getting an estimate on the 'Stang, and getting a car that makes more sense for the family."

Jenny blinked, unsure if she'd heard his words correctly. He'd brought her here for a new car? But he loved the Mustang. Had rebuilt it from scraps. Adam doted on this car. He'd refused to even consider the idea of a trade-in, or getting a second car, from the moment Frankie was born.

He opened the door, signaled the dog to follow, and started walking the lot. Jenny quickly caught up.

"But you don't want a new car. You want the Mustang." This was too weird. Like he was taking her grievances one by one and tossing them out the window. They couldn't afford a new car. Insurance had taken care of most of the hospital bills, but there was still a big chunk to deal with, and more coming down the road from checkups and the surgery for his hip. She'd been annoyed about the Mustang a couple weeks ago, yes, and she did want more of a family car.

But this felt too much like how her father would do what her mother wanted, to appease her. Jenny didn't need Adam to get rid of the Mustang for her. She would not be selfish like her mother, living for bridge games and gossip and anything else that was superficial and insincere.

Jenny didn't want to be appeased, and she didn't want Adam to give up his favorite car. For her. That wasn't what she wanted. Not at all. What she wanted—

"It's not really practical, though, is it?" he was saying. "With two kids, and now a dog. Besides, I wanted the Mustang. You never did."

Except she did love the classic car. The sleek lines and red color were pretty. It was fun to drive. It held a lot of their memories from high school, then bringing Frankie home from the hospital. Impractical, yes, but the car was also part of them.

She wanted the car. Not for him. For herself. Because it was a part of the person she'd been before the tornado. It was the last physical piece of the Adam she knew before the storm and epilepsy tore their pretty world apart.

Adam stopped before a row of minivans in different shades of blues and reds, with a couple black and gray options, too. "Now, I've read the ratings, and this is the most sought-after option on the market. You've got automatic sliders and trunk, it seats seven comfortably and even has these little hanger things on the back of the front seats that you can hook grocery bag handles through so they don't tip over in transit."

She had to stop this. It wasn't fair. Life had taken Adam away from her, had taken her dreams away. Letting go of the memories the Mustang held… It was just too much. She would make do with the Mustang, or they would figure out a payment plan for a second car. "You don't have to do this, Adam. You don't have to pretend you want a minivan just to make me happy."

"I'm not pretending, and this isn't about making you happy. It's about making your life easier. Tell me school drop-off and pickup won't be better in this? Winter's coming, Jen. We can't walk with the boys through five feet of snow."

"We've never had five feet of snow all at once. Not in Slippery Rock."

"It could happen. I read that the *Farmer's Almanac* is calling for the worst winter in a hundred years."

"The *Farmer's Almanac* always says it's going to be the worst winter ever. Adam—"

"Let me do this, Jenny. I can't drive the Mustang, anyway, and you hate it."

"I don't hate it." She didn't like hauling all the paraphernalia that came with having a family in it, but that was beside the point. She could deal with those annoyances. This was Adam's car. It was their past. Giving it up…was like giving up on everything they had promised one another in that justice of the peace office. For better or worse. She'd never imagined just how *worse* things could be, but that didn't mean she gave up. Not now. Not when things were beginning to go so well between them.

"That makes two of us, then. But you have to admit it's not practical."

"I don't care about practicality. The Mustang, it's…it's us. It's our past. I lost my virginity in this car. We brought the boys home from the hospital in it." She took Adam's hands. "You can't trade it in."

Adam squeezed her fingers and rested his forehead against hers for a moment. "The memories we have aren't in the Mustang, they're in us. They'll always be in us."

"But—"

"No buts. Better gas mileage, more room, family friendly. You say you want to build a future. Let's ride into that future in something more comfortable than a classic Mustang."

Jenny closed her eyes, trying to imagine a future without the annoyances of the Mustang. Adam kept talking, as if the trade was a done deal. "Now, I talked to Vince earlier, and he quoted me thirty grand on the Mustang. Which means we can almost buy this baby—" he smacked his hand against the hood of a black van "—outright. Smaller payment. We won't even feel the extra bill."

It was tempting. Not the minivan. Jenny hated minivans more than she hated hauling the boys and all their gear around in the Mustang, and listening to them complain that there wasn't enough room in the backseat for both of them. One of the SUVs in the next row, though, would be nice. Roomy. Terrible on gas mileage, but the thought of not having to wrestle Frankie's football stuff or another art project or Adam's wheelchair into the trunk was definitely tempting.

Vince, a balding man who habitually wore khaki pants and plaid shirts, came out of the sales office door. He had a thick black mustache, and short cropped black hair. "I see you got her here. Are you ready to take this beautiful family van for a spin around the neighborhood?"

"We are."

"No, we aren't," Jenny said, and put her hand on Adam's arm. "Would you excuse us, please?" When Vince backed away, Jenny focused on Adam. "I don't want you giving up the Mustang. We can afford two cars."

"What's the point of two cars when only one of us drives?" He held up a hand when Jenny started to speak. "I will drive again, but it's not going to be tomorrow or even next week. And when it does happen, I don't think my doctors will agree that a Mustang is the best option. I want to do this, Jenny."

"You don't have to impress me with this kind of gesture." But it was a nice gesture, and the comfort of a larger family car would be appreciated. And Adam seemed very relaxed about the whole trade-in. He wasn't clenching his fist the way he did when something upset him. He wasn't talking too fast, although he'd talked over her a couple times. Jenny blew out a breath. "I don't want the Mustang to be something we fight about when we should be fighting about something else. We can't trade it in."

"This is my decision, my choice. Yeah, it's something that is important to you, but I realized the other day that my name is the only name on the title. I can do this with or without you—I'd just rather it was with you. That we choose a car, together, that is right for our family." He brushed his hand over her hair. "Trading the Mustang isn't just a gesture. I've been listening to you, watching you. That day in the rain, I thought you'd never get the boys safely inside. And I worried about the three of you until you were home. A minivan is safer, it's more practical. Let me do this, Jen."

Jenny pulled her lower lip between her teeth. He was right about the practicality. And she'd nearly lost her patience and her sanity that day in the rain. The Mustang wasn't a good choice for a family car, but it sure was pretty. Fun to drive. She couldn't bear to trade the pretty car in for a minivan, though. That seemed like an insult to the sporty little car.

"You know how I don't like cut flowers?"

Adam frowned. "Yeah?"

"I don't like minivans, either."

"But you said—"

"I said we needed a more practical car." She ran her hand over the cool metal of the van and shook her head. "I meant an SUV, one of the medium-size vehicles, not the gigantic ones. Plenty of cargo room. Plenty of space for the boys."

Adam watched her for a moment. "You want an SUV?"

Jenny nodded. "If it's my choice, then, yeah. An SUV. In blue."

Adam motioned to Vince, who hurried over to them. "She'd like to see something in blue, in an SUV," he said, making the salesman chuckle.

Jenny reached for Adam's hand and squeezed. "Thank you," she whispered.

"You're welcome," he said.

Jenny felt some of the heaviness around her heart lift. She wasn't the same girl who had lost her virginity on the cracked vinyl seat, or who had been petrified at the thought of bringing Frankie home from the hospital. It was time to let that girl go.

No one said anything about the dog sitting on the floor beside their regular booth at the Slope. Adam found that odd. Levi, Collin and James had had plenty to say about him finally showing up to darts. Even Aiden had joined in. But none of them said diddly about the dog now sitting beside him.

Or the three women—Jenny, Mara and Savannah—who kept stealing glances at the table.

Levi took aim at the board on the wall and landed a fifteen pointer. James stepped up to the throwing line next. The guys didn't seem to notice the looks the women were sending in their direction. Probably, if this was a few months ago, he wouldn't have noticed, either. Savannah said something, all three women drank, then Jenny went to the jukebox to slide quarters into the slot. Aiden pulled James's darts from the wall, then crossed to the line to take aim. He landed a fast forty-five points with three darts. Obviously, darts were big in California.

After the old Merle Haggard song—a particular favorite of Merle the bartender's—stopped, Jenny chose another. Keith Urban's voice filled the bar, singing about wasted time. Adam had been good at filling up his days before the accident, and although he didn't regret the time spent with his friends or his kids, he did regret that he hadn't included Jenny in all those things, too. Look how well Collin and James had adjusted to life with a woman at the center. Meanwhile, Adam had kept his life mostly separate—events with friends, events with Jenny. Only on holidays had his life included both, and even then he'd tried to keep those lines firmly drawn. As if the wife and kids across the yard were one entity and the friends surrounding the grill or sitting around the fire pit in the backyard weren't at the same party.

Why had he done that? Adam couldn't understand what he had been thinking. His friends loved Jenny and the boys. Jenny loved the guys. The boys saw Levi, Collin and James as heroes. Why had Adam tried to keep things so separated?

He had no answer.

"You're up." Collin dropped a few darts before Adam. Aiden slid into the booth across from him.

"Remember, you're aiming at the round target with the numbers on it, not the wood paneling to the side," his brother said. Adam flipped him the bird, and the guys chuckled.

His doctor probably wouldn't like him playing with darts any more than he wanted him handling kitchen cutlery, but Adam figured if the dog wasn't freaking out, he could handle a little dart throwing. He slid from the booth, took aim and scored a ten. Not bad. He hadn't thrown a dart since before the tornado hit Slippery Rock.

Collin scored a fifteen and smirked. "Two more throws," he said.

Levi and James sat in the booth, watching as Adam took aim again. "About time you came out with us heathens," said James.

"And with a dog, no less," Levi said, just as

Adam threw. The dart went wide, thunking against the wood paneling and clattering to the floor. "Not sure what Merle was thinking when you walked in with Beulah there."

"Her name is Sheba." Adam picked his dart off the floor and threw again, hitting five this time. "And she kind of goes where I go."

"You need her to throw for you, too?" This from Collin, who stood at the throwing line with Adam. "Because your game is off tonight." Collin took aim and landed another fifteen score. "No way you're coming back from that ten. And there are no second throws, so don't even think about that five you were getting ready to write down."

"Second throws are valid when another player tries to distract the thrower. Rules are rules, gentlemen," James said.

"I don't see any gentlemen at this table," Adam grumbled as he handed his darts to James.

"So what's the deal with the dog?" This from Levi, who'd been watching Sheba off and on most of the night. "Service animal?"

"Like an early warning system, or something," Aiden offered.

"She's not Doppler radar." Adam rolled his eyes. "But she can tell when my system is off, even before I can."

"So she's like a nurse?" This came from James, who landed a twenty shot, pushing his score to the number one spot. Adam's score was firmly at the bottom.

Adam shook his head. "No, she's not like a nurse. She can't dispense medications or bandage a cut." He caught the look James sent Levi and that Levi passed on to Collin and Collin shared with Aiden. Worry mixed with genuine interest and bit of gentle ribbing. Okay, so maybe he'd lost his sense of humor over the past few months. He took the darts and stepped to the throwing line with Collin. "She did come with a nurse's uniform, though, if any of you need to spice up your love lives."

Collin landed another fifteen-point shot. "Mine's good, thanks."

Adam aimed and threw, landing a fifteen. Not enough to overtake anyone, but a solid showing for his first night at darts in over three months. "James?"

"I carry my own handcuffs, thanks. That's all the role playing Mara needs."

Collin playfully punched James. "That's my sister you're handcuffing, you know. And I don't need to know about it."

Levi tallied the scores. James finished first, Aiden second, Collin and Levi tied and Adam placed last.

"That's all for me, boys." Levi stood and tossed a few bills on the table. "Good to see you're back."

"Good to be back." Or at least making his way back. Adam wasn't sure things would ever feel as comfortable as they had been before the tornado. He didn't think he wanted that level of comfort, because all he'd cared about then was his routine, his schedule. Everyone else came second. Knowing he'd put Jenny on a back burner rankled.

Levi offered a wave to the table and left. Aiden went to the jukebox where a woman Adam didn't recognize was studying the music options.

Collin and James caught Juanita's attention and ordered another round of beers.

"You're off the night shift?" Adam asked James. The last time the four of them had been here, his friend had been working nights at the police department. Since the tornado, he'd been turning split shifts so that he could help with some of the renovation projects around town. Those were mostly finished by now, though.

"For a while. If I win the election, it'll be days only. If I don't, who knows where the new chief will place me."

"You'll win." Collin sat back and sipped his beer. The women had left the dance floor, and returned to the bar and their glasses of wine. "People here appreciate your work ethic. All those split shifts, the work on the farmer's market and the new grandstand, they noticed."

James shrugged. "I want to be the police chief,

but it's out of my hands at this point. Besides, I have Mara and Zeke to think about. Being an officer won't take up as much time as being the chief."

James had been working toward becoming the next chief of police for Slippery Rock for as long as Adam could remember. He'd gotten the right degree in college, attended the right conferences, done all the right things. And now he acted as if not becoming chief was no big thing. Adam couldn't imagine.

All he had wanted was to run the cabinet shop, build things with his hands. Now he couldn't, and he was trying to adjust to that, but the knowledge that he might never work a band saw or sander still rankled. Maybe that was the difference in choosing to let something go and being forced to. The three of them finished their drinks—beers for Collin and James, water for Adam—listening to the songs Jenny, Savannah and Mara had chosen not long before. Aiden returned to the table, a longneck in his hand.

"Shot down?" Collin asked.

"Like a clay pigeon on a target range." Aiden grabbed an empty chair from a nearby table and sat.

"I never wanted to be the boss." The words slipped from Adam's mouth before he could stop them. Collin, James and Aiden stared at him. "I mean, I wanted to run Buchanan's, but I wanted to build the things we sell, not just push papers."

"That's my point. Being the chief would mean more paperwork, less interaction with people."

"At least you have the choice. Kind of."

James shrugged. "Not sure how much choice I have in the matter. But I'm okay with it."

And somehow, Adam would learn how to be okay with not being involved with Buchanan's the way he'd always envisioned. And he would win Jenny back. Like James said, he had a family to think of. Less time at work would mean more time with Jenny. With Frankie and Garrett. That wasn't a bad thing.

"Adam?" Jenny returned to the booth and slid into the seat beside him. James offered his seat to Savannah, then grabbed two chairs so he and Mara could sit to the side of the booth.

"A bunch of healthy men, amazing music on the juke—by a local singer, no less," Mara said, grinning as Savannah's voice filled the bar. "And here we are sitting at a table instead of scuffing up Merle's dance floor."

James took her hand and led her to the floor. Collin and Savannah followed.

"Do you want to dance?" Adam put his arm over the back of the bench seat, catching a lock of Jenny's hair around his finger.

"Sure," she said.

Sheba stood when Adam did, but he gave her the signal to stay. The dog obediently sat, but kept her attention focused on the dance floor. Adam put his arms around Jenny's waist, pulling her close. He couldn't remember the last time the two of them had gone dancing. Before Garrett, he thought. Whenever it had been, it was too long ago.

He pulled her closer, smelling the coconut fragrance from her shampoo. She'd worn jeans and a light cotton top that skimmed over her hips. Her arms wound around his neck as they swayed to Savannah's song. "Having a good time?"

She nodded against his shoulder. "You?"

"Yeah." He couldn't think of a single valid reason he hadn't brought Jenny with him before. The weekly dart game began as a way to draw Levi out of his post-football slump, but both Levi and Collin had brought women from time to time. Now that the truth about James's long-term affair with Mara was out, Adam understood why his friend had never brought a girl to the Slope. Adam didn't have the same excuses as the other guys. He'd simply not considered that Jenny would want to come to the bar once they had the boys.

Now he couldn't imagine coming to darts and not ending the night right here on the dance floor with her. Savannah's song finished. Collin tossed a few bills on the table and waved as he and Savannah turned to go. James and Mara were talking quietly, but looked like they might be ready to leave, too. Which would leave only Aiden, him and Jenny from their little group.

It had been a quiet night, with just a few other tables being used. He recognized the mayor and his wife eating burgers at a corner table, a few other regulars watching baseball, muted, on the TV behind the bar. Adam didn't want the night to end, but he admitted it would be nice to go home. With Jenny.

"Time to head out?"

She nodded. "Sadie has a geometry test tomorrow. And it is a Wednesday night," she said. "The boys have school, too."

It was still early, barely eight o'clock, but it had been a long day. Buying the SUV, talking to Aiden, getting to know the dog. Adam didn't want to go back to the RV, but he could deal with that.

Jenny sidled a bit closer to him. "Also, I'd like to spend some time with only you."

Adrenaline stabbed through his body. Jenny wanted to be alone. With him. "Then let's go home."

ALL SHE WANTED was to keep kissing him. To feel the rasp of his stubble against the sensitive skin of her breasts. To have him inside her again, because when they were like this, none of the rest mattered. She was just Jenny and he was just Adam. There were no doctor schedules to figure out, no worry about medication changes, no kids, no work, no interfering or uninterested parents. Just his skin against hers. Her hands on his body.

They'd barely paid Sadie and gotten the boys up to their beds before Adam had drawn her into his arms. She liked being in his arms again. Wanted to be in his arms here, in their house, and not in the RV.

Adam's hands cupped her face, and he speared his tongue into her mouth. Jenny met the rush, liking the fierceness in his kiss. He growled, and she liked that sound even more. It sent a skittering of awareness up her spine. She liked Adam like this. Open. A little desperate. A lot focused.

He pushed her back against the wall, and she could feel his erection hard against her belly. She pulled his shirt from his jeans, allowing her hands to roam over the ridges of his abdomen. His mouth found the sensitive spot just below her ear, and Jenny forgot to breathe. Her head slammed against the wall, but she didn't care about the pain, she just wanted more of this moment.

More of Adam's hands and lips on her. More of the heat of him surrounding her.

More, more, more.

But if they kept bumping into walls, either

Frankie or Garrett would wake up and then this would be over.

"Upstairs," she whispered, taking his hand in hers.

Sheba followed close on their heels, and whined gently when Adam shut the bedroom door, leaving her in the hall.

"She's going to wake the boys."

Adam opened the door. Gave her the signal to stay, then patted her head. "Good girl," he said, when she took position to one side. "Who would've thought we'd have to consider the feelings of a dog when we want to have sex?"

Jenny grinned. "And she's such a nice dog, too."

Adam reached toward the door. "Want her to come in? We could have an audience."

Jenny covered his hand with her own. "Not on your life. Just you. Just me." She reached up to lay her mouth on his, enjoying the feel of him against her. Then she wound her leg around his, wanting him closer still.

It wasn't enough.

His hand slid under the soft fabric of her shirt, pushing the heat between them higher. Her stomach muscles clenched as he caressed the skin of her lower back, while his mouth continued to devour her. He kissed his way down her neck to her clavicle. Jenny's hands found his shoulders and squeezed, trying to push her body higher against the wall, wanting his mouth, that stubble, his hands on her breasts.

Instead, his hand found her center, and despite the layer of denim between his flesh and hers, Jenny felt her pulse skyrocket.

"This isn't going to work against a wall," he said, his voice as unsteady as her body felt.

"It's working just fine." He needed to keep touching her, needed to push her harder against the wall.

But his hand left her, and Adam lifted her away from the wall, walking her across the room. She pressed her lips to his, buried her hands in his hair, then giggled when he tossed her onto the big bed as if she were a doll.

He hadn't been in this room since the tornado. Hadn't been up the stairs, in general, until a couple nights ago when he put the boys to bed. No. She wasn't going into mom zone. This was about her, about Adam. About hot sex and nothing else.

Adam grabbed his shirttail, pulling it over his head to reveal that familiar sprinkling of hair over his pecs, shoulders that made her mouth go dry and a set of washboard abs that her hands itched to explore. She pulled off her own shirt, glad she'd ignored the bra on the dresser earlier, when his tongue darted out over his lips. Jenny unbuttoned her jeans, pushing them over her hips. The sandals she'd worn had fallen off at some point, probably when she'd tried to wrap her body around his at the wall. Adam kicked off his shoes, then tossed aside his jeans, leaving him wearing only a pair of boxer briefs.

He crawled across the bed to her, putting one knee between hers. Jenny reclined on her elbows, sighing as his skin slipped across hers. Adam's hand cupped the back of her head, holding her close to him, and this time when he kissed her, she thought she might actually burn through the duvet and mattress from the heat his touch evoked.

His erection was hot and thick against her hip, and she let her hands wander. Taking in the highs and lows of his abdomen, she flirted with the band of his boxers. She drew her thumbnail along his ribs and felt his body shiver at the touch.

Adam settled her against the soft pillows, then explored her body, his hands burning fire along her sides, his thumb dipping erotically into her belly button, and she thought she could feel the thumping of her pulse right there between her thighs. Which was silly. She'd never felt anything like that in her life. It wasn't as if this was her first time having sex with her husband.

Of course, he'd never been this focused before.

He dragged her panties down her legs, and his green eyes lit with fire as he looked at her. Jenny sucked in an unsteady breath.

Adam kissed his way up her body, settling his

hips between hers. Jenny wrapped her legs around him, and his mouth finally found her breast. His hot, slick tongue toyed with her hard nipple, sucking and biting until she thought she might lose her mind.

She pushed her hands past the cotton of his briefs, sliding them over his hips, and he managed to wriggle out of them while keeping most of his attention focused on her breasts. He tweaked one nipple with his hand while he gently nipped the other with his mouth. He soothed the first with his tongue and settled in to torture the other with his hand. Jenny reached between them to find his length, hard and hot.

She closed her fist over him, and he sucked in an unsteady breath. A drop of liquid seeped out, and she massaged it into his length with her thumb.

Adam reached between them, and his thumb found the bundle of nerves between the slick folds of her flesh. Jenny couldn't breathe for a moment, could only feel the pulse between her legs building, building while his hands and mouth made her body feel wondrous things. One finger, then two slipped between her folds, and Jenny couldn't stop her hips from jolting upward, driving his thumb more vigorously against her.

"Adam." His name slipped from her mouth as wave upon wave crashed down on her. She felt her inner muscles squeeze his fingers as the orgasm crested, then she was floating. Absently, she realized his penis was still in her fist, but she couldn't seem to make her hand move over his length. Adam pressed a kiss to her sternum, then the base of her neck, then those wicked lips were against hers, and all Jenny could do was hold on while he stoked the embers of heat in her veins back to burning flame.

He needed to be inside her. She needed to feel him there, but he withdrew. He reached over the side of the bed, took a packet from the wallet in his jeans and tore it open with his teeth. When he had sheathed himself, Adam pressed kiss after kiss to her belly, until it was a mass of quivering nerves, then he took her breast in his mouth, and all Jenny could do was clutch the soft duvet cover in her fists as he pushed his fingers back into her body.

"Yes." The word was like a prayer on her lips, then his mouth was against hers once more.

Adam thrust his thick length into her, and all she could think was that if this moment never ended, it would be too soon. Bliss made the edges of her vision hazy, drove her nails to score his back, and made her wrap her legs more tightly around his hips, riding another wave of orgasm with him.

That growl sounded again, making her belly clench, then Adam emptied himself into her.

He collapsed on the bed, breathing heavily, his sweaty forehead resting against her shoulder.

"My Jenny," he said when he'd caught his breath.

Jenny wrapped her arms around his neck, burying her face against his chest. Adam rolled to the side, taking her with him, and she let her legs tangle with his.

His hand caressed her arm, and his breathing softened. Jenny settled against his shoulder, ignoring the fact that she should get up, find her clothes and send Adam to the RV.

Her eyelids drifted closed.

Just for a little while, she was going to be a woman who did whatever she wanted, without a thought to the consequences.

CHAPTER TWELVE

JENNY TWISTED AND untwisted the paper clip that had separated Frankie's spelling homework from his math. It was only three sheets, and she wasn't sure why his teacher sent them home separated. At least the paper clip gave her something to do with her hands, though, because it seemed as if she needed something to keep them busy. Ever since that night at the Slope with Adam, she had needed to be busy. Needed something to occupy her time so that she didn't spend it daydreaming about him.

The paper clip wasn't doing its job, though, because here she was, twisting and untwisting it and still thinking about him. About what was happening between them. The closeness was good. Spending time that wasn't just about work or the boys. So why did she feel as if everything in their lives was precariously balanced and just waiting for the slightest tip to throw everything topsy-turvy again?

Frankie pushed the paper across the table. "Okay?" he asked, and the boredom in his voice was palpable. Last week, his class went from complicated addition and subtraction to multiplication, and he didn't like the change. Like Adam, their son preferred the life around him to be familiar, and multiplication was anything but familiar.

She checked over the work, complimenting him on his attention to detail. "You're doing great, kiddo. Multiplication is just another way to think about addition and—"

But Frankie was already pushing away from the table. "Don't care," he said, and sped from the room. Jenny couldn't blame him. Math had never been her favorite subject, either.

She checked his spelling paper, then put all the homework back into the green folder he carried home each day. The right pocket bulged and she reached inside, pulling out a carefully folded piece of paper. Jenny considered putting it back in, but then thought about all the late-night worries the little boy had had. About the drawings Garrett had made. She unfolded it.

"My Dad" was written in messy handwriting across the top. She sat back in her chair to read.

One time, I went to work with my dad. He made a chair, and he hit his hand on the saw. It bled a little, but he said it was no big deal. I think it hurt, but he just wrapped his hand in a handkerchief and finished his work. He didn't cry. He took the chair home to my mom and it made her smile. When I grow up, I want to be like my dad so I can make things for people that make them smile.

The back door slammed, and Jenny hurriedly put the piece of paper back in the folder, then slipped the folder into Frankie's backpack. The boys rushed into the kitchen, grabbing bottles of juice from the fridge as they chattered about the dress-up days during the homecoming celebration the following week.

"The football players will come tomorrow after lunch, and we'll cheer," Frankie was saying.

Garrett's eyes rounded. "Can we talk to 'em?"

"Nope, just the principal and the coach talk, but they'll be there. And then we'll go outside for the parade."

"And they'll throw candy?"

"Usually. And the girls will be in fancy dresses." Frankie sounded disgusted at the thought of the homecoming court wearing dresses during the parade. "But the girls always throw candy."

"I can't wait for the candy."

"Have you two decided how you'll dress for Hero Day tomorrow?" Jenny asked. She craned her neck, but didn't see Adam in the hallway. She wanted to bring up Frankie's paper, to tell him she was proud of him, but didn't want to embarrass the boy.

"I'm gonna be Iron Man," Garrett said, slurping his juice. The boys sat beside her at the table.

"I thought you were going to be a firefighter."

Garrett shrugged. "Frankie said I could wear his Iron Man costume. We forgot about the firefighter stuff."

Jenny frowned. "I'm sorry, baby, we did, didn't we? If you really want to be a firefighter, we could go tonight." They usually had some toy things at Mallard's, and if not, the dollar store downtown might have a few things. She'd have to push dinner back a bit.

"S'okay, Mom. Iron Man is a real hero. He even has a movie about him."

"Three movies. Plus the Avengers movies," Frankie corrected.

Garrett counted on his fingers. "That's five movies. That's a lot of hero."

Jenny moved to the counter, pulled potatoes from the bin, then began peeling. Frankie had requested meat loaf for dinner, and the potatoes were the last of the prep work.

"Who will you dress up as?" she asked, pinpointing Frankie over her shoulder.

He studied his juice bottle carefully. "I don't know yet."

Jenny turned from the peeling, and leaned her

hip against the counter. She studied the boy for a minute, but he didn't seem upset or even concerned about Hero Day. "Well, I think it's decision time. Tomorrow is the big day, after all. We won't have time to go to a store before school in the morning."

"It's okay. I'll just wear something from here."

Jenny ruffled Frankie's hair, then returned to the counter and the potatoes. "Just let me know. The stores won't close until about eight."

The boys continued talking, with Frankie explaining how the homecoming parade worked, and the assembly beforehand. It had been too long since the two of them had talked in the kitchen while she prepped dinner. Hearing their childish voices was nice. Knowing that Adam was just outside was even better.

She could live like this. Could build a life around these three men. Work was going well; she'd sent the contracts off to the distributor last week, and the first house with the Joplin builder would begin after the Christmas holidays. Plenty of time to build up their stock and get the new hires trained. Then there was Adam, who seemed to be returning to his old self more every day.

Scratch that. Not his old self. The old Adam didn't invite her to the Slope, didn't send her a green plant for her office. The old Adam had left the fence materials languishing in the backyard for more than six months.

Frankie tugged on her T-shirt, bringing her back to the kitchen. Garrett had disappeared.

"I need my football stuff from the garage."

"What for? You don't have a game until next week."

"We're supposed to take everything to school. For a fitting. Or something."

"And you need it tomorrow?"

Frankie nodded.

"I'll get it down in a minute, okay?"

He nodded again, then hurried out of the house. She heard the back door slam shut behind him. Jenny put the meat loaf in the oven, then set the potatoes in the pan to boil before going into the garage.

After digging the football things out of the attic when practices began in August, Jenny had put the shoulder pads and other gear in one of Adam's old duffels and hung it on a peg. She grabbed the bag now and set it on the floor of the laundry room so Frankie could go through it later, then opened the door to the backyard.

Aiden and Adam sat at the patio table, talking, with Sheba at Adam's feet, while Garrett ran around making airplane noises and randomly holding out his right hand in what looked like an Iron Man gesture. Practicing for tomorrow, no doubt.

The lowering sun was turning the tops of the trees surrounding the lake to fire. Water gently lapped against the shore, and in the distance, a fishing boat motored past. This was the backyard she had dreamed about. The ground around the newly installed fence would need replanting in the spring, but the rosebushes bloomed red and green, and the chrysanthemums were beginning to flower. Leaves on the red maple in the corner would begin turning in another week or so.

She crossed her arms over her chest and joined the men at the table. "Dinner in about an hour. You staying?" she asked Aiden.

"What's on the menu?"

"Meat loaf, mashed potatoes and green beans."

"With bacon bits?"

"Is there any other way to cook green beans?"

"I'm staying."

Jenny grinned. "Have you seen Frankie? He came out here a few minutes ago."

Adam shook his head, but didn't seem concerned that their eight-year-old was nowhere to be found in the yard. Jenny frowned. The fence was supposed to make corralling the boys easier.

"Probably went around front. Hey, what do you think about running the ad starting next week?

Now that we have the first contract with the builder, we need to get started on the hiring."

"Sure." Jenny was only half listening to Adam as he continued talking to Aiden about the changes at Buchanan's. Where had Frankie gone? She remembered hearing the back door slam. Then she went to the garage. He could have come back inside then, but she should have heard the door. Unless he went out the gate and...where? To a friend's house? To the beach on the other side of the fence? "He wouldn't have gone to the beach, would he? It's too cool for wading."

"The gate's locked. He's probably in the front yard. He said something about uniforms." Adam continued talking to Aiden about contacting the college in the next town to see about placing an ad in their student paper or contacting one of the professors in the design department. He didn't seem concerned about Frankie at all. Typical.

And getting mad at Adam, who was in the backyard with their other son, wouldn't solve this problem.

Jenny fisted her hands. It was okay, Frankie wasn't the type of kid to just wander off, but he did sometimes get distracted. It was possible he'd gone to the garage for his football stuff on his own. But she'd been there, in the garage, then in the kitchen. She'd have seen or heard him. Jenny pushed back at the panic beginning to clog her throat.

Just then, the side gate opened and Frankie ambled through. Relief washed over Jenny, while Adam and Aiden continued talking as if she hadn't just been mentally going through the process of calling the police to search for the little boy.

"Where have you been?"

Frankie blinked at her and a guilty expression crossed his face. "Just, ah, walking."

"You're supposed to tell us when you leave the yard."

"Sorry." But he seemed more annoyed that he'd been caught than sorry he hadn't followed the rule about leaving the yard. "Did you get my stuff?"

"Yes. Why didn't you tell me or your dad where you were going?"

"Because I wasn't going to be gone long." The answer was reasonable, if totally and completely wrong. Time wasn't the point. Not knowing where her son might be was the point. It also didn't explain that guilty look on his face a moment ago.

"In the future, no matter how long you're going to be gone, you need to tell us you're leaving." Jenny pointed to the door. "Inside. You can help me set the table."

"Mo-om," Frankie said, drawing out the word.

"Listen to your mother, Frankie. You know how you like to know where we are? Same goes for us about you," Adam said, his voice firm but kind.

Jenny stared at Adam. She couldn't remember him ever correcting either of the boys, not even in agreement with her. She smiled at him and mouthed *"Thank you."* Adam shrugged, as if his standing by her was not a big deal. But it was. To Jenny, it was everything. More than his sending the right flowers or backing up her decisions at work or trading in the old Mustang for the new SUV. Those were things he did because she told him what she wanted. This was Adam being a parent to their child, and she loved him for it.

Frankie frowned, but didn't say anything more before stomping inside.

The door slammed behind him, and Adam reached out, touching his hand to hers. "Is he going to be mad at us for long?"

She shook her head, grinning at him. "He'll be over it by dinner. Even if he isn't, it's not always our job to be their friends."

"I know," Adam said sheepishly.

"Have Garrett come in to wash up in a little while, okay?" She went inside, to find Frankie sitting at the kitchen table with his chin in his hands. "Hey, sport," she said, ruffling his soft brown hair as she passed.

"Hey."

"I brought your football stuff inside." She handed plates to him, then checked the potatoes while he set them around the table. Jenny opened a can of green beans, added a few bacon bits to them, then set them on the stove to heat. "You want to tell me why you left the yard?" She glanced at Frankie, who set his mouth in a hard line. "It's not that I don't think you can take care of yourself. It's that when I know where you are, if there is ever a problem I can get to you quickly."

"I just walked over to Mrs. Hess's house. She has a new puppy," he said. "She's just across the street. I'm not a baby," he added, in a mumble.

"Mrs. Hess likes it when you visit, but I still need to know where you are." Jenny handed him napkins, and he placed them beside the plates while she laid out the flatware. "I worry about you, you know. And Garrett."

"And Dad?"

Jenny nodded. "Yeah, I worry about Dad, too."

"He's better now."

"He is, but I still worry."

"Because he can have another seizure?"

Because of the seizures, because of that dark place he'd been living in. Because, although she liked the man she was now getting to know, she still felt as if the man was more of a myth than a real person. And that was on her. She had to start trusting him again. If she didn't, no matter how many changes he made to his life or she made to hers, it wouldn't be enough for them.

"I worry about Dad because I love him. Just

like I worry about you because I love you. And Garrett and your grandparents. Love means putting someone else's safety and needs above your own."

"And that's why I have to tell you when I go see Mrs. Hess?"

"Yeah. That's why. Just like that's why I let you know where I'll be every night. So you don't have to worry."

The timer for the potatoes went off. Jenny dumped them into a colander to drain, then into a bowl to mix with milk and butter. She gave the beans a stir while she waited for the hot potatoes to melt some of the butter.

"I don't want you to worry."

She turned. Frankie had shoved his hands into the pockets of his jeans and was scuffing the toe of his sneaker against the floor.

"I know."

"I didn't mean it."

"I know that, too. Tell you what. You have my permission to visit Mrs. Hess and her puppy anytime you want. You just need to let me know where you're going first. Okay?"

He nodded.

"Why don't you go wash your hands before dinner?"

Frankie nodded once more before disappearing upstairs.

A few minutes later, the five of them sat around the kitchen table, talking and eating. Adam and Aiden were discussing the football team's chances at the homecoming game the next night, while Garrett chattered on about the merits of Iron Man versus a firefighter. Frankie seemed content to let his younger brother take the conversational lead. No one spoke to Jenny, but it didn't matter. This was her family.

She wasn't alone.

ADAM'S ALARM CLOCK BUZZED, waking him from a deep sleep. He turned over, slapping at the clock on the nightstand in the RV. The night before, after Aiden left and they got the boys down for the night, he'd been tempted to ask Jenny if he could stay in the house. But he wanted her to make that move.

Returning to the house, to their bedroom, on a full-time basis needed to come from her. God, he hoped it came from her soon.

Adam sat up, stretching out the kinks in his back from sleeping on the slightly too short mattress. When Nancy had outfitted the trailer, she'd customized it for herself and Owen, not Adam. He stretched his hands over his head, pulled a clean T-shirt on and walked to the house and inside. Jenny stood in the kitchen, making pancakes.

Adam slid his arms around her waist, kissing her neck.

"Good morning," he said, his mouth enjoying the feel of her soft skin. Jenny chuckled, put her hand over his and leaned against him for a minute.

"Good morning. Ready for the craziness of a dress-up-day Friday?"

The sound of the boys' footsteps clattered against the hardwood stairs. "Can't be much different from any other Friday, can it?"

"You have no idea."

"I have to go see Mrs. Hess, Mom," Frankie yelled, and before Jenny could react, the door slammed behind him.

"Well, he did tell you before he went."

"Mrs. Hess has a new puppy. We're going to have to revisit that 'any time you want to go see the puppy' thing."

Garrett reached the kitchen, the plastic of his Iron Man suit scraping with each step. The little boy held out his right hand. "Pancakes," he said, his voice sounding hollow as it came from behind the mask. "Please," he added, before continuing to the kitchen table.

"Do you want syrup or peanut butter?" Jenny asked, setting a plate of dollar-size pancakes before him.

"Syrup."

She returned to the counter, craning her neck.

Adam couldn't see the little boy, but he did hear Jenny's slight intake of breath.

"Everything okay?" He pushed past her, but saw just a flash of what looked like a little boy and small dog before the gate to the backyard closed behind Frankie.

"Everything is fine," Jenny said, but she looked at something behind him as she spoke. Adam wasn't sure what that was about. At least the kid was back and breakfast could go on without interruption.

Adam turned from the counter and stopped dead.

Frankie stood in the doorway. He wore his football pants, tennis shoes and shoulder pads, but instead of the jersey for his Saturday league, he wore Adam's old jersey from high school. The numbers were a bit ragged from the wear and tear of the games, and there was a small rip in one shoulder. Adam couldn't remember how the tear happened, but seeing the jersey brought back a host of other memories. How it had felt to make a touchdown-saving tackle. The dread of two-a-day practices in August. The thrill of running through whatever sign the cheerleaders made for that first Friday night game. The sadness in watching his best friends raise the state championship trophy while he stood on the sidelines because of the injury to his neck.

That jersey wasn't him anymore.

"What are you doing?"

"I'm, um, ready for breakfast," Frankie said, practically hugging the doorway instead of coming into the kitchen.

"Syrup or peanut butter?" Jenny asked, the words sounding too chirpy to Adam's ears. Like she was trying too hard to be happy. If it was this hard for him to see Frankie in the old jersey, how much harder would it be for her?

Because she'd lost the man who wore the old thing, too. The man who could take care of her, who had a purpose to his life. Who wasn't sidelined, permanently, from life.

"Peanut butter," Frankie said, but he didn't come into the kitchen, even when Jenny set the plate of pancakes at his usual seat.

"Why are you wearing that?" Adam was still trying to wrap his mind around why Frankie had his old jersey on. What did an old football rag have to do with Hero Day?

Jenny put her hand on Adam's shoulder and squeezed, as if urging him to do something. Sit down and have breakfast? He wasn't hungry. In fact, he felt like he might vomit. Frankie needed to take the old jersey off. Now.

"I, um, it's Hero Day." Frankie's voice was quiet and he still hadn't moved from the doorway.

"Heroes save people. Like Iron Man," Garrett added.

For the life of him, Adam couldn't figure out how his old football jersey equated to saving people. All it represented was an old football season and Jenny's packing abilities. The thing should be moth-eaten by now.

Jenny picked up the backpack that had been hanging from Frankie's seat. She pulled a folder from inside and handed him a piece of folded-up paper. The words *My Dad* in Frankie's handwriting made his heart stutter in his chest.

Adam looked at his son, who had taken one step into the kitchen. His left hand remained behind the door jamb, though, as if he was ready to bolt. Adam read the few lines on the page, then swallowed.

"I remember this day. It was last summer."

Frankie nodded. "It was before," he said, and his gruff voice was barely more than a whisper.

"Cutting my hand on a band saw doesn't make me a hero, Frankie."

"You were trying to save us. When you were hurt, you were trying to save us." Frankie took another step into the room, and Adam saw the leash twisted around his hand. "Mrs. Hess got a puppy."

The little yellow puppy yipped as it stepped into the kitchen behind Frankie, drawing Sheba's attention. The older dog focused on the younger, but didn't move from her position beside Adam.

"You're his hero, Adam," Jenny said, squeezing his hand in hers.

It was as if his heart squeezed in unison with Jenny's hand, and it hurt to breathe. Adam watched the words on the creased paper blur.

"But I didn't save you," he said.

"But you would have. You ran into that building because you thought the boys were inside. You thought other children were inside."

"I want to be like you," Frankie said. "A hero like you."

Adam couldn't find any words that would make sense of what he was seeing. His youngest son happily pouring more syrup over his pancakes, wearing an Iron Man costume. His other son looking miserable, holding the leash of a puppy while wearing Adam's old football uniform. A puppy that looked like a miniature version of his service dog. A son who wanted to be like him, despite the fact that he was no longer the fun, football-playing dad. Despite the fact that he might never be the fun dad again.

Frankie wanted to be like him.

"Is this why you disappeared yesterday afternoon?" Jenny asked, and Frankie nodded.

"I thought about using one of Garrett's stuffed animals, but then I'd have to carry it. Dad doesn't carry Sheba. She's a working dog. Mrs. Hess said it was okay, so can I bring him as part of my dress-up day?"

"Unless the school objects, I'm okay with it," Jenny said.

Adam swallowed hard. "It's, ah, okay with me, too," he said. The words sounded hoarse to him.

God, what had he done to deserve a kid like this? Adam let the paper drop to the floor, stepped forward and enfolded him in a hug.

"Dad, you're smushing me," Frankie said after a long moment.

Adam loosened his grip on the boy. "I love you, kiddo."

"Love you, too, Dad."

He glanced at Jenny, unsure what to say next. She glanced at the clock. Almost time to leave for school. "We have to get a move on. Eat, eat."

Frankie grabbed one of the pancakes from his plate and began slathering peanut butter over it with a butter knife. Then he folded it over and started eating it like a sandwich.

Jenny offered a small smile. Adam took her hand, holding it close to his heart. How could he have been so stupid as to think he should walk away from this? From Frankie and Garrett? From her? He'd been such a fool.

"I love you," he said.

"I love you, too." Jenny rested her head on his shoulder. "I love you, too."

The six of them walked to school together, Garrett hurrying ahead to pick flowers from the neighbors' yards, Frankie leading Mrs. Hess's puppy, and Sheba pushing the little dog ahead with her nose from time to time. Adam held Jenny's hand, enjoying the feel of warm fall sunshine on his face. He nodded to a few of the other parents.

None of them seemed to notice the cane or the dog beside him. Of course, none of them had paid too much attention to the wheelchair, either. Maybe the curious glances and pitying looks had been figments of his imagination. Or exaggerations. He'd been so uncomfortable in the chair he had to have made the people around him uncomfortable, too.

Garrett divided the bouquet he'd picked in half, offering part to a girl wearing a Princess Leia outfit and the other to a girl wearing a firefighter's hat.

Their little caravan turned the corner, and the school block spread out before them. Older students wore team hoodies or held fake badges. Several of the elementary students wore superhero-themed Halloween costumes, like Garrett. A few wore football jerseys. Only Frankie hauled a small dog as part of his costume.

For the first time, Adam went up the steps to the school, stopping his older son before he went inside.

"Let's check in with the office before you go to class. Deal?"

Frankie nodded. Garrett launched himself at Adam, hugging him. "See ya after school, Dad," he said, and disappeared into the crush of little bodies going inside.

Jenny took the leash from Frankie. "I'll just hang on to Kujo here, while you get approval from the office."

"His name is Gandy, Mom," Frankie said, shaking his head. "Come on, Dad."

Sheba circled Adam, almost seeming to prance. Adam used the hand command for heel, and the dog settled down. She kept looking back to the puppy, though. Probably worried it would follow.

Adam held the school door open, nodding to the teacher watching the kids flood through. "We need to approve part of his costume before school," he explained.

The teacher pointed them toward the office, at the other end of the entryway.

"Hand, Frankie," Adam said, and the little boy tugged on it.

"You already have my hand, Dad."

Funny, he hadn't felt like he was holding on to anything. Probably just the distraction of Gandy and Sheba and the surreal quality of this morning. He glanced at Frankie, and the little boy's face seemed to waver before him.

"Sorry, kiddo. Let's go get that approval."

Adam and Frankie continued through the entryway, and waited at the sliding window of the office while the secretary went to find the principal.

"You think it'll be okay and Gandy can stay?"

"We'll see." Adam blinked, trying to bring the office into focus. Everything seemed blurry, which was odd, but no matter what he did, focus seemed just beyond his reach. Sheba whined behind him and he reached to pat her head. But she wasn't there. "It's okay, girl. Just a few more minutes."

"Dad?" Frankie's voice seemed to come to him from a long way away, but Sheba's whining seemed louder, as if she were right in his ear. Which was wrong. The dog was louder than the boy, but not that much louder.

"Dad?" Frankie's voice again, only this time there was a tremor.

Tingling started in Adam's fingertips, which was a relief because until the tingling started, he couldn't feel Frankie's hand in his. The little boy squeezed, and repeated, "Dad."

"It's okay, buddy."

But it wasn't okay. Adam's hand still tingled, and the brick of the office wall seemed to waver like Frankie's face had done a few minutes before. The voices in the hallway were loud, but Sheba's bark was louder, and seemed almost frenzied. Which was odd. Sheba was the calmest dog Adam had ever known. He shook his head, trying to clear it, but that only seemed to make things worse.

"Dad?"

He needed to sit down. Maybe he should have eaten breakfast with the boys this morning. Usually, the medication cut his appetite, but this morning he'd felt hungry. He'd been too distracted by Frankie's costume to eat, though.

"I'm just going to sit down for a second," he said. There was a bench against the wall. He needed to sit there. On the bench. Adam turned, but the wall was a blur of brick and mortar, and he couldn't make out where the bench might be. Still, he stepped away from the wall.

Adam's knee buckled under him, and he tried to catch his weight with the cane, but his hand couldn't grip the curved top. He felt himself falling, saw Frankie's eyes widen in terror as the floor rushed up toward him.

Then everything went black.

CHAPTER THIRTEEN

JENNY PACED THE hallway of Springfield Regional Hospital, cell phone to her ear. She could still hear Frankie's screaming voice echoing in that damned entryway.

"Yes, I'll call you as soon as I know anything. Right now, all I know is that he's stable."

Nancy sighed audibly over the phone. "We can come. All of the projects are on schedule. Shutting down the business early won't hurt anything."

A single day wouldn't hurt things; Jenny knew that. What she didn't know was if this was a single day or another long-term stay. What if Adam seized again while getting the MRI? The paramedics had gotten him stabilized quickly, but epilepsy was different in every patient, especially those who contracted it because of head injuries.

"Thank you, I appreciate that. But I'd appreciate it more if you could stay. Frankie and Garrett are going to need familiar faces around them." She pinched the bridge of her nose. Seeing Adam on that floor had been terrifying. Seeing the horror on Frankie's face had nearly undone her. Then she'd had to leave him.

Jenny blew out a breath. "Would you pick them up from school? Take them to your house—it might be easier for them."

"Jenny, I need to do something. I can't just sit on my thumbs here while my son—"

"What you can do is take care of the boys until I can get there. Adam has the best doctors in the state. They're familiar with the injury. He's stable. I'll call you when I know more." She hung up, put the phone in her purse, then continued to pace.

He would be okay. The doctors would figure out a new drug regimen. This was bad, but it wasn't the end of the world. She'd known, they'd known, more seizures were not just possible but probable because of the scarring on Adam's brain. It was just a setback, something that had to happen so that the doctors could find the thing that would cure him. That was all.

Jenny took a deep breath.

It wasn't all. While the paramedics had stabilized him, he'd still been unresponsive in the ambulance. What if he'd hit his head hard enough to cause more scarring? What if this wasn't just the last seizure before the doctors found the right medication for him? What if this was the start of something much worse? The epilepsy had been semicontrolled before this morning. What if this meant it was now out of control?

How did she explain that to the boys, who were just now getting used to the changes in their father?

How did she make sure Adam knew, no matter what the doctors said in the next few hours, that it didn't have to change anything for them? Whatever this was, they were stronger now than they had been three months before. Rough edges? Sure, every couple had them. But the bond she felt with him now was so much more than it had been when the tornado struck.

They had so much to live for. And so much to lose if this setback thrust Adam back into that dark place that had nearly taken him before.

The doctor rounded the corner, wearing his familiar lab coat. His collared shirt was wrinkled and the khakis he wore were stained at the bottom. Not an overall inspiring look. Then again, this was how he had looked every other time she'd seen him. She had to stop thinking in negatives and focus on the positives.

Like the fact that he seemed relaxed. How the hell could the man be relaxed at a time like this?

"Mrs. Buchanan, I'm sorry for the delay. There was a traffic accident on the south side of town, putting Adam on a wait list for the MRI machine."

She didn't care about a car accident, and Jenny

knew that was heartless of her. But the doctor hadn't added the word *fatal*, so she assumed the people involved weren't in dire need of medical attention. Not like her husband.

"Is he okay?"

"The seizure has stopped, and we're not seeing any abnormal brain activity. For now, he's fine." He motioned for her to follow, and continued talking about the treatment course as they moved through the maze of hallways between the waiting area she'd been assigned and the private room where Adam rested.

Once in the room, Jenny focused on Adam. His eyes were closed, and he looked so still. Beeping machines sent a fresh shot of adrenaline through her system. There were pads and cords hooked up to Adam's chest, his forehead. An alligator clip was snapped onto his index finger. And he looked so very still.

She wanted him to move, just a little, but Adam remained immobile.

For now. Not the clean bill of health she wanted, but she would take those two simple words.

"Is he awake?"

"He's had a sedative, but will wake up in a little while." The doctor wrote something on Adam's chart before focusing on her. "I know you want answers, and right now I don't have any. We're going to make a small adjustment to his meds, but until the full results are back from the MRI, we won't know what triggered this episode. Even after we have the results, we may not have a clear indicator."

Right, she remembered this part. The part where the doctor said brain injuries rarely responded in typical fashion. That each patient was unique. That what worked for patient A wouldn't necessarily work for patient B.

"But he's okay?"

"Pressure is stabilized, he responds to stimuli. Yes, he's okay."

Jenny closed her eyes. At the side of the bed, she reached for Adam's hand. It was cold in hers, and she rubbed it, hoping for some kind of reaction. The machine's beeping didn't change, and Adam didn't open his eyes.

"Can I stay?" she asked. "I want to be here when he wakes up."

"Of course," Dr. Lambert said. Jenny focused on Adam's breathing.

He wasn't hooked up to a breathing machine, like he'd been after they'd found him in the rubble. That was a positive sign, she told herself. Breathing on his own was definitely positive. The numbers on the machines were similar to the numbers that had bleeped in the few days before his initial hospital release. Another positive sign.

"He can have visitors later this evening."

Adam would hate visitors.

People staring at me like I'm some kind of carnival exhibit.

His voice echoed in her mind. His parents and she had taken turns sitting with him and staying with the boys after the tornado. When he woke up, his parents had been on duty. When she came to relieve them a few hours later, the first thing he'd said was that he didn't want them to come back. That they made him feel like he was on display.

"Do you think he can come home soon?"

"We'll monitor him for the night, but barring any major changes, I'd say we can release him tomorrow. I'm going to check on a couple of things, but I'll be back in a half hour."

One day. It was better than the three weeks he'd spent here before.

She nodded and the doctor took off, leaving Jenny alone in the room with the beeping machines and her sleeping husband. She knew she should call Nancy. Aiden. Adam's friends. But she couldn't let go of his hand, not even for the few seconds it would take to fish through her bag to find her phone. She squeezed, but there was no response from Adam, only the beeping of the machines monitoring his condition.

NOTHING FELT RIGHT despite both Jenny and Dr. Lambert insisting that things were fine.

He was in the hospital. How fine could any of this be?

"We'll do another MRI next week, but for now, this is very promising."

Promising. Right. After more than a month without a seizure, he'd been knocked to the ground—in front of his kid—by his malfunctioning brain. Didn't seem very promising to him.

"Adam, it's just a drug adjustment," Jenny said. She sat beside him in the familiar plastic chair with the gray-and-blue striping on the back. He hated plastic chairs. No design, just hard surface. Utility.

Wooden chairs, now they had style. Grace. Smoothing lines, surprising features. Like the chair he'd worked on with Aiden in the shop, made from different types of wood. He supposed hospitals didn't care much for design elements. They wanted function for their patients, their patient's families.

Both Jenny and the doctor stared at him, and he realized they were waiting for an answer. "Right. Simple adjustment." The two exchanged a glance that Adam didn't need clear vision to read. Pity.

Worry.

His two least favorite emotions.

The two of them started chatting again, but Adam tuned them out. He didn't need to hear their positive talk about drug interactions or the promise of the MRI taken earlier that afternoon. None of that mattered.

This wasn't going away.

He'd fooled himself into thinking that the epilepsy didn't matter. That the longer he went without a seizure, the less likely it was to happen again. He couldn't block out the look of terror on Frankie's face as Adam had fallen in that hallway.

It didn't matter if the seizures were far apart or back-to-back. He wouldn't put the people he loved through that. Not when he could prevent their pain.

Not even if preventing their pain meant opening a bottomless pit of his own. He had to let go of them, all of them. His boys. His parents.

Jenny.

God, he didn't want to let her go.

Seeing her with the distributor, having a slice of pizza, had nearly killed him; it still made him feel pain in parts of his body he didn't want to feel pain. And that was after he knew the pizza was only a business lunch.

"Tomorrow morning, assuming there are no more setbacks, I'll release you to go home."

Home, ha. The RV wasn't his home. Jenny's bedroom certainly wasn't his home. Slippery Rock wouldn't be his home for much longer, because staying there would only keep the wounds open and bleeding. He needed to staunch the blood, and to do that he would need distance.

So would Jenny.

"And I'll see you in my office in three weeks. If there are any more incidents, or if the medications feel off—they give you pain, blurred vision, anything at all—I'm only a phone call away."

"Thank you," Jenny said, a relieved smile playing over her face. She looked expectantly at Adam.

"Thanks, Doc," he managed to say. Thanks for nothing.

That was unfair, and he knew it. Doctors weren't miracle workers. They did their best with the machines and treatments and knowledge that they had. Sometimes, those things just weren't enough. He should have known that by now.

A WEEK LATER, Adam dumped hot spaghetti noodles into a colander to drain, dropped a pat of butter into the still-hot pan and set it back on the stove. As the butter melted he turned on the burner under the spaghetti sauce and put garlic bread in the oven. The boys were with his parents for the night, and for that he was glad. Because he had to tell Jenny goodbye. He couldn't keep doing this to her. He'd already done enough.

Over the past week he'd watched as the circles under her eyes returned, darker than ever. Seen her hands tremble over the simplest tasks. Because she was exhausted with taking care of him, with keeping things normal for the boys, keeping the business running smoothly.

While he sat in the RV with the service dog, waiting for the next seizure.

Last time, she had asked him to move out. This time, he knew she wouldn't. She had always been a strong woman, stronger than he gave her credit for, but over the past couple weeks, he'd seen that strength and determination grow even more. Jenny wouldn't give up on him; the thought both terrified and awed him. Which meant he had to do this final thing for her—not because he was afraid of her leaving him, but because he knew her life could be so much more if he wasn't in it. Pulling her down. Making her afraid.

God, he'd thought things were getting better, had hoped the doctors were right. The rational part of his mind told him that people with epilepsy had fulfilling relationships all the time. The emotional part didn't want to ever see the looks of fear from Jenny or his boys again. Not ever.

So he was letting them go.

He just needed one more night with her. First.

"Dinner will be ready in five," he called.

"I'm not hungry." Jenny's voice was quiet behind him. "At least, not for food."

Adam's mouth went dry and blood rushed from his brain to his pants. He turned slowly and saw

Jenny set her juice glass down deliberately. The denim of his jeans tightened around his hips. She reached behind her to tug the zipper of her dress down, down, down.

"And I don't want to talk." She slipped one strap over her shoulder and then the next. She pulled her arms free from the dress, but held it to her breasts with one hand. "Why don't you turn off dinner?"

Adam reached behind him, flicking the burners into the off position. "I wasn't hungry, either," he said, his voice rough.

Jenny turned and let the dress fall as she started up the stairs toward their bedroom. The room from which he'd been banned when she'd asked him to move out just a few short weeks ago. The room which, after tonight, he might never see again. He pushed that thought from his mind.

She didn't wear a bra, but her lacy panties were hot pink. Her hips were full, and those long legs tapered down to bare feet that were still a little bit tan from the long summer months.

Jenny's curly hair swayed side to side as she walked, beckoning him to follow. Adam did.

He had to let her go, for real, this time. They'd given this a good run. Had nearly made it back to the Jenny and Adam they'd been before the tornado. It killed him that they hadn't made it all the way back, but after the seizure at the school, he'd realized they could never be the same people they had been. He would never have full control over his body, over his mind, again. She would always be afraid of what might happen next.

But he could give her tonight, then he would walk away.

Jenny sat on the bed, pushing herself to the pillows. "I—"

"You said you didn't want to talk. So don't talk." He reached the bed, rested his knee on the mattress and his hands on either side of her body. "Just be with me," he said.

Jenny's pupils dilated, making her hazel eyes look nearly black in the dwindling evening light.

"I don't think I can be completely silent," she teased, then pressed her mouth to his jaw.

"Try," he said, and covered her lips with his.

Adam took his time, exploring her mouth the way he had a hundred times before, but it felt completely different. As if they hadn't been here, in their bedroom, just a few days before. She tasted sweet, like the best parts of a crisp Missouri fall.

She tilted her head, giving him better access to her mouth as he thrust his tongue inside. He nipped the corner of her mouth and she sighed before running the tip of her tongue along his bottom lip. Her fingers played with the hair at his nape, urging him closer and closer. Adam knelt on the bed, taking her face in his hands. He pulled back a fraction.

"I'm just going to say one thing before we go back to the no-talking thing." He kicked his Nikes off his feet. "You are the best person I have ever known." Tears glinted in her eyes. "I love you, Jennifer Anne Buchanan. I always have."

Then he pressed her back against the pillows and stripped off his T-shirt, and because he didn't think the words would be enough, tried to show her with his hands and his mouth how much she meant to him.

SHE WAS LOSING HIM.

All the progress the two of them had made over the past month was gone, as if it had never existed.

Jenny rested her head on Adam's chest, listening to him breathe. He hadn't said anything, but she could tell in the way his hands rested loosely over her back. The Adam she had come to know over the past couple weeks held on. He comforted. He encouraged.

That Adam was gone, even though he was still with her in their bedroom. Even though he'd told her he loved her. She hated him for that.

He'd made her believe. In him. In herself. In their marriage. And when the first obstacle came, he was ready to duck out. Again. Well, she wasn't going to let him get away with that disappearing act again. She deserved better. No, she *demanded* better. For herself and for their boys.

She sat up, pulling the sheet around her body as she did. Adam let her go. Pain radiated around her heart, but Jenny forced herself to ignore the flashes to focus on Adam. She had to make him mad. Mad enough to fight, the way he'd started fighting after he saw her having lunch with Mike Harrison.

Only what did she have to fight with?

"I'm going to finish dinner," she stated.

He didn't respond, just lay there in their bed, the bed he'd made for them, staring at the ceiling.

Jenny grabbed a pillow from the chest at the foot and heaved it at his head. Adam blinked, like a baby owl seeing sunlight for the first time.

"What was that for?" He rubbed his palm over his head and supported himself on his elbow.

"Because you are the most obtuse, frustrating man on the face of this earth."

He blinked at her.

"Well?" she said.

"Well, what?"

"Well, what do you have to say to that?"

"That you're right."

Jenny stomped her foot on the floor and winced as a shaft of pain shot up her leg. Well, at least it wasn't only her heart that was hurting now. "No, I'm not right. I'm being just as obtuse and frustrating as you are. No one person is *always* this or that or *the most* of anything else."

"Sure they are. You're the most beautiful woman I've ever known. You're smart and kind and funny. You're an amazing mother and a generous lover." Adam sat up, and hope blossomed in Jenny's chest. Maybe she'd gotten the signals wrong, God knew she'd done so before.

"Then why aren't—"

Adam held up a hand, stopping her. "That's why I have to leave."

The hope trying to find purchase in her heart plummeted to her feet. "You don't have to leave."

"Yeah, I do." Adam pulled his jeans over his hips, grabbed his shirt off the floor and pulled it on. "Because if I don't, you never will, and you deserve better than me."

Jenny bit down on her lip to keep from crying out at his words. *She* deserved? What about what he deserved? What about what they deserved, together? What about the boys? And, goddammit, what did deserving have to do with anything?

As far as Jenny was concerned, people deserved dessert after every meal, preferably of the darkest, richest chocolate variety. That didn't mean they always got it.

"So all of this, the coming to work, the dinners out, the new car. Those things were what? Devices to trick me into thinking you were changing? Things you were using to set me up so you could pull the rug out from under me?" Jenny reached for a pair of jeans, pulling them on before grabbing a top from the dresser. She let the sheet drop, then put her hands on her hips. "You are one colossal piece of work, you know that?"

"I didn't do any of this to hurt you."

"Sure you did. This was all a game to you, wasn't it?"

"It wasn't a game. I wanted you back. I still want you back, Jen, but I can't make you walk through this life with me, not now. Not when I don't control it."

"News flash, Adam, no one controls life. It's a combination of destiny and hard work and a lot of error. We make the best choices with the information we have at the time—"

"Well, the information I have is that I'm broken. That not only don't I have control of this life, but that there's something inside me that is controlling me." Adam picked up the pillow she'd tossed at his head, and squeezed it until she thought the little buttons might pop off. They didn't.

"Then we figure out how to control—"

"We? What we? You and me? Me and the doctors? You and me and the doctors? And where does that leave Frankie and Garrett? Waiting at home while *we* go to doctor appointments and play with drug regimens and take ugly little pictures of my brain that we'll never show another living person because the scarring makes it look

like some kind of monster has left claw marks
on it?"

"Stop." Jenny took a step back. She'd wanted
him to fight, but to fight *with* her, not just fight
her.

"Why? Why don't we go even further. What
happens when I'm not swimming in the lake because it's too dangerous, but the boys are? What
happens when a seizure puts me facedown in the
sand, and they're crying and screaming for it to
end, but I can't stop it? What happens then?"

"Stop."

But Adam kept going. "Because I know what
happens then. I've seen the horror wash over
Frankie's face, I've heard the terror when he calls
out for me, and I've felt the helplessness as I try
to keep the seizure from happening. And guess
what? I can't, Jenny. I can't stop it. I didn't ask
for this, and I can't stop it." He threw the pillow
to the floor, where it landed with a soft thud. "I
can't stop any of it, but I can stop it from affecting you. The boys. My family. I can stop that, and
goddammit, I'm going to."

"Adam, don't," Jenny said, reaching out to him,
but he was too far away. Adam shoved his hands
into his pockets, as if her touch might brand him.
"The doctor said—"

"The doctor said? He said they'd found the
right combination. He said a service dog would

detect the seizure. He said do the physical therapy, strengthen the hip, get ready for surgery. And he said no surgery until the seizures were under control. And guess what? They're not."

"It was just a setback."

"And there will be another. And another. I can't do that to you, Jenny. I can't put you through this over and over again. I won't do it to the boys. I can't control my body, but I can control who my body hurts. Right now, it's hurting you. It's hurting the boys."

He couldn't mean that. If he meant that, then this was really over. The strides they'd been making, the feelings he'd awakened in her…it was all for nothing. She was a twenty-six-year-old, single mother who had failed at the only thing she'd ever wanted to do in her life. She had failed at loving another person.

"Then why this?" She waved her hands at the room, at the bed. Why hadn't he just walked away? Why get a sitter for the boys? Why plan the whole dinner and sex thing? "Why not just let me go?"

Adam swallowed. "Because I'm a selfish bastard in addition to being a colossal piece of work. I wanted one more memory of you to take with me."

She wouldn't cry. Jenny refused to cry, not now. Not when he was already gone. Tears would only make things worse, though how things could feel worse than they did right now, she wasn't sure. She only knew she wouldn't cry in front of Adam Buchanan. She wouldn't cry for him.

She'd done enough crying over the past three months.

"Then take your memory and get out."

CHAPTER FOURTEEN

ADAM DRAGGED A duffel down the narrow, retract-able steps from the attic. Jenny had left a few min-utes ago for work, and for the first time in several weeks, she'd taken the boys to school on her way. Because he'd hidden in the RV like a scared little boy instead of facing his family.

Instead of facing her.

Adam knew what he had to do, but he also knew the more he was around Jenny, the more he would waffle. He'd talk himself into staying, just like he'd talked himself into fighting for her after spotting her having lunch with the developer. If he did that, if he stayed, she would be the one to be hurt by it. After a seizure, he was left with a bit of a headache and a feeling that things weren't quite right.

For the people he loved, it was a hundred times worse. Frankie had avoided being in the same room as him since the seizure at the school. Gar-rett was back to drawing ominous clouds in his pictures. Jenny was exhausted and pretending everything was fine.

At least, she'd been pretending before last night. Since their fight, she'd simply ignored him. Which was fine. If he didn't exist, he couldn't hurt her.

The last person Adam wanted to hurt was Jenny. That was why he had to leave. No question about that. He'd find some other place to live, somewhere he didn't know anyone. Somewhere he could be anonymous and alone.

Inside the RV, Adam stuffed the duffel with his clothes. The bag was nowhere near full, but he didn't have anything else to take with him. He took the keys from the visor and started the engine. Pulled carefully onto the street, ignoring the soft whine of Sheba. Probably he should release her back to her trainer. Maybe there was a person she could actually help somewhere in the world. It was comforting not being alone in the RV, though, so Adam kept driving until he reached the ranch house where his parents lived. They would be at work by now, which was good, because he didn't know how to tell them he was leaving.

Adam parked the oversize vehicle, hefted the duffel over his shoulder, then wrapped Sheba's leash around his palm a couple times. He could call them once he was settled, and in the meantime, he'd keep himself too busy to become a burden or a bother. To anyone. Before he actually left town, there were a few things he needed to do to make sure Jenny was cared for.

He walked to the B and B, tapped his hand on the bell and waited for the desk clerk to come out of the office. The clerk handed an oversize gold key to him, and didn't seem to recognize him. A weird feeling, when everybody knew everybody else in this town.

Out the side window, he could see the bulk of Buchanan's. Jenny would be inside, finalizing some sale or contract. Aiden would be overseeing the workers building Adam's furniture designs. His father would be loading a truck, with a handful of other workers. His mother would be answering the phones.

Everyone at Buchanan's had a place. Everyone except him.

He called a number from the phone book, waiting until a pleasant female voice answered the phone. "Dilgaard Law, how may I direct your call?"

Adam cleared his throat. "I need to talk to someone about dissolving a partnership."

"I'll connect you," she said, and then Muzak filled the phone line.

Step one—find a way to leave the business in Jenny's hands, completely. Adam didn't want her to buy him out, and he didn't want to leave enough room for anyone else to get into the company ownership. Jenny knew what to do; Aiden had decided to stay in town so he could hold down that portion of the business. If Jenny decided she needed a new partner, Adam's brother could fill those shoes. If she didn't want another partner, Adam would ensure she didn't have to take one on.

A series of clicks sounded over the line, then the receptionist's voice came back. "It will be a few minutes, unless you'd like to leave a call back number?"

"No, I'll hold." Because if he didn't do this now, he might not do it.

Step one—give Jenny the business.

Step two—walk away.

"He walked out?" Mara's eyes widened across the table. Her arm paused, the glass of tea she'd been drinking frozen halfway to her mouth.

It had been a week since Jenny had made love with Adam, and he'd walked out of her life. Seven days that felt like seven years. Or maybe seventy.

"More or less." Minus the pillow squeezing and throwing, but Jenny didn't want to get into exactly how childish she—and Adam—had been the other night. It was hard enough telling her friends that he'd gone. If either Mara or Savannah realized how ridiculous the fight had been, they might jump to the conclusion that things between Jenny and Adam weren't really over. And they were. This time, she was well and truly done.

She'd been afraid of being alone. Now she realized alone wasn't the worst feeling in the world. The worst feeling in the world was the one she'd been carrying around for the past week: the feeling that she would never be enough.

She should have been used to it. Adam wasn't the self-absorbed person her mother was, or at least, if he was self-absorbed, it hadn't been in a selfish way. Adam simply hadn't considered that his way of doing things wasn't always the best.

Then the tornado trapped him in the rubble of that church. She had thought he was finally learning that lesson.

"Jenny, what can we do?" Savannah reached across the table and squeezed her hand.

She offered a thin smile. "Nothing. He doesn't want to burden anyone with his problems. He doesn't want to feel powerless in any situation. I could fight if he were simply afraid. I can't fight against what he sees as his inadequacies." Not when she had plenty of those on her own. "He moved into the B and B." It had taken all of an afternoon for that news to spread through the warehouse, and most likely through the rest of the town. Somehow, everyone had missed that Adam had been living in his parents' RV for a few weeks. But as soon as he took a room at the Slippery Rock B and B it was front-page news.

"Wow." Mara leaned back in the booth. "You're way too calm for this to be the whole story."

Jenny shrugged. "Calm or not, this is the whole story. After that whole flower debacle, he started to pay attention to the things I like. He traded in the Mustang, he sent me potted plants. He was there. In the house, with the boys, at work. I had him back. Then that seizure hit, and now I have to face the fact that he was never really back. I'd projected all of that onto him. Made him feel guilty or something."

"It wasn't wrong for you to demand that he wake up. I barely knew Adam, but even I could see that he was not himself after the tornado," Savannah said.

"I don't know." Jenny sipped her tea, wondering. In theory, she knew that it was not wrong to demand to be heard, to want to be understood. In reality, though, weren't demanding and wanting selfish motivations?

No, it had to matter that she'd demanded to be heard for his sake as much as her own. So that he could take his life back. So that they could find some kind of balance as a couple, as a family.

"What will you do?"

She had no idea. "Go to work, make sure our employees are cared for. Go home, show my boys that I'm still here, that they aren't alone. Make sure my parents and his don't place the blame solely on his shoulders. Adam might be the one walking away, but he's also the one who is hurting. He's walking away from a job he loved, friends he could depend on and a family who always encouraged him." She finished her tea, but decided not to order another. She didn't need the caffeine to stay awake. It had been impossible to sleep since he'd walked out, even the night she'd taken two over-the-counter sleeping pills, hoping to shut out the voices in her head.

"You're not in this alone," Mara said, compassion lacing the words.

"I know. Thanks for meeting me for early drinks. I know it's a pain, but the boys will be out of school soon, and I don't want to leave them with a babysitter just yet."

"How are they dealing with Adam's leaving?" Savannah pushed her index finger against the lip of her glass, making a high C sing across the table.

"Frankie is back to needing to know my every move during the day. Garrett drew another attack tornado in art class this week. Neither of them has really put it together that Adam isn't coming back." When they did… She would figure out how to rebalance their lives. Again.

God, she wanted to hate Adam for making her balance and rebalance their lives. Instead, she felt nothing.

"I want to be angry at him. Why do I just feel

numb?" Anger would be so much better than the helpless feeling she'd had for the past few days. Almost any emotion would be better than that.

"Because you love him." Mara reached out to squeeze Jenny's hand. Savannah rested her palm over theirs.

"I don't want to love him." Why couldn't she stop? He'd hurt her before, and she'd been able to stop herself then. Or at least to keep her heart from completely breaking open. Why couldn't she do that now?

Mara and Savannah offered small smiles, but no words of comfort.

CHAPTER FIFTEEN

ADAM PACED THE small room at the B and B, unable to sit still. It was Friday, nearly a week since he'd moved out of Jenny's house. He'd tried watching TV, but during the day the only options for television seemed to be soap operas filled with lying, cheating and lovemaking, or scripted talk shows about real people who lied, cheated and loved making their significant others feel like dirt.

He'd had enough of lying, had no desire to cheat and couldn't stop replaying that last night with Jenny in his mind. He didn't need the manufactured drama of either the soaps or talk shows. He had his own soap opera going right now.

What he needed was a drink, but drinking wasn't allowed in his condition. Of course, neither was living alone, and he'd managed that just fine for the past week. Adam pocketed the key to his room and signaled Sheba to follow him. The dog kept pace with him through the streets of town until they reached the Slippery Slope.

Adam ducked inside before he could talk himself out of it.

Sliding onto a bar stool, he ordered a draft from Merle.

Adam was the only patron at two in the afternoon, and after Merle slid the icy glass over the bar, he considered dumping a few dollars' worth of quarters into the jukebox for company. He knew just what he'd play. Darius Rucker on repeat, with maybe a twist of Tim McGraw, just to keep things going. He crossed the floor and began dropping coins into the slot.

"You going to drink that?" Merle eyed Adam from across the bar. Out of quarters, Adam returned to his stool and sat. "You know, I was okay with you bringing a dog into the place, but if you're just going to keel over and die, I'm going to have to ask you to take that outside."

"I'm not trying to kill myself," Adam said, but he didn't pick up the glass. He only watched it, daring himself to take that first drink.

The door opened, and Collin and Levi walked in. Adam shot Merle a look, and the old bartender just shrugged. Darius Rucker's smooth voice began singing about a drunk who had walked out on the woman he loved. Perfect song for his situation. His friends joined him at the bar, each ordering a beer.

"Figured we'd find you here, sooner or later."

Collin was the first to speak. "You know, moving the RV into your drive to win back Jenny was odd. Moving into the B and B was downright stupid. But mixing alcohol with the drug cocktail you're on is perfectly moronic."

"I didn't ask for your opinion."

"Well, you're getting it anyway." Aiden joined them at the bar, and Adam wondered how long his brother had been there. The door hadn't opened since Levi and Collin entered a moment before. Had Aiden been watching him? Why couldn't they just let him be? He was doing the right thing here.

He was doing the only thing he could do.

"Fine, say what you have to say and get out." Adam picked up the mug of beer and sipped. Hops and barley slid down his throat, making him feel as if he'd finally taken a step forward. He knew it was childish and dangerous, but Adam didn't care. He'd already had everything that mattered taken away from him. Why shouldn't he drown these lingering feelings of loss, too?

Aiden jerked the beer mug from his hand, and liquid sloshed over the gleaming mahogany of the bar. "You're an ass, how's that for starters?" his brother said.

"I've heard worse."

"You're an inconsiderate child who is acting

like some other inconsiderate child has stolen his favorite toy."

"What would you know about it?"

"Nothing." Aiden went behind the bar and stared at Adam across the expanse of gleaming wood. "I don't know anything about what you're going through—you've got me on that one. What I know about is running away from problems, and running away doesn't solve anything."

"What have you ever run away from?"

Aiden just stared at him. "Slippery Rock." He crossed his arms over his chest. "I didn't have a scratch on me after that crash. I walked away. They had to cut you out of the car, and then life-flighted you to the hospital in Springfield while our mother held on to our father's arm as if it was the only solid thing she could find. I saw what that did to them. What I did to them, and I vowed then and there to walk away as soon as I could."

"You left because of me?"

"No, I left because of what I'd done to you. I knew I shouldn't have driven that night, but I didn't care."

"It wasn't your fault there was black ice on the road."

Aiden shrugged. "It was my hubris that made me leave the house that night, all because I wanted to see a girl."

"You didn't make me come along."

"I didn't stop you, either."

But that didn't make what had happened in high school the same as what Adam was dealing with now. He hadn't caused that accident any more than he had caused the tornado a few months before. Years ago, he'd needed surgery and a long time to heal. Now, there was no amount of surgery or healing that could fix what was wrong with him. No matter what anyone else said.

"That was different. A neck injury isn't the same as epilepsy." He hated that word. It meant he was weak. He didn't want to be weak.

"The difference between now and then is then you took back your life. Now you're letting your life be taken from you." Levi's deep voice seemed loud in the quiet bar. Darius Rucker's voice had faded into silence, and Tim McGraw's hadn't yet begun to fill the space. "This doesn't have to be the end of everything you want."

"Like that tackle a few years ago wasn't the end of everything you wanted, Levi?"

"That was different. Football is a game that I walked away from. You're planning on walking away from your life."

They made it sound like he planned to walk into Slippery Rock Lake with a weight locked around his neck. Adam didn't want to kill himself; he only wanted to not hurt the people he loved.

"I'm giving her space to move on."

"What if she doesn't want to move on?" This time Collin spoke up. "What if she wants to be right here with you?"

"She deserves better." Maybe if he kept repeating those words, his brain would finally take them in. Jenny deserved all the best things. Good job, good kids, a husband who could take care of her. Adam couldn't work, he'd scared the hell out of their kids and he couldn't even do laundry without messing it up. He was useless to Jenny.

"Who said anything about what she deserves? What about what she wants? What she wants is you, you big jerk," Aiden declared.

None of this mattered. Adam slipped off the bar stool. He walked out of the place without another word.

Adam didn't have a destination in mind; he just wanted space. Space and time. His feet had other ideas, though, because ten minutes later, he stood before the house that used to be his home. Sheba sat beside him, staring at the blue front door.

He was right. Jenny did deserve better than him. It didn't matter what anyone else said or thought. He knew he was right in this. That was what mattered.

Adam went around to the backyard, slipped through the gate and in the back door. He knew what he needed to do: stop waiting around and leave already. He wanted one thing to take with him before he left.

He found the picture on the mantel, a snapshot he'd taken of Jenny and the boys the summer before everything fell apart. They'd been building sand castles on the narrow beach when he got home from a softball game. In the waning sunset, he'd watched the three of them measure sand, add walls and begin to decorate. He'd been torn between watching them and joining in the fun. In the end, he'd slipped inside the house to grab the camera. He'd snapped fifteen pictures before any of them realized he was there. Once they saw him, they'd drawn him into their sand castle building.

If he stayed, he'd get drawn back into their lives, little by little. And little by little, he would watch all of them give up something they wanted or needed. For him. He couldn't let that happen. Adam picked up the picture, slid it out of the frame and put it in his back pocket.

The door banged open, and Frankie ran down the hallway. He held a certificate in his hands and had an excited look on his face. The expression dimmed when he saw Adam standing at the mantel.

"Hey, buddy," Adam said. "How was school? And where's your brother?"

"School was good. Garrett will be here in a minute. He was right behind me."

"And your mom?" He didn't hear Jenny's footsteps in the hall, but she had to be close. She wouldn't let the boys walk home from school alone.

"She's with Garrett."

"Oh." Adam should go before she got home, before he talked himself out of leaving, just like he'd done before. He needed to be stronger than that.

Frankie slid his backpack from his shoulders and held out the piece of paper.

"For Creative Excellence" it read, along with a handwritten notation on the line below.

"The principal said I had the most unique costume on Hero Day. She said Mrs. Hess's puppy put it over the top. What does 'over the top' mean?"

"It's kind of like an exaggeration, or like what you did was better than what anyone else did."

"Cool."

It *was* cool. There had been several other kids wearing sports uniforms, but Frankie had been one of the few to dress up like an actual football player instead of a football fan. And the dog had been cute, even if it made it inside the school for only a few moments before everything went crazy.

"It is cool."

"Are you home now?"

Adam wasn't sure how to answer that. Saying no felt wrong, but saying yes didn't feel any more right. "I just had to pick something up."

"Oh." Frankie put the sheet of paper on the coffee table. "I wasn't afraid."

"Frankie…"

"Well, maybe a little."

"It's okay. The seizures scare me a little, too." More like a lot. More like fear the size of Australia. Frankie didn't need to know that, though. Adam knelt before his son, ignoring the slight twinge in his hip as he hunkered down on the living room floor.

"Mom says the doctors are trying to fix you."

"They are."

"When they fix you, will you come home?"

Adam shook his head. "I don't think that is a good idea, buddy." The words seemed inadequate, but Adam was unsure how to explain the feelings of inadequacy and fear to a little boy who saw him as a hero. Heroes weren't afraid of anything, and although he was trying to step quietly out of their lives, Adam wanted to be the hero that Frankie saw him as.

"Why not?"

"Because they may not be able to fix me."

"But maybe they can."

He wanted that sentiment to be true. So badly. Adam's heart squeezed at the serious expression on his little boy's face.

The back door opened and closed again, as Frankie threw his arms around Adam's neck.

"They can fix you, I know they can. But even if they can't, you should come home. So we can take care of you," he whispered.

Adam closed his eyes, concentrating on breathing in and out.

"Dad!" Garrett squealed when he saw them in the living room, then launched himself into Adam's arms, too. "You're back. We missed you."

"I missed you guys, too." Adam's gaze clashed with Jenny's across the living room. He untangled the boys' arms and stood. "I need to talk to your mom for a minute, guys."

"'Bout what?" Garrett asked, but Frankie was already pulling his brother up the stairs.

When they reached the top, Adam turned to Jenny. "Hi."

"Hello," she said, her voice frigid. She unzipped her hoodie and hung it in the closet near the front door, along with the boys' backpacks.

"I didn't think you'd be home."

"I figured."

"I'll get out of your hair," he stated, unsure what else there was to say. *Hi, I broke into our house to steal a family photo?* He didn't think Jenny would find that amusing. Pathetic, not amusing.

"What are you doing here, Adam?"

He started to tell her the truth, but changed his mind. "I thought I'd left something behind."

"We have your old football stuff, your collection of Steve McQueen movies and chipped Elvis glassware. Take your pick." She crossed her arms over her chest. The circles under her eyes seemed even darker than they had the night he'd walked out. Adam's chest squeezed.

"I didn't mean to hurt you, Jen."

She shook her head. "Well, congratulations, you accomplished something you didn't mean to."

He hated to see that defeated set to her shoulders, the exhaustion on her face. He wanted to wipe it all away. Take on all that stress and pain. If he could do that he would, but he didn't know how to without also opening her up to more pain in the future. Adam refused to do that.

"If I could change it—"

"You would. I get it."

Adam crossed to the hallway that would take him to the backyard. Maybe he would be able to breathe once he was outside. "I am sorry, Jenny."

She drew her lower lip between her teeth, but didn't say anything. Adam walked out the door, then paused, leaning against the fence for a moment, trying to draw air into his lungs.

"You can't just go, Dad," Frankie said. He'd come outside and now stood at the edge of the patio, that certificate in his hands. "In class today we read a story about heroes. And after the story, Mrs. Kelcher said real heroes are afraid."

Adam didn't think the boy had heard his teacher

correctly. Courage meant being braver than whatever fear tried to hold you back. He'd lost his courage the day he woke up in that hospital bed.

"That was just a story, buddy."

"No, it wasn't. She took the book off the nonfiction shelf in our classroom. That means it's true." Frankie frowned and crossed his arms over his chest. "In the story, the general was afraid, but he asked his men to fight with him, anyway, because what they were fighting for was more important. She said that is what real courage is. Being afraid, but knowing that what you want is more important than being afraid. She said it. She said a real hero fights even when he is afraid. It's okay to be scared."

Adam had no idea what book the kid had read in class, but it didn't matter. Nonfiction or fiction, that story had been about soldiers. Not an ex-football-playing woodworker.

Frankie launched himself forward, wrapping his arms around Adam's waist. "You're still my hero, Dad. You just have to remember."

Adam wasn't sure what to do. Push his son away? He couldn't do that. He patted the little boy's shoulders. "Remember what?"

"That it's okay to be scared."

"Frankie," Adam began, but stopped himself. He loosened the boy's arms, then sat with him at the table.

"It really is okay to be scared, Dad," Frankie said earnestly.

Adam didn't want to be afraid. He didn't want his sons to be. Or Jenny. But he had no idea how to stop.

"I don't want to be scared," he admitted, and it was as if those few words loosened the fear that had been choking him since the seizure. Fear that had insisted Jenny and the boys would be better off without him. That he would be better off alone, independent. Without any of the ties that could lead to the pain of those moments he'd been stuck under the rubble of the old church.

Love for his boys and his wife had sent him out into the tornado.

Fear of the pain that came from the destruction had made him hide from them for the past few months.

"I don't, either."

Adam sighed. He was positive of one thing: it was too late to fix the mess he'd made of his life by letting fear rule his actions. But if Frankie's teacher was right, courage meant a person chose to fight not because he wasn't afraid, but because there was something greater than fear on the other side of the battle.

"Kiddo?" He caught Frankie's gaze and chucked the little boy under his chin. "You're *my* hero."

CHAPTER SIXTEEN

THE DAY OF Adam's follow-up MRI, Jenny pulled the SUV into the parking lot of the doctor's office in Springfield with two minutes to spare. The secretary had left three voice messages and sent one very long email, ignoring Jenny's insistence that Adam A) no longer lived at the house by the lake and B) had a different phone number than hers.

When those things didn't work, she decided to remove her phone number and email from his charts in person. The last thing she needed right now were more phone calls and emails reminding her of the man who'd walked out on her.

Twice.

Inside, the receptionist pointed her down the hallway and into a waiting room. Jenny sat in the hard plastic chair and folded her hands in her lap. She swiveled when the door opened, and her heart seemed to stutter in her chest.

Adam was here.

How had he gotten here? The office had been calling the house nonstop for three days, looking for him.

Jenny stood. "I was just leaving."

"Don't go. They have the results for the MRI. You might as well hear them, too."

She would rather be anywhere than in this small, sterile room with Adam, but she did want to know that he was all right. Or at least as all right as he could be, considering his diagnosis. Jenny sat.

Adam took the chair across from her and rolled a magazine from the rack in his hands. "How have you been?"

"Peachy. You?"

"I've been better."

"Pity." She knew she was being mean-spirited, but she didn't care. Seeing Adam had set her world off balance once again. Not that it had been all that balanced before she walked into the doctor's office, but it had been getting there. She'd gotten through two whole days without breaking down in tears or throwing that stupid pillow at the wall.

The door opened again and Dr. Lambert walked in. His pants and shirt were as wrinkled as ever, and his hair looked a little windblown. Not the picture of steadfast intelligence. Maybe the doctor was the problem. Maybe Adam needed someone who didn't look as if he'd just stepped out of some crazy lab test.

"Jenny, Adam." He sat across from them and pulled a stack of papers from the folder on his desk. "This marks the third week since the last seizure. How have you been? Blurred vision? Weakness?"

"Not since last week." Adam reached out to pat Sheba's head. Funny, Jenny hadn't noticed the dog when he'd came into the room. Or when he'd surprised her at their house a couple weeks before. *Her* house, she reminded herself. Adam had walked out of it, leaving her with the mortgage and a paper saying he was releasing her from sharing any of the profits of the home, should she choose to sell it.

As if selling was an option. The boys had been through enough. She wasn't going to sell the only home they'd known out from under them. She would continue dealing with the mortgage payments and upkeep schedule. It shouldn't be much harder than the schedule she'd had this past summer.

The doctor was talking again, about more of the warning signs. He checked Adam's vitals while they spoke, marking a few things down on the tablet beside him.

"As you both know, we have the final MRI results in." He put the slide on a screen on the wall and flipped on the light. The image of Adam's brain filled the space, dark scarred areas scoring it. Jenny shivered, wondering if she would ever get used to the sight.

Not that it mattered. This was going to be her

last visit to this doctor's office. If Adam didn't want to share his life with her, she was certainly not going to partake in any of these checkups.

The doctor clicked the keyboard and another image of Adam's brain was illuminated. He pointed from one to the other. "As you can see, the scarring is beginning to recede in the newest image. The recession may not seem like a lot, but it is a significant improvement over what we saw after the last seizure." He typed on the keyboard again, and a third picture appeared. "And from the images taken after Adam was found in the rubble."

Jenny concentrated on the screen. The ugly scars still dominated the images, but Dr. Lambert was right. The tentacle-like scars were smaller, and seemed less dense now. She glanced at Adam, but couldn't read his expression.

"What does this actually mean?" she asked. Maybe he couldn't see the differences in the MRIs. After the last seizure, he'd said things were fuzzy. Maybe his vision was still impaired a bit.

"The more the scarring dissipates, the less likely Adam will have another incident. Now, we can't say it will completely disappear, but the reduction is enough that I feel confident there is a chance of a full recovery."

"Full?" The word squeaked out of Jenny's mouth.

The doctor beamed. "It will take a while, and you should remain on the medications, continue taking all of the precautions and working with the service dog. But there is a chance that the seizure you just had will be the last."

Adam cleared his throat. "And if it isn't?"

"If it isn't, we consider other medications. We keep an eye on the scarring. Time is our friend in this case. The longer you go between seizures, the better the chances of your brain healing."

Jenny swallowed. *Healing.* That was the best word she had heard in a long time.

LONG AFTER THE doctor left the room, Adam sat in the chair, trying to process what he had heard.

The words *full recovery* echoed in his mind. That meant he might get his life back. He looked at Jenny from the corner of his eye. The only problem with getting his life back was that she might misunderstand just what he wanted. He wanted her. He wanted to choose her, and work through whatever came at them, together.

And now he didn't have a hope in hell of making her see that he'd been ready to move forward before hearing what the doctor had to say.

Jenny rose from her chair. Sheba sat up.

"Well, that was good news."

"The best." Adam took a deep breath. Whether she believed him or not, there were things he needed to say to her. Starting with his five hundredth *I'm sorry*. Somehow, the apology didn't seem like the right place to start.

"I love you." The words slipped from his mouth before Adam could stop them. Jenny stared at him for a long moment. "Loving you is the best thing I've done in my whole life."

"Adam, I can't. I can't go down this road with you again. You love me, you don't. You want me in your life, then you walk away. I'm happy for you, I really am, but I can't let myself get pulled back into this again."

"I'm not trying to pull you back in. I just wanted to explain that I was trying to protect you, and before you get mad about that, I know you don't need protection. You're a smart woman and you're stronger than me. But my instinct is to protect the people I love, especially from myself."

"Oh, Adam." Jenny shook her head and closed her eyes.

"I have loved you for nearly half of my life. I never wanted to hurt you, Jen, and I'm sorry that I did. I was so afraid of hurting you that I tried to shut you out, because I thought if there was distance between us, you wouldn't wind up hurt." He paused. "You deserved better than that. So did the boys. I'm sorry."

Jenny held her bag to her chest like a shield. "I'm sorry, too."

"I don't want to be alone, and if you're not

with me, no matter who else is around, I'm alone. You're my level, Jen. You're what holds me true."

She shook her head, slowly, then faster. "I can't let myself fall back down this rabbit hole with you," she said, and fled from the office.

JENNY DROVE HOME in a fog. She didn't remember taking the highway out of Springfield, or seeing the big sign announcing the city limits of Slippery Rock, or making the turn from downtown to their quiet street along the lakefront. A mixture of echoes filled her mind. The doctor saying Adam might have a complete recovery. Adam saying that without her he would always be alone.

He'd nearly gotten her with that one. Because she didn't want to be alone, either. Since he'd walked out of their lives, she'd done everything she could to fill the time. She spent most of her days at Buchanan's, had started volunteering at school activities, had scheduled play dates with the boys' friends. She'd accepted every invitation from Mara and Savannah, which meant she'd paid about a semester's worth of fees and books to Sadie for babysitting. Through all of that, she remained alone.

Not just lonely, but alone. As if she were locked in some kind of bubble and no matter who she was with, no one could break through. She heard her friends talking, listened to the boys, to her in-laws. No one seemed to hear her, though.

Jenny put the car in Park and walked through the backyard gate. She blinked, thinking she had to be hallucinating, but the scene remained.

Fairy lights hung from the trees. Enlarged pictures of her, the boys and Adam were propped on easels and hung along the fence. She swallowed. Some of the best moments of her life were spread out before her, and she wanted to die.

"I love you, Jenny." Adam spoke from behind her and she whirled around.

"What are you doing here?"

"I paid a fortune to an Uber driver to get me here before you. He missed the window by about two minutes. I'm late."

She gestured to the yard. "How?"

"The guys hung the lights while we were at the doctor's office."

"I don't understand." Her heart beat fast in her chest. This didn't make sense. And that Uber driver had to have cost a fortune.

"I thought, when we ran away to that justice of the peace nine years ago, that we were joking when we said the for-better-or-for-worse part. I mean, who expects worse at age nineteen?"

Jenny certainly hadn't. She'd thought they would get married and have a couple kids and live the charmed life of TV sitcoms. Boy, had she been wrong.

"Most of the worst can be laid at my feet. I didn't listen to what you wanted, I didn't know what you needed, and after the tornado, I tried my hardest to shut you out completely because I was afraid you would finally realize that you didn't want or need me."

Jenny shook her head. "I've always wanted you. Always needed you." She didn't care if admitting it made her weak. It was the truth.

"We got some good news today, and as I was listening to the doctor tell me things were going to get better, I couldn't help thinking they weren't. Because without you in my life, nothing is better. Nothing is okay. It's like those moments after a seizure. The colors are a little too bright and the shapes are too fuzzy and everything sounds a little too muffled. I'm there. I can feel myself going through the motions, but without you there, I don't really know what's happening."

She knew that feeling, all too well.

"I gave you nine years of worse, but if you'll let me, I'd like to give you sixty or seventy years of better." He knelt in the grass and pulled a small box from the pocket of his jeans. "Will you marry me again, Jenny?"

She put her hands over her mouth, trying to take in what was happening. "It wasn't all bad," she managed to say. With trembling fingers, she reached to open the box. Nestled inside was a ring, encircled with diamonds.

"I can get you a whole new ring, if you want. But you know, there is that old-and-new thing that goes with weddings."

And it was the perfect symbolism for them. He'd given her a small diamond when they eloped nine years before. The ring in the box would stack nicely below it. Close to her heart. Just as Adam had always been.

"What about the borrowed and blue parts?"

"The SUV is blue."

That made Jenny laugh.

"And all these twinkle lights were borrowed from our friends. Who are quietly waiting on the other side of the fence to hear if we're going to have a wedding."

Jenny looked around, taking in not only the lights and the pictures, but the people. Aiden, Levi, Savannah and Collin stepped through the side gate. Her parents and Adam's had been standing near the door on the patio. Mara, James and little Zeke stood near the gate to the beach.

"Oh, my God."

"No pressure, but they're all rooting for a yes," Adam said, a smile in his voice. Jenny laughed, and the laughter quickly turned to tears.

"Don't cry, Momma." Frankie and Garrett

rushed from their position on the porch with their grandparents.

She hugged them close. "It's okay. Happy tears," she said.

"Is that a yes to the proposal?" Adam asked.

Jenny nodded—she couldn't force words past her lips.

"We're going to need one of you to go after a justice of the peace," Adam said. "She said yes, and I'm not giving her time to change her mind."

Their friends laughed, and Jenny saw several phone screens light up the evening sky.

"I do love you, Adam Buchanan."

"And I love you, Jennifer Anne Buchanan. I just forgot for a while that love isn't just a feeling." He kissed her gently on the lips.

"What is it, then?" she asked, smiling up at the man she had loved for most of her life.

"Love is what you do."

* * * * *

Get 2 Free Books,
Plus 2 Free Gifts—
just for trying the
Reader Service!

HARLEQUIN *Presents*

YES! Please send me 2 FREE Harlequin Presents® novels and my 2 FREE gifts (gifts are worth about $10 retail). After receiving them, if I don't wish to receive any more books, I can return the shipping statement marked "cancel." If I don't cancel, I will receive 6 brand-new novels every month and be billed just $4.55 each for the regular-print edition or $5.55 each for the larger-print edition in the U.S., or $5.49 each for the regular-print edition or $5.99 each for the larger-print edition in Canada. That's a saving of at least 11% off the cover price! It's quite a bargain! Shipping and handling is just 50¢ per book in the U.S. and 75¢ per book in Canada.* I understand that accepting the 2 free books and gifts places me under no obligation to buy anything. I can always return a shipment and cancel at any time. The free books and gifts are mine to keep no matter what I decide.

Please check one: ☐ Harlequin Presents® Regular-Print ☐ Harlequin Presents® Larger-Print
(106/306 HDN GLWL)   (176/376 HDN GLWL)

Name _____ (PLEASE PRINT)

Address _____ Apt. #

City _____ State/Prov. _____ Zip/Postal Code _____

Signature (if under 18, a parent or guardian must sign)

Mail to the Reader Service:
IN U.S.A.: P.O. Box 1341, Buffalo, NY 14240-8531
IN CANADA: P.O. Box 603, Fort Erie, Ontario L2A 5X3

Want to try two free books from another series?
Call 1-800-873-8635 or visit www.ReaderService.com.

* Terms and prices subject to change without notice. Prices do not include applicable taxes. Sales tax applicable in N.Y. Canadian residents will be charged applicable taxes. Offer not valid in Quebec. This offer is limited to one order per household. Books received may not be as shown. Not valid for current subscribers to Harlequin Presents books. All orders subject to approval. Credit or debit balances in a customer's account(s) may be offset by any other outstanding balance owed by or to the customer. Please allow 4 to 6 weeks for delivery. Offer available while quantities last.

Your Privacy—The Reader Service is committed to protecting your privacy. Our Privacy Policy is available online at www.ReaderService.com or upon request from the Reader Service.

We make a portion of our mailing list available to reputable third parties that offer products we believe may interest you. If you prefer that we not exchange your name with third parties, or if you wish to clarify or modify your communication preferences, please visit us at www.ReaderService.com/consumerschoice or write to us at Reader Service Preference Service, P.O. Box 9062, Buffalo, NY 14240-9062. Include your complete name and address.

HP17R2

Get 2 Free Books,
Plus 2 Free Gifts—
just for trying the
Reader Service!

HARLEQUIN

HEARTWARMING™

HW17R

HOMETOWN HEARTS ♥

YES! Please send me **The Hometown Hearts Collection** in Larger Print. This collection begins with 3 FREE books and 2 FREE gifts in the first shipment. Along with my 3 free books, I'll also get the next 4 books from the Hometown Hearts Collection, in LARGER PRINT, which I may either return and owe nothing, or keep for the low price of $4.99 U.S./ $5.89 CDN each plus $2.99 for shipping and handling per shipment*. If I decide to continue, about once a month for 8 months I will get 6 or 7 more books, but will only need to pay for 4. That means 2 or 3 books in every shipment will be FREE! If I decide to keep the entire collection, I'll have paid for only 32 books because 19 books are FREE! I understand that accepting the 3 free books and gifts places me under no obligation to buy anything. I can always return a shipment and cancel at any time. My free books and gifts are mine to keep no matter what I decide.

262 HCN 3432 462 HCN 3432

Name _____ (PLEASE PRINT) _____

Address _____ Apt. # _____

City _____ State/Prov. _____ Zip/Postal Code _____

Signature (if under 18, a parent or guardian must sign) _____

Mail to the **Reader Service:**

IN U.S.A.: P.O. Box 1867, Buffalo, NY. 14240-1867
IN CANADA: P.O. Box 609, Fort Erie, Ontario L2A 5X3

* Terms and prices subject to change without notice. Prices do not include applicable taxes. Sales tax applicable in NY. Canadian residents will be charged applicable taxes. This offer is limited to one order per household. All orders subject to approval. Credit or debit balances in a customer's account(s) may be offset by any other outstanding balance owed by or to the customer. Please allow 4 to 6 weeks for delivery. Offer available while quantities last. Offer not available to Quebec residents.

Your Privacy—The Reader Service is committed to protecting your privacy. Our Privacy Policy is available online at www.ReaderService.com or upon request from the Reader Service.

We make a portion of our mailing list available to reputable third parties that offer products we believe may interest you. If you prefer that we not exchange your name with third parties, or if you wish to clarify or modify your communication preferences, please visit us at www.ReaderService.com/consumerschoice or write to us at Reader Service Preference Service, P.O. Box 9062, Buffalo, NY. 14240-9062. Include your complete name and address.